Project Jennifer

Project Jennifer

JILL AMY
ROSENBLATT

KENSINGTON BOOKS
http://www.kensingtonbooks.com

KENSINGTON BOOKS are published by

Kensington Publishing Corp.
850 Third Avenue
New York, NY 10022

All Kensington titles, imprints, and distributed lines are available at special quantity discounts for bulk purchases for sales promotion, premiums, fund-raising, educational, or institutional use.

Special book excerpts or customized printings can also be created to fit specific needs. For details, write or phone the office of the Kensington Special Sales Manager: Kensington Publishing Corp., 850 Third Avenue, New York, NY 10022. Attn. Special Sales Department. Phone: 1-800-221-2647.

Kensington and the K logo Reg. U.S. Pat. & TM Off.

ISBN-13: 978-0-7582-2358-6
ISBN-10: 0-7582-2358-7

First Kensington Trade Paperback Printing: August 2008
10 9 8 7 6 5 4 3 2 1

Printed in the United States of America

For Mrs. Danvers

Acknowledgments

There are so many people to thank:

My editor, Danielle Chiotti, for her patience, support, and encouragement.

My agent, Agnes Birnbaum: thanks for taking me on and looking out for me. You're the best!

David Joy, Annie Dunn-Watson, and Bruce Ross from Burlington College. Your support is so much appreciated. Thank you for encouraging us all to hold on to our dreams.

Glenn Franklin, Martin Gringer, and Ken Sutak for their legal advice.

Frank, for the info on the workings of the police department.

And, most important, thank you, Mom, for passing down your love of reading and writing gene to me, for your suggestions, for telling me when something "needs work" and for always being there.

JOAN

Chapter 1

It was Nietzsche's fault.

For the record, I knew it was bizarre to blame the disasters of life on nineteenth-century lunatic philosophers. But, when my fiancé, Michael, dumped me and married Jennifer six months later, I had two thoughts on the subject. First, I was in love with a man whose knowledge of relationship etiquette was as deep as a wading pool. Second, it was Nietzsche's theory of the superman—and I use the term generically—come to pass. The strong fearless individual, living on her own terms, taking what she wanted by will, or will to power. That was Jennifer.

It was Saturday, exactly one week since Michael's wedding. My boss, Fred Lutz, was a friend of Michael's family. I had eavesdropped, caught shreds of conversations, and put together a complete picture: the ceremony in the gazebo, the ice sculptures at the reception, and let's not forget the symbolic releasing of the doves. I put on a brave face Monday and Tuesday; Lutz wouldn't make eye contact. By Wednesday, I gave up and called in sick. I spent the rest of the week curled into a fetal ball on my royal blue couch where Michael and I had once cuddled, talked, and watched movies together, sniveling into my Long Island Iced Tea. It was Saturday night and I was reciting the wedding details for the hundredth time to Carrie and Louise, the Athos and Porthos of our trio. Who was I? I wasn't Aramis and at the moment, I sure as hell wasn't the scrappy D'Artagnan. I had the foresight to lay in a lavish buffet. Why shouldn't my friends eat well while I wallowed in misery? I thought they came to commiserate. It soon became clear they didn't come for tea, sympathy, or the shrimp platter. This wasn't a pity party; it was an intervention.

"The ice sculptures were mammoth," I blubbered. "And there were three of them. Oh my God," I cried out, the irony finally hitting me, "a melting hunk of ice—that was our relationship. That was my life with Michael." And then I began bawling again.

"Joanie—honey—forty-two percent of women say they're sorry they ever walked down the aisle," Louise comforted. This from my childhood friend who married out of high school and had been confessing her happiness to me ever since.

Carrie's advice was a bit more direct, and delivered as she polished off the last of the shrimp platter. "He's a useless insensitive shit, Joanie, forget him." That has been Carrie's mantra for the six years I've known her. I heard it the first day we met at the Mane Event, her black smock a shocking contrast to her spiked platinum blond hair. As she moussed, gelled, and volumized, she made her signature pronouncement about her ex-boyfriend Randy. Randy then proved her correct by arriving and insisting the stereo in her apartment belonged to *him*. When it was over, Randy needed hair plugs, I posted Carrie's bail, and we've been friends ever since.

Although their advice was appreciated, it didn't help. I looked around the apartment; all I saw was Michael. Our quiet dinners, Michael picking me up to go for walks in the park; he loved to take walks. He always wanted us to spend time together by ourselves. He talked about his dreams for the future, our future. Floating in my special place of cosmic cluelessness, thinking everything was fine, I was blissfully happy until I found myself out in the cold without any explanation, unless you count the arrival of Jennifer as the explanation. Why didn't I see Jennifer coming? If there were signs, I didn't see any. What did she have that I didn't have?

It was all a hideous déjà vu. Before Michael there had been Steve. I thought Steve was The One. He had that 1970s Alan

Alda sensitivity. We had deep soulful conversations, comfortable silences, we shared a lot of the same interests, and he was hot. And then we fell apart. And I didn't understand what happened then either. I was sensing a disturbing trend.

"He's a useless, insensitive shit, Joanie," Carrie repeated, as she picked the peanuts out of the mixed nuts. "Forget him."

"But he was my useless, insensitive . . ."

"Don't start that, Joanie. Remember when Carl was cheating on me? You said love hurts but you gotta move on and it'll all work out. Remember when you said that?"

I hate to admit this, but at that moment, I was drawing a blank on Carl. "Vaguely," I slurred. I had spent my life dispensing sage, psychoanalytic social work babble to friends and strangers alike. All of which had worked beautifully—for them. The irony was not lost on me.

"So I dumped Carl, moved on, and it was the best thing for me," Carrie finished.

I had a moment of clarity. "He dumped you," I corrected.

"He did? Whatever. Anyway, it was the best thing for me."

"Him, too," Louise said, her cherub-cheeked face lighting up with a smile.

Carrie glared at her, but said nothing. Carrie and Louise were united only in their loyalty to me. If I disappeared tomorrow, there would be one ugly throw down. And Carrie would win. Long live the Musketeers.

In my alcoholic stupor, I tried to refocus and decided Carrie was right. I was going to have to get over this. For almost six months, I had wallowed in my childish fantasies, my favorite being Michael coming to his senses, abandoning the beautiful, polished, and disgustingly perfect Jennifer and returning to his plain Joan. That was fantasy number thirteen, not to be confused with fantasy number seventeen, which was the same except Jennifer had boils and sores.

I stood up, because life-changing pronouncements cannot be made while sitting down.

"I am moving on," I announced. "I am an educated, intelligent individual, and it's all going to work out."

The Musketeers chimed in—all for one, one for all.

"Damn straight," Carrie exhorted. "Tomorrow you'll go out and show that useless, insensitive shit you don't need him and start a new life."

Hours after they had gone and I had cried myself into exhaustion, my last thoughts were that it was nutball Nietzsche's fault, and if I had only seen Super Jennifer coming, none of this would have happened. And I wondered if everything would've been different if I had been a Jennifer.

Chapter 2

Six A.M. Monday morning: I was standing in the middle of my living room, my hangover replaced by the headache from hell. Not an auspicious beginning to the first, no, second day of the rest of one's life.

On the other side of the wall, my landlord, Christine, was making way too much noise. With a groan, I surveyed the mess of plastic cups and empty platters. The refuse reminded me of Michael's parents' gold-plated, overpriced, and underwhelming parties.

During our sixteen months together, Michael's mother was always throwing a fabulous fete at some restaurant, and Michael had to be there to meet and greet. The first time his mother, "Patricia" as she insisted I call her, gave me directions, I arrived at my destination to find the Goldberg bar mitzvah. Can you say passive-aggressive hostility, boys and girls?

Michael laughed it off, gave me a kiss and a promise to pick me up from then on. After our engagement, "Patricia's" disdain for me fell off my radar. I was too busy anticipating my life with Michael as one continuous Kodak moment. We'd have a home in Dix Hills, summers in the Hamptons, enjoy a Palm Beach retirement—the good life. God knows everything was already planned for Michael. His parents had mapped out his existence from birth to death and what was planned for Michael was planned for me, too, or so I thought.

It was at one of these mandatory soirees that I'd first seen Jennifer. She was having an animated discussion with Michael's mother. His mother beckoned to Michael but after a few moments he drifted back to me. I looked over to find "Patricia" laughing and talking with Jennifer. That should have set off an alarm; she was way too happy.

I snapped out of my stupor to crawl into my clothes and get ready for work. *Note to self: post-alcohol residue acts as clarifying agent.* I could've spent the last six months getting loaded and achieving a Zen state of awareness. Who knew?

But at the moment the fact that my life was in ruins did not excuse me from performing gainful employment. Decked out in black, with sunglasses concealing the dark circles under my eyes, I slunk out into daylight like Nosferatu, slumped into my car, and drove to work.

I arrived at the office and slithered to my desk. My boss, Fred Lutz, was a small, nervous man who could always be counted on to agree with the last person who spoke to him. Michael had encouraged me to apply for the job. And what exactly was my job? As a special assistant, I used my interpersonal skills to creatively problem solve, communicate, compose correspondence, not to mention order lunch and make photocopies.

I wish I knew where my college advisor was at this moment. I had been an English major during sophomore year. My advisor assured me that it was the optimum career path: "It demonstrates that you are a well-read, well-rounded individual," he exhorted. As he was the head of the English department I sensed his natural enthusiasm. Unfortunately, I had difficulty translating his rationale into hard cash and gave it up as a bad idea. After a while I gave up school, too. Since I now made a very nice living with those well-read, well-rounded skills, if I saw him today I would repent my poor judgment and offer to read *Moby Dick* for penance.

After Michael's de-engagement to me, I became the office pariah, suffering the obligatory "tut-tut" comments and the furtive whispers that suddenly stopped when I approached. Eventually it settled down, and then Michael got married so I could once again enjoy the "pathetic loser chick" glances I had always been so fond of. I slouched at my desk trying to blend in with the cabinets. Twenty minutes into the day, Lutz called me into his office.

I settled in my usual spot, the guest chair to the left of the impressive oak desk. Lutz sat behind the desk, folding, then clenching, then wringing his hands.

"Well," he said.

I sat, pad and pen at the ready. "Do you have anything special for today?" I asked.

"Well," he said again, "well."

That was three *wells*. *Houston, we have a problem.*

"Joan," he began. "I'm afraid . . ."

Oh no. While my brain shifted into fight, flight, and freak out, Lutz fired me.

"I don't understand," I said. "Why?"

Lutz continued wringing his hands. *Why are you wringing your hands, you moron? I'm the one without a job.* "Well, Joan—let's look at the situation. You don't do much."

I needed a clever comeback, but even if I hadn't been in the throes of relationship and occupational crises, verbal sparring had always been a problem. I longed to give a heartfelt and eloquent speech that would convince Lutz to keep me on, but all I could squeak out was, "You could change my responsibilities. . . . I'll do more." *Bravo, Joan, bravo.*

Pulling out a handkerchief, Lutz mopped his face. I would've felt sorry for him, if it wasn't for my looming unemployment problem.

"Well, Joan, I can't do that. You know I gave you the job as a favor to Michael. It was an—arrangement."

"An arrangement?" I sputtered.

"Yes, one where I overpaid and underworked you."

Okay, to be fair, I knew that. It was easy to buy into Michael's "valuable asset to any organization" shtick because I wanted to. Now the world was veering off its axis again. Not a problem. I could always stop at a liquor store on the way home. I did a quick mental recap: true love I'd been waiting for entire life dumps me, six months later marries impossibly gorgeous Super Jennifer. Current job that was no more than secret handshake deal for worthless position is gone, too. *Note to self: Sign up for self-esteem-building course, pronto.*

Now, if I only had a brain, I would've come up with a superb comeback such as: "Instead of phasing out an underworked, overpaid position, why don't you turn it into a useful, properly paid position?" And then that semester of prelaw would not have been wasted. Unfortunately, the extent of my negotiating skills was, "Could you—maybe—keep me on for another month or so, until I can find something else?" *Excellent, Joan, you've got him now.*

Lutz leaned back in his chair with a heavy sigh. Maybe I did have him?

"Joan, I need this position—for someone else."

"Someone else?" I could feel the blood draining from my face. "A friend of Michael?"

Lutz cleared his throat, avoiding my gaze. "A friend of Jennifer."

Even though my stomach flipped like a high diver, I was not shocked.

I should have gone out in a Bon Jovi blaze of glory, bringing Lutz to his knees with, "You're pathetic. Don't you have any pride? Your practice of secondhand nepotism is deplorable." I imagined the office staff crowding at the door yelling: "You go, girl! Tell him, Joanie!"

Instead, I melted into a puddle of passivity.

"Oh," I said finally.

"Good luck, Joan," he said.

I got up and walked out.

I didn't breathe until I hit the parking lot. I was in trouble. Big, big trouble.

I drove home, too stunned to cry.

Inside my apartment, I collapsed onto the couch to review the emotional flotsam that was my life. Eventually I forced myself off the couch and headed for the kitchen; you can't do a proper survey without chocolate.

I didn't make it; there was a knock at the door. I opened it to find my landlord, Christine, standing there.

"Hi, honey," she said. "Got a minute? I need to talk to you."

I knew that look of shy embarrassment. I had seen it an hour ago.

Uh—oh . . .

Chapter 3

According to me, there are two theories of life. There is the "Third Time's the Charm" theory wherein things may be tough but they work out in the end. And then there is the "Everything Comes in Three's" theory wherein not only does everything go south, but it does so times three. If you had asked me six months and one week ago, I would have said I was a "Third Time's the Charm" kind of girl, but I revised this viewpoint as Christine sat at my expensive Pier 1 dining room table explaining why I had to move out.

"You remember I told you my niece was getting married."

I vaguely remembered a niece. I had been floating in pre-marital euphoria when we discussed it. I nodded.

"And how we talked about her taking the apartment after you . . . got married."

"I'm not getting married," I said, in case she missed the memo—or the hysterical crying that went on unabated for months.

She took my hand. "I know, honey, I know. It's just that, well . . . my niece . . . she eloped suddenly and my sister is a little upset, so they need the apartment now."

I felt sorry for Christine—I did. It wasn't her fault my life had gone to hell. I tuned her out as she did a rerun of the obligatory "you'll recover and forget Michael" speech. I was thinking about that party again.

This time I didn't focus on Michael or his mother. I zeroed in on Jennifer. The perfect hair, the porcelain skin, the prima ballerina posture, and of course, the impeccable couture clothes. It was a tape playing in my head, rewinding, and playing again. His mother beckoning to him, Michael walking away from me to stand at Jennifer's side. Her relaxed, easy delivery while touching his arm, and the charming easy laugh and hair toss. Turning to look at me, she smiled. I didn't get it then. I got it now. Michael was smiling, too. A smile I thought was forced; I was wrong. Nor was it forced from the other men standing nearby. Forget how all the world's a stage—Jennifer was the stage, and everyone else was the audience. *How does she do it?* I asked myself over and over again. Christine's next question brought me back to earth.

"Do you have a Plan B?"

I smiled. "I didn't need a Plan B. I had a fiancé. I was getting married."

Christine fiddled with her coffee cup while I brought out the Drake's Coffee Cakes. I prefer a nosh and a beverage with a catastrophe. It gives the experience that little something extra.

"You can go to your mother's, can't you?"

A shiver ran up my spine. "Can you give me a month?"

She took my hand. "Oh, honey, I would if I could, you know that."

A moment of silent panic followed. I decided some congratulations were in order even though the entire world was getting married except for me. Okay, that wasn't true. But it felt like it was.

"Congratulations to your niece, Christine. I'm sure it will all work out. Eloping is so romantic."

"It is—Jennifer has always been spontaneous," she said.

I nodded over my mental scream. *Another one! How do they do it? What is it about Jennifers?*

It was a thought I would have to return to another time. Right now I had to figure out my Plan C so I didn't have to resort to the dreaded Plan B—living with Mom.

Chapter 4

I am convinced that as the universe was formed, a manual was written that was standard issue to all mothers. This manual contained all the phrases poor unfortunate daughters have been subjected to down through the ages: "If he doesn't see all the beautiful things I see in you, that's his misfortune." "Worry about the inside and not the outside." And my personal favorite, "All of my friends tell me what a beautiful girl you are." Isn't that the problem in a nutshell? When only middle-aged women think you're beautiful, something is definitely wrong. And what exactly were the grading criteria? Pinchable cheeks? Retention of baby fat?

In the fifteen-minute drive to my mother's house, I tried to mentally conjure a Houdini solution to my problems. No luck. Now I was standing in my mother's living room, my bare feet sinking into the plush carpet as my mother completed the five-year-wrap-up at the top of her lungs. She was already in my room removing the dust covers from the furniture.

". . . and after you get your bachelor's you can go on to graduate school." I swear she never took a breath.

"Ma, please—" I called out as I headed toward the kitchen. Only Godiva dark chocolate would soothe my frayed nerves. "I haven't decided anything yet."

My mother followed me and began filling the tea kettle. "I don't understand a beautiful, intelligent girl with excellent grades not having a career." This was chapter six of the manual. Express great confidence while noting lack of success. This is why counseling centers are not run by Jewish mothers.

She was out of Godiva, so I settled for a double-fudge brownie. "Why are you speaking in the third person? I'm in the room."

I admit I have tried almost every major imaginable: business, education, marketing, history, prelaw, psychology, sociology, even philosophy, which I took only to sound more interesting at the parties given by Michael's parents. I had studied count-less career paths and then left them behind; I was not prepared to be the one left behind.

"I want you to find something," my mother went on. "Do you remember Melissa from your father's office? Her daughter finished Katharine Gibbs and she works in Manhattan." My mother paused to drop an octave. "Makes a small fortune."

"Ma!" I cried, "who's here that you're whispering?"

"They pay for her lunch *and* a gym membership."

I rooted around in the fridge: Chinese food, fried chicken, a salami roll. How did I miss Katharine Gibbs?

"That's definitely worth three hours on a train every day," I said.

I swallowed hard. Discussion of my many academic adven-tures was not why I had come. I had to do it. I had to ask for money. As in, "Hi, Mom, I don't want to live with you, I just want you to loan me hundreds of dollars." Okay, not exactly like that.

"Mom, I need to borrow some of the money Daddy left me."

She turned to me. "Joanie, your father left that money specifically for your education—he made wonderful provi-sions, thank God—and you still don't have your degree." She brushed a piece of lint from her sweater. I could see it now. Mom's friends from the old days, also known as the Brooklyn Brigade, would be regaled with new Joan tales of woe at the monthly canasta game. Oy vey.

"Ma, I know, but I need to get another apartment—" I took

a closer look. My mother was wearing a brand new outfit. My mother hated shopping. And she had a new do. My mother had worn the same style since Reagan was in office. And hello, when did she wash that gray right out of her hair?

"Joanie, what is it?"

"What's with you?" I asked, peering more closely.

"Nothing is with me." She smoothed her skirt and began searching the cabinets for tea bags. "Don't be ridiculous."

I picked up the box from the counter. "Looking for these?" I definitely detected a faint rosy glow on her cheeks. "Let's try again. What's with you and the new hair and clothes, Ma?" A lightbulb went on. "You're seeing someone," I said.

My mother threw her arms around me. "Oh, honey, I didn't want to upset you."

My *mother* had a boyfriend. I'd been dumped, my life had fallen to pieces, and now my mother had a boyfriend. I was a romantic pariah; my mother was a stud muffin magnet. I was sure that now was the perfect time for that leftover Chinese food.

"Who is he?"

"You know Dave who fixes any home repair problems I have? His wife's sister's husband's friend. He lost his wife last year."

"How lucky for everyone. What if he finds her?"

"Don't be fresh, Joanie. Your father—God bless him, he made such wonderful provisions—has been gone for a long time. Maybe Dave knows someone your age—"

"Ma!"

"Just thinking." She gave me another hug. "You're going to find someone, you will. If Michael didn't see all the wonderful qualities I see in you—then it's his loss."

I'm sure he's suffering.

"You have to get over him, Joanie."

"I am, Ma," I said through gritted teeth. "Ma, I need to borrow that money."

"You don't want to move back home?"

I could feel the guilt oozing out of me. I couldn't look at her. She gave a heavy sigh and turned back to the stove.

"I'll loan you whatever you need. But not your college money. That's for you to finish school, which you will. Now don't stuff, we're going to eat dinner soon."

I shuddered at the thought that one day, if or when I had children, the manual would be mine and I would recite the same nonsense to them. They would hate me for it and well they should. I thought about Jennifer. Did she have a manual? Where did she get it? What did it say?

I have always measured current life experiences against previous encounters. When I studied social work, we learned how to help people do this in order to recognize progress. In the dark days after Michael's wedding to Jennifer, I put my own spin on the process and employed the technique as a retrospective of decay.

For example, Michael used to pick me up at my pleasant, well-lit apartment, with its blue and white curtains, cream-colored carpeting, and large plasma screen television, as opposed to walking down into a basement and standing in a small, dark, claustrophobic, depressing Mole Hole with threadbare carpet, which was my new apartment a week later. I was expecting a groundhog to spring up and tut-tut about how they let anyone in nowadays.

Before the downward spiral began, I had a nice landlord, a kind landlord. Now I had the Addams family, complete with the terrier from hell. As I handed over the first month's rent and security—thanks to Mom's Savings and Loan and the sale of the plasma screen television—to my landlord, a large man with a larger belly whom Carrie christened Kong, the terrier attempted to gnaw my ankle to the bone. As the children heaved destruction around us, Kong counted my money and asked for repeated assurances that *I* wouldn't make any noise. *Except for my wretched cries of despair, I'll be quiet as a mouse.*

Louise and Carrie helped me schlep my boxes down into the pits of hell while Carrie's latest boyfriend, Scott, did the heavy lifting. Scott was nice—he seemed nice—Carrie said he was nice. Actually, Scott rarely spoke. I wondered if that was the reason Carrie was so happy. Despite my intense almost two-year relationship with Michael and my intense brief relationship with Steve, coupling dynamics were never my area. I always felt like I never knew what to say, so I talked too much. That's probably why I was the romantic success I was at this moment.

Carrie dropped a box onto the floor. "If you had stayed with your mother, you would've saved on rent. It wouldn't have killed you."

"Yes, yes, it would have. Twenty-nine-and-a-half-year-old, ditched brides-to-be do not move in with their mothers. I would need therapy and she'd be paying for that, too."

Louise came down, her arms wrapped around a carton. "Joanie," she huffed, "seventy-eight percent of women go home after a failed relationship."

"They forgot to tell you sixty percent were on Zoloft," I said.

"They'd have to be," Carrie said.

Scott teetered down the stairs with a wicker chair I couldn't bear to part with, mainly because it was Michael's favorite chair. He planted it in the corner of the living room, then himself in it, and ceased to be helpful.

"You know, I never went home after I left Adam," Carrie said while rummaging in a paper bag and bringing out a bagel and a cup of coffee for Scott.

"*He* left you," I said.

"The point is I didn't go home."

"They wouldn't let you in," Louise said.

Carrie's lips tightened. A tense air of repressed dislike hung in the room.

Then the cacophony began, like a symphony playing above our heads. First the mother screamed, then the children cried, then the dog barked. Finally, Kong bellowed at someone to get out of the house.

"Is he throwing the wife out?" Louise was appalled.

I sank onto the floor. "Probably the eight-year-old."

Carrie flipped open a box to unpack. "My money's on the toddler."

After a few moments, silence.

Carrie looked around. "Well," she said, "this is nice."

I smiled. Everyone said our friendship wouldn't last, but Carrie could be okay.

"It's a hole," I said.

"Yes . . . yes, it is," she answered.

I sat there, looking around. This was my new life. I missed my old apartment, my old life, but most of all I missed Michael. And then I thought of Jennifer. Even before I was handing back the ring—before it was over, she knew she'd won. How did she do it? I repeated it in my head until I uttered it out loud.

"Who?" Louise asked me. "Do what?"

"Jennifer," I said. "How did Jennifer get Michael? No matter what his parents tried, he was never interested."

Carrie sat up. "What? You never mentioned this."

Realizing my butt was numb, I shifted. I also missed my plush carpeting. I never mentioned it because I didn't think it mattered. I was too naive to realize everything mattered.

"Michael told me that before he started law school his parents had tried to hook them up, but he wasn't interested."

"And then he met you and took you to parties where his parents treated you like Ebola."

"I was wearing them down," I said without conviction. "Michael and I were happy. No matter what Adolph and Eva said, he never paid any attention to them. He had them under control. He had everything under control."

"Sure he did," Carrie snapped. I knew that lilt of sarcasm in her tone. Michael was not her favorite person. I had only to ask, "What does that mean?" and she'd be only too happy to tell me. I didn't ask.

Carrie stood up, smoothing her clothes in preparation for her closing statement. "Joanie, for the last time, there is no such thing as a Jennifer Persona."

This was a charge I could defend. "I beg to differ. They have an . . . aura . . ."

She snorted. "They're just chicks with expensive wardrobes."

"I have a cousin Jennifer," Louise piped up. "She had three marriage proposals in one year."

"You see!" I cried.

"She turned them all down. She married a doctor. He's a proctologist."

"See, Joanie, even a Jennifer can wear expensive threads and still have bad taste," Carrie said through a mouthful of bagel.

"You don't understand." I had to prove my point. "It's like the difference between Grace Kelly, Jackie O, and . . . everyone else. It's inbred. They're not like the rest of us."

"Come on, Joans, don't get yourself in a twist."

I ignored her. "She hooked him and reeled him in. Right under my nose. She stole him because she could."

"Joanie, it's got nothing to do with women. Men lie, cheat, and then they rip your heart out and step on it. You can't trust any of them."

Scott crumpled the bagel wrapping, stuffed it in his empty cup, stood up and, snaking his arm around Carrie's waist, gave her a kiss on her cheek. "I gotta go," he said.

She ran her hands up and down his arms, brushing her lips against his. "Okay, baby." He shuffled out without another word.

Louise patted my shoulder. "Joanie, forty-six percent of women say there is a formula for recovering from bad relationships."

Louise had her finger on the pulse of women's issues by way of extensive reading of popular magazines. In high school it was *Mademoiselle* and *Young Miss*. As she got older, *Cosmopolitan* had all the answers. Any hot woman's issue would elicit a knowledgeable response as to what the women of America were thinking. Perhaps she could tell me what percentage of American women had found themselves in my situation and worked their way out. Better yet, how many looked at themselves and thought they had the IQ of Bozo the Clown? I couldn't speak for anyone else, but I'd been feeling more than a little stupid lately. I decided that rather than dabbling in introspection, it

was better to stick with depression. There were no requirements for improvement and the hours were better, leaving
plenty of free time to spend under the blankets with the lights
out.

I refocused as Carrie piped up. "She's right, Joans. There *is*
a formula. Rebound sex, chocolate, and booze. Not necessarily
in that order."

"That wasn't in my textbooks."

Carrie patted my shoulder. "You were reading the wrong
ones."

"Exercise, eat right, and find a new interest." Louise countered triumphantly.

"I found an interest after Adam," Carrie shot back. "I studied witchcraft, and stuck pins in the balls of his anatomically
correct voodoo doll."

"You forgot to exercise," I said absently.

Carrie turned her back on Louise to face me. "Look, I'll
give you a haircut, put in some highlights; you'll be a new
woman."

Hours after they had gone, I was still thinking about Carrie's
offer. A new do wasn't going to cut it, so to speak. Depression
wasn't going to do it either. I had screwed up. I had followed
my mother's advice: developed my mind, personality, and kept
reasonably thin thighs. I did everything the "right" way, and
then waited for my prince to come. And he came. And then
Jennifer came and walked off with him, leaving me to wave
good-bye. I concede Michael was a shit for leaving me and he
was an übershit for ducking my calls afterward. But obviously I
must have screwed up as well. What was it? We spent time
watching movies. Too mundane? What about the walks on the
beach, the home-cooked meals. Too tame and "old married"?
Had it been our decision "to wait" until after marriage? He
suggested it. Why? Because he had decided to pursue Jennifer
and her bag of tricks, that's why. If discovery was the key to
knowledge, then I needed to discover what Nietzsche knew all
those years ago. How had Jennifer overcome the ordinary to
become the ideal woman—and take the man I loved?

As I crawled into bed on my first night in my new Mole Hole, I closed my eyes to the fugue pounding overhead and knew I had to get the hell out of here. I also knew that something else had to be done first. I needed a job. A good job. And I needed it fast.

Chapter 5

A job search required a carefully constructed arsenal: one *Newsday* Help Wanted section, three "good suits" for interviews, and one highly creative résumé.

I knew what my problem was right off. I had years of education, in countless subjects, but knew nothing that would help me acquire a job. Pouring over the ads, I realized there was no need for someone to explain the tactics of the Battle of Bull Run, no high-powered executive wanted an in-depth explanation of Shakespeare's themes of love and power politics in *The Tempest,* and no one in any boardroom cared how the pyramids were constructed. I was an untapped well of useless information. Marketing? I had taken one class. Train to become a stockbroker? I needed to make money now. And any jobs I did find interesting required something I didn't have—a degree.

So what *did* I have? I could type, use a computer; my phone skills were excellent. Administrative assistant/secretary was the way to go. I faxed out my résumé. Then came the interviews. . . .

Who among working women hasn't learned the stock answers for surviving interviews? *Greatest strength? Multitasking of course. Efficiency! Cooperation! Team player! Greatest weakness? Perfectionist. What do I want, what are my long-term goals? To stay with this company for the rest of my life. I love it here. I can tell already. I never want to leave. Top priority? Making a contribution to your company. How can I help you? How would I rate my skills? Excellent! Fantastic! Top notch! Quick learner! Show me once, I'm set for life.*

I would have relayed all of this critical and highly factual information during my first interview at a plastics manufacturing company, a fascinating industry for the single woman, but I didn't get a chance as my prospective boss, Attila the Hun, kept interrupting our chat in order to abuse various members of his staff. I didn't see any hunchbacks but there must've been a bell tower somewhere in the office. I kept waiting for some poor drone to schlep past the office crying, "Sanctuary! Sanctuary!" Attila said he would call me. God forbid.

Interview Number Two took place in a medical billing office; here the drones were confined to minuscule cubes. Dilbert country. Prospective Boss Felix Unger was consumed with my organizational capabilities. That's all he talked about while spraying an oil slick of Lemon Pledge on his desk and scrubbing compulsively. I considered knocking over his coffee cup to see if he'd go postal. As the interview progressed, I amused myself with a mental game of "Guess which cabinet has the cleaning products?" While examining me through narrowed eyes, he lamented that the last four secretaries did not have organizational capabilities. How did I like to organize my desk? *I don't keep anything on the desk; I keep everything on the floor so you can trip over it when you come out to talk to me.* But I couldn't bring myself to say it. Carrie always said that was my problem. I'm nice Joan, always a kind word and a helpful phrase Joan. Felix seemed less than satisfied with my assurances of orderliness. Perhaps if I had produced a can of Lysol from my purse that would've helped.

Next I entered the high-powered arena of commercial real estate. I interviewed with Madame Van Winkle, the head of Human Resources. She asked questions and I poured out my laundry list of talents. Not only was she not impressed, she proceeded to close her eyes. After an uncomfortable silence, I leaned forward to take a closer look. My interviewer was napping. She had gone sleepy-bye—dreamland—night nights. I faced a dilemma: Did I keep going and risk waking her or should I let her nap? Lucky for me I didn't have to decide as suddenly her eyelids shot back up. She didn't ask if I was interested and I didn't bring it up. I consoled myself: my career path did not include Narcoleptics, Inc. *Memo to me: Keep open mind re: future career in HR. Plenty of rest—guaranteed.*

I closed out the week with a twenty-minute interview with a man named Wells. He was medium height, with dark hair and a ruddy, healthy complexion. A little thinner, a little taller, and a little more handsome, and he could've been a Ken doll. But he wasn't hard to look at. He glanced over my résumé and talked through the whole interview. I managed to squeeze in a few bits of my spiel. The company sold insurance. He needed a secretary. He told me how much he was paying and asked if I was interested. I said yes and walked out sure I'd never hear from him.

My first week of job hunting was a complete washout. Damn.

I had just gotten back to the apartment when the phone rang. It was Carrie. I had to take the phone into my bedroom because overhead the children were ripping up the floorboards to build a panic room as Kong roared and stomped.

"What's going on over there?" Carrie asked.

"They're practicing for their audition for *Eight is Enough: The Psychotic Generation*," I yelled.

"Look, I called every contact I have. I got the info, but I gotta tell you I don't think this is a good idea."

I wasn't listening. "Where will she be?"

"She's having lunch tomorrow in Port Jefferson. Joanie, this isn't like you—this is like me. Let it go."

"Meet me at Danford's. Noon tomorrow."

I heard a sigh on the other end of the line. "Okay."

Thankfully, my noncareer would be on hold for the weekend. I had resolved to find out how Jennifer had stolen my fiancé. It was time to get started.

The sun was shining, the air smelled warm, and a salty breeze was funneling in off the sound. In short, a perfect summer day in Port Jefferson. Crowds filled the quaint streets and the bellowing horn of the ferry meant more day-trippers were on the way from Connecticut. I used to navigate the narrow sidewalks with Michael, stopping to buy knickknacks, sampling seafood and ice cream, enjoying the festival for the eye and palate. And where was I now? I was crouching behind a bush, thinking about all the great heroines of literature I had done term papers on over the years. None of them had stooped to hiding behind an evergreen to size up their competition.

Not fifty feet away from me, Jennifer was sitting down to lunch. If that wasn't bad enough, I was tormented by the sweet scent of Michael. This had become a problem ever since he left me. I would be out somewhere and I caught his scent or the sound of his voice and then it was gone. I canvassed the area and sighed. No Michael. Just Jennifer. Hair? Perfect. Clothes? Pastel, tailored, elegant. I couldn't see the nails; no problem, I had brought my binoculars.

I was taking in the French manicure and checking for matching pedicure when out of the corner of my eye, I saw Carrie approaching carrying a book.

"Get down," I ordered hoarsely.

She rolled her eyes, did a Groucho crouch and parked herself next to me. "Well, I'm sure nobody noticed that," she said. "Let me take a look."

"No," I said, training my binoculars on Jennifer and marveling at her dining skills. No fork flying to the floor, no glass tipping over. I was sure when she finished the tablecloth would be spotless. That was just wrong.

"If you're not going to let me look, why am I here?"

"You're my alibi in case I'm arrested."

Carrie opened the book and flipped the pages. "Have you thought of moving on with your life?"

"She even eats perfectly," I muttered.

"I guess not," Carrie said.

Jennifer's companions were engrossed in her narrative. While they too had matching everything from head to toe, something was missing. That Jennifer grace and polish, that devil-may-care

Jennifer style. Her posture was straight, yet never stiff. Her eyes were calm, serene, her expression a cross between bemused and tolerant when someone else spoke. She never rushed, never hurried. It was easy to imagine she was never on the receiving end of anything except a compliment.

Louise suddenly appeared and scrunched down next to us.

"What are you doing here?" I asked. "You can't afford to get arrested."

Louise giggled. "I can't stay long. I have a birthday party at three."

Carrie was still flipping through the book. It took a moment for me to realize it was a high school yearbook. Jennifer's yearbook. I snatched it out of her hand.

"You got it! How'd you get it? Is she in there?" Feverishly I ripped through the pages. Somewhere in this book there must be evidence that Jennifer had been a scrawny, pimply faced teenager with braces, mousy hair, and a scoliosis back brace.

"Try the bent down page," Carrie offered dryly.

I found it and barely suppressed a groan. No such luck. Just a younger version of her present self. There was no God.

"Do you see this?" I moaned. "This is wrong. Just wrong. Even in high school, she wasn't a geek. How is that possible? Everyone is a geek in high school. It's mandatory."

Looking up I found Jennifer finishing her delightful story. I'm sure all her stories were delightful. Her companions laughed, delighted by her delightful story. So did the two guys sitting at the table next to her. Then, as if on cue, she glanced over at them, and with a slight tilt of her head, gave them a coy smile. They leaned in as a unit and grinned. *Can you say Pavlov's dogs, boys and girls?* Would it be wrong if I went over and punched her lights out? *Memo to me: Take that anger management class you never thought you'd need.*

"Did you see that?" I cried.

"A little louder, Joanie," Carrie said. "They didn't hear you across the street."

Scott joined our little party, carrying a brown paper bag. He removed a sandwich and presented it to Carrie.

"Thanks, babe," she said, giving him a kiss.

I continued watching as Jennifer launched a combination clever comment, alluring leg cross, and world class hair flip. A trifecta. The two guys at the next table were now drooling.

"Did you see the trajectory of that hair flip?" I asked, losing my balance and nearly falling backward.

"How can I see it when you won't let go of the damn binoculars," Carrie shot back.

At that moment "Patricia" arrived at the table, wearing her standard issue cream-colored suit. I wondered, would it be wrong if I went over there and let her have one up side the head as well—probably. She gave Jennifer the flying "kiss-kiss" routine.

"This is unhealthy," Louise said. "It's like the time you followed David Rand around all through twelfth grade—"

"I did not follow David Rand," I protested. "And it wasn't the entire year."

"So you did follow him around," Carrie said.

"I thought he liked me. I tried to provide opportunities to cultivate a possible relationship."

"And have your picture taken with him for the yearbook." Louise giggled.

I shrugged. At least it would have *looked* like I was with someone. Of course, I didn't say that. Twenty-nine-and-a-half-year-old women recently dumped by their fiancés did not admit to such things.

David had been in my history class. He was impossibly handsome and on the football team. When I found out he was my assigned project partner, my drool meter went through the roof. Our presentation was "Winston Churchill: Why He Wasn't Just Roosevelt's Flunky." We talked, he smiled, and I did the entire project for both of us. I thought we had something.

A week into the project, David began complaining to me about his problems with his girlfriend, the übercheerleader, Jennifer. My helper instincts kicked in and before I knew it, Jennifer was squealing with joy, hugging me at my locker because she and David were back together and better than ever. I did get a picture for the yearbook with David—and Jennifer. I marveled that it never occurred to them that they were taking romantic advice from someone who was alone.

"Forget David, Joanie," Carrie said. "You had Steve in college. You should look him up. Maybe he's a psychiatrist now. He can treat you when you have your nervous breakdown."

"You could be a little more supportive," I retorted. "I helped when you stalked Paul."

Louise gave me a wide-eyed, openmouthed look.

"I didn't *know* she was stalking him. I thought I was helping her work through her issues," I defended, returning to 007 mode.

Jennifer was still talking, her devoted audience still hanging on every word. What could she possibly be saying? What earth-shattering information could she possibly be imparting? Her quest for the perfect eyeliner? Unbelievable. The waiter was handing out the dessert menus. I would've liked a cheesecake and tea myself. Watching other people eat makes me hungry.

"I did not stalk him," Carrie clarified. "I went to his house to spray paint *shithead* on his car."

Scott pulled out a bottle of soda from the bag and opened it for Carrie.

"Thanks, baby," she cooed as she took it.

Louise was gaping now.

"It started as a healthy exercise," I said. "She hid the paint cans until we were there. She made me an accomplice."

Carrie sat up. "Hey, that *was* a healthy exercise—of revenge. Speaking of which, I wish you'd move on to the anger stage already."

I resumed Jennifer-watching. "I know. Wanton destruction is so much more fun than schizophrenic depression."

My gaze moved to Michael's mother. "I should have spray painted *bitch* on his mother's car," I muttered.

"Yes, you should have," Carrie said, as she polished off the sandwich.

"Why would you do that?" Louise asked.

Only Carrie knew the whole story. Only Carrie could truly appreciate the depths of my humiliation.

"She took the ring back," I said stiffly, while everyone at Jennifer's table broke into laughter at her big finish.

"Oh my God, Joanie, why didn't you tell me?" Louise cried. "Fifty-two percent of women said someone other than the fiancé asked for the ring back."

"You can tell 'them,' whoever 'they' are, they can make it fifty-three."

I went to the house expecting to meet Michael for lunch and instead found "Patricia," in that same damn cream-colored pantsuit. She must have one for each day of the week, the witch. She stood over me as I sat on the living room sofa, explaining fate and destiny to me and how Michael and I had neither in common. We weren't "meant" for each other. That's what she said. Thinking this was just another ploy to get rid of me before Michael showed up, I asked where he was. She ignored me, held out her hand, and demanded I give her the ring. I just slipped it off my finger and handed it over. I don't remember leaving the house. I called him, expecting anger and indignation, even an unconcerned chuckle and, "Don't worry about it, baby, I'll take care of it." What I got was the answering machine. I left messages. There were no return phone calls. After a while all I got was the continuous ringing of the phone. His mother had done a breakup by proxy. I didn't know you could do that. My shock and humiliation stepped aside to make way for good old-fashioned anger and infuriation. If he was done with me, he could have at least looked me in the eye and said so. When I wasn't wondering why I was still upset over a man who would do such a thing, I still missed him. I missed our train rides to New York City, the Knicks games, the trips to the Metropolitan Museum because he knew how much I enjoyed it. Good old clear-thinking Joan. I may be screwed up, but it was comforting to know I was consistent about it.

Now watching Michael's mother laugh with Jennifer, I swallowed hard, holding back the tears. "I would've liked it as a memento," I said.

"Screw that," Carrie said, "you could've sold it."

"You know a recent survey said sixty-two percent of all

women stalk their exes at one time or another," Louise said. "But, Joanie, they usually don't stalk the ex's wife or girlfriend."

Louise was right. I'd been crouching here for over an hour. *Well, Joan, what have you learned?*

"Besides the supermodel figure, man magnet personality, perfect skin, and flawless table manners, what does she have that I don't?" I whined. The answer was all too clear. "My fiancé. I hate her."

"That's the spirit," Carrie chimed in.

Louise patted my shoulder. "Someday you are going to find someone like my Stan. You will. Just give it time. You'll find the same kind of happiness, Joanie."

"Yeah, Joanie," Carrie snapped. "That's something to look forward to."

Louise shot Carrie a sharp look. I sensed we were on the brink of one nasty bush incident when a familiar scent filled my nostrils. My nose always knew. I felt a jolt as Michael came into my binocular view.

Strolling up to the table, he kissed his mother, kissed his wife, and settled in next to Jennifer. He smiled. He smiled as Jennifer spoke. He smiled as they got up and said good-bye to everyone. He was happy. Perfectly happy.

Unexpectedly, my anger stage kicked in. I looked for something, anything to throw. I knew heaving an object and having it land on his head with a satisfying thud would make me feel so much better. I looked down at the binoculars.

I got up, stretching into launch position, and then felt myself sailing to the ground as Carrie tackled me from behind.

As we rolled away from the shrubs, I saw Louise behind us, wildly waving her arms. All I wanted was one chance to bean him, just one chance. In the scuffle, the binoculars slipped away from us. I lunged for them and came up with—feet. My gaze moved upward past black shoes, blue pants, handcuffs, baton, and stopped at the gun. I gave an internal groan—Suffolk County PD.

For once my brain didn't drain. "My contact lens!" I cried. "Don't move!" *Excellent, Joan. Pathetic and yet demonstrates quick thinking.*

He hooked his baton through the binocular strap, hoisting it in the air. I abandoned groping around for the nonexistent lens. The officer, in his early forties, with salt and pepper hair, wasn't smiling.

"I guess you won't be needing these," he said. He wiggled his fingers, indicating that we should get up.

His eagle eyes fastened on Carrie. "Don't I know you?" he asked.

Carrie did a half turn hoping for sun glare. "I don't think so," she said.

He focused on me. "Making a public nuisance, disturbing the peace, and possibly"—he held up the binoculars—"attempted assault." His stern eyes bore into mine.

I gave him my best pathetic look.

"A warning this time, ladies, understood?"

We mumbled "yes," as he strolled behind us. We turned in unison to see him hand the binoculars to Scott, who was now seated comfortably on a bench, eating an ice-cream cone.

I looked back at the restaurant in time to see Michael walking away with Jennifer, his mother gazing after them, wearing a self-satisfied smile.

It was two in the afternoon. For me, the day was over. It was obvious that Jennifer was the pied piper—she led and Michael followed. He held her chair, he poured her coffee, he listened, he smiled. He was totally whipped, and who did that remind me of? Me. I had been so happy to have him, I became his faithful schnauzer. Now that I had seen them in action I could carry the weight of realizing how ridiculous I must have looked. Excellent. I was yet to discover the Holy Grail of Jennifer, but I knew if I kept searching, I'd figure it out. Tomorrow, it was back to the Help Wanted section. Beyond that, another cloud was hanging over my head, an event that I was looking forward to like a root canal. Next week—I turned thirty.

Chapter 6

A week later, I found myself where I had least expected: outside Tim Wells's office. By noon I had the lowdown on the previous secretary. Words like *nightmare* and *horror scene* were freely thrown around, making me feel much more secure; following a disaster left nowhere to go but up. The job offer had come in the nick of time and saved me from the dismal Plan B I had found: a night shift job doing data entry with a group of pasty faced people who never ventured out until the sun went down. Count Dracula's clerical sweatshop.

I sat at my desk, shuffling papers, trying to appear busy. I didn't have a clue. As usual my mind drifted to Jennifer and Michael, and I lapsed into deep internal debate as to whether he had left me over my tableware faux pas or the fact that I ate. Jennifer was a size six. I was a size six at birth; I hated her. I was mentally constructing two dolls when I realized someone was standing over me. I looked up. *Mr. Wells, I presume?*

"Don't you hate that?" he asked quietly.

I looked around. "What?" I answered timidly. I was out of the loop on the new employee pop quiz.

"The first day, when there's nothing to do."

Think, Joan. This could be a trick question.

"I already have a list," I sputtered. "I have filing to do and I've already started answering the phone. I can do both—at the same time."

"And chew gum?" he asked.

"Absolutely," I answered. *No, Joan. Wrong answer.* "Not that I would chew gum at work or while speaking on the telephone," I stumbled.

"Of course not," he said, handing me folders and a sticky. "File these, and call this person back. Tell him I need to move dinner to six."

He walked away, and then turned back. "You can do that separately or at the same time," he said with a wink.

I answered him with a relieved smile and watched as he disappeared into his office and closed the door. *Okay, Joan, not getting fired today. This is good.*

On Friday, I left work and drove to my mother's to celebrate my new job and my thirtieth birthday. What is it about women and thirty? Isn't it a little ridiculous to think your entire life hinges on one number and will irrevocably change because of that number? It's not like you'll go to sleep at twenty-nine and wake up at thirty to find your breasts saying hello to your belly button and your hips morphed into shelving units. And yet you're afraid it's going to happen. I often thought men and women were not so different. A woman's thirty was like a man's forty, only with obsession over cellulite. The number meant something. It was the shining beacon of the first milestone of your adult life, the crucial measuring stick of how well you had navigated the murky waters of being a grown-up. The education, the car, the job, the house, and the man. Did you get it all? Some? None? Beyond, the glaring spotlight on the mother of all questions: you're thirty, have you got your life together? Of course, you don't think of any of this if you're too busy having a life. Which at the current moment, I was not.

I pulled into my mother's driveway and sat there, staring at the small round flowerpots dotting the walkway. I thought about my father, Mark "he was a good provider, thank God" Benjamin. I thought about him every year at this time. I remembered our Sunday lunches; my parents would take me out. Before we left the house, my father would hold my coat and help me find my way into it, one arm at a time. Of all the things to remember, I never understood why I should remember that. When I started first grade he had a cough, at Thanksgiving he was in the hospital, by December he was gone. Every year, I always wondered what he would think of me if he were here. I slouched out of the car. This year, I didn't want to ask that question.

"How's the plumber?" We had finished a dinner of chicken cutlets and pasta. Ignoring the carb overload signal, I went to work on the chocolate pudding and whipped cream.

"He's not a plumber, Joanie; he's a friend of a plumber."

"Whatever. How is he?"

"Joanie, he has a nephew."

"No, absolutely no way," I cried. "You are not fixing me up. Do you remember what happened last time with the bodybuilder?"

My mother's expression turned indignant. "You didn't give him a chance," she accused. "He was very nice!"

"I can't have a relationship with a man whose first question is 'What's your body mass index?' Besides, his breasts were bigger than mine. Oh, and how about the accountant? Remember him?"

She got up and waved her hand at me as she snatched the shrieking tea kettle from the stove. "Patrick was a lovely man," she said. "I don't know why you stopped seeing him."

"Yes, he was lovely, Ma. Lovely—and married."

She sank into the chair. "He was married?"

"Didn't you wonder why he was only available for an early dinner Monday or Thursday?"

"Well, yes, I did." She pondered this as I brought the cups to the table. I observed my mother's luminous skin and was about to ask what new makeup she was using when I realized she wasn't wearing any. She had the whole stupefied glowing thing going on.

"You're having sex, aren't you?" I accused.

She took my hand. "I didn't want to upset you."

My mother was having sex. And I wasn't.

My mother placed her hand on mine. "Joanie, honey, you know, it's going to happen for you and when it does—"

I held up my hand. Discussion of my nonexistent sex life was so yesterday.

We sat in silence for a moment. "You know your father would be so proud of you, Joanie."

I doubted that but let the comment slide.

"He had such plans for you. He even had your name picked out before you were born."

"Daddy wanted to name me Joan? Why?"

"Oh, honey, I don't know. He just said you were a Joan, not a Jennifer."

My chi unhinged. "Who said anything about Jennifer?"

"I wanted to name you Jennifer," she breezed, as if none of this was really important. "But your father insisted." I sat there stunned. I had been inches away from nirvana.

She got up and crossed the kitchen, removed a white envelope from the drawer and handed it to me.

"Happy Birthday, Joanie."

Inside the envelope was a gift certificate to the mall.

Mental recap: fiancé lost to Malibu Jenny, evicted, living in hole, fired, broke, thirty, single, celibate, Mother having sex. Dead Father caused bad karma. Name meaning "God is gracious" equals life in shapeless garments suffering or praying vs. Jennifer meaning "white wave" equals life on sandy beach, size six bikini, long blond hair flowing in breeze, gorgeous man at side. Current life worth summed up by mall gift card.

I gave her a kiss. "Thanks, Ma," I said.

"Things will get better, Joanie. You'll see. I want you to go back to school."

"I will, Ma. I promise."

I drove through the quiet tree-lined streets, making my way to the Long Island Expressway.

The fog of the last few weeks was finally burning off, and my mother's revelation of the history of my name was the cool breeze that finally cleared the air. Darwin wrote of the process of natural selection; some people were inherently strong, others not. This led inevitably to "survival of the fittest," which ironically was not coined by Darwin but by his friend, Herbert Spencer, another philosopher who believed that those who didn't rise above were just out of luck. Yet again, my extensive education provided no true insight save this: some are born to be Joans, others Jennifers. But if evolution happens, then why couldn't I evolve from the one to the other? And furthermore, if we are the masters of our own fate, engineering our own destiny, which is somehow all causally related to sex (according to Freud, another nutball), then I had made a terrible mistake. I wasn't having any sex and I had engineered myself into a disaster. So, since I had evolved into this, there had to be a way to evolve out with the exact results I wanted.

I was driving on autopilot and before I knew it, had rolled into my driveway. I checked to make sure no one was around. Every time I pulled up the kids opened the front door and two-pound Cujo raced out, making a beeline for my lower extremities. Carrie suggested kicking it and seeing if it would make a first down. The coast was clear.

I made my move and the key was in the lock when I heard the door creak. The dog barked and tore off with screaming children following. I slammed the door and checked the clock. Seven-thirty. Carrie and Scott were coming by to celebrate my birthday. She had promised to give me a new do for my new decade but I was in no mood for a haircut. Having visitors would interrupt my yearly habit of introspection in order to assess where I was in the journey of life, and where I was going. Usually, I didn't do this while someone was giving me an angle cut with her boyfriend crunching potato chips and watching my fourteen-inch secondhand television.

Carrie tried to put the kibosh on the entire introspection process and move directly to the planning ahead part.

"Scott and I have been talking about you all day," she said, bringing the scissor down on a hank of my hair; it made a shearing sound and the locks fell, clinging to the smock.

I glanced over at Scott, attempting a mental picture of him actually speaking.

"What have you decided?" I asked as she made another life-changing snip.

"This new job is a good move for you. Insurance is a good business to be in. Everybody needs it."

"I'm a secretary. I don't sell insurance." More cutting and snipping.

"You're a secretary *now*," she went on, "but as soon as you learn the ropes you'll move ahead. You'll see. Weren't you like the only kid taking eight periods in twelfth grade?"

"I had nothing else to do."

"I should've gone to class," she mused, while slathering my hair with mousse and gel for that carefree wind-blown look. "Too bad smoking by the handball court wasn't worth a credit. Anyway, you're dedicated. And remember what you always told me? It's all going to work out. You always said that."

She was right. I did always say that. I had to stop saying that—look where it got me.

"So," I sighed, "I'm facing a bright future pushing life insurance policies and the value-packed benefits of accidental death and dismemberment, which brings to mind every relationship I've ever had. If I didn't impale them with flying cutlery or crush their toes dancing or spill coffee in their laps—"

"Except Steve," she interjected, trying to settle me down.

While Michael had a few small scars, Steve *had* escaped unscathed.

"He's probably a doctor in Manhattan. I could've been the wife of a prominent physician. I could've helped him work his way through med school."

"Yeah, so he could've dumped you for someone else after he graduated."

The loud whirr of the blow-dryer stopped the conversation but my mind kept churning. Yes, he would've. For who? A Jennifer, that's who. Because he would have had me; I wouldn't have had him. That was the secret. Were there not untold amounts of women who spent their lives snared by this very concept, the idea of waiting to be loved, that love was something to say please and thank you for? Darwin, Nietzsche, they knew—we are masters of our own fate—it's up to us to rise above, make it happen, not wait around for it to "work out." So what if Nietzsche lost his mind at age forty-four? Does winding up a babbling lunatic preclude one from having had any useful thoughts? I think not. Survival demands action. Carrie was right. It was time to stop taking inventory and move on. I was master of my own fate. I should have been a Jennifer. My father had been wrong. He gave me the wrong name.

I bolted out of my chair. Carrie switched off the dryer. Scott remained glued to the television. Apparently lack of sound hadn't broken his concentration.

"What?" Carrie said. "Your hair's not done."

I paced the floor, stepping over Scott when necessary. "It's not just the hair," I said.

"What the hell are you talking about?"

"You heard me," I said. "It's not just the hair, the smile, or the clothes. It's the whole package—the one I don't have. That I *should* have. I should've been a Jennifer. My mother wanted to name me Jennifer."

"Joan—my mother wanted to name me Angelica. Do you really think that would've made a difference?"

I wasn't listening. I paced, hands on hips, the plan coming together. I think I may have been running a fever.

"Jennifers are in control, they lead, they do what they want, get what they want, and take any man they want. Jennifers are a complete success," I pronounced.

"Joans, don't get twisted. A name doesn't make a person," Carrie answered.

"Carrie, throughout history, Jennifers have lived up to this standard—Jennifer Love Hewitt."

"Dumped by Carson Daly."

"Old news. She has a hit TV show. . . . Jennifer Lopez."

Carrie threw up her hands. "An ass the size of a parking garage!"

"That all men in the Western Hemisphere want to get their hands on."

"Jennifer Aniston," Carrie said thoughtfully.

"Proves my point! She blew the Jennifer code and lost Brad Pitt because she was *not* in control."

"But, Joanie, your name has been connected with successful, important women."

I strode back into the dining room, if you could call it that, and sunk into a chair. "Such as?" I asked.

Carrie searched and I waited.

"Joan Crawford."

"A freak with a wire hanger fetish. This is what you're giving me."

"Joan Baez," she tried.

"Adored by a generation of wasted druggies. When is the last time anyone heard of her?"

Carrie began to pace. I had her on the ropes. She stopped, stood over Scott and peered down at him.

Eyes glued to the television, Scott mumbled something.

Carrie turned to me, a beacon of hope for Joans everywhere gleaming in her eye. "Joan of Arc," she repeated triumphantly.

I stared at her, eyes misting. "Burned at the stake," I murmured. "Died a virgin."

I stood up. "If I had been Jennifer, none of this would have happened. There never would have been a Michael because I would have been with Steve. I could've had Steve or Michael. I could've had anyone I wanted. And they would've wanted me."

Carrie nodded but said nothing. I had made a decision and there was no going back. It was time for a change. It was time to reclaim my lost heritage and become the woman I was meant to be. It was time for Project Jennifer to begin.

BECOMING
JENNIFER

Chapter 7

It is a well-known fact most solutions to most problems are closer in proximity than one thinks. As I conducted a 360-degree virtual tour of my apartment the next morning, I found mine. I took in the books cascading out of the bookcase, including a dog-eared copy of *Sociological Trends in Ancient Mayan Culture* listing off a shelf. I had read these books, and they told me nothing. Obviously I was reading the wrong books. It was time to read the right books, and the next time I met a man I liked, I would use what I learned, and before I could say "Hello Jenny," it would be a done deal. I broke it down like a term paper. Above me, Kong and the Mrs. were having relationship issues at the top of their lungs. A door slammed, followed by Kong's pitiful bellowing pleas to "come out of there." *Don't do it*, I thought as I polished off my list.

My reeducation syllabus looked something like this: Men: Who are they? What do they think about? What do they want? What will make them run the other way? I knew what Carrie would say. "That will take five minutes, no, four. Next." Then there was the all important topic of the self. I made a list of the information I hoped to find.

    A. Personality Transformation:
        1. How To Become Someone Other Than Yourself
        2. Learning To Choose Style Over Substance

    3. Creating The Come-Get-Me Persona
    4. The Gift-o-meter: How To Get The Most Out
        Of Your Man

  B. The Joys of Body Image:
    1. The No-Sweat Way To A Brand-New Body
    2. Building The All-Spandex Wardrobe
    3. Taste: Who Needs It? Learn To Love Foods
        That Are Good For You

Okay. I probably would not find those exact topics. But I knew what I was looking for. Next stop: library. I rushed a shower and threw my hair up. I was almost out the door when the phone rang. It was Carrie. I babbled my plan with the ardor of a physicist discovering a new molecular structure, expecting the Nobel Prize committee to polish up my award. I was greeted with:

"Joanie, you don't need to do this."

I was incredulous. "Of course I do. How else am I going to get this right?"

"Joanie, forget the research. Guys are simple. Eat, sleep, sex, and sports. That's it."

She went on, telling me how I just needed to be myself and everything was going to work out. Being on the receiving end of my own advice, I hated myself for poisoning her with that nonsense. *Memo to me: Never give anyone advice again. Ever.* Mentally, I was already out the door.

"I know what I'm doing," I breezed, "I'll call you later."

The library stretched out before me, beckoning me into the hallowed halls of wisdom and truth that would set me free. It was quiet for a Saturday. I strode purposefully to the computers and punched in every combo I could think of: relationships, self-improvement, relationship improvement, improve self in order to have a relationship. The list was endless. After running between the upper and lower levels for forty-five minutes, I teetered to the checkout desk, my arms wrapped precariously around a pile ending just below my nose. I found myself in front of the quintessential library lady: small, thick gray hair in a bun, wire-frame glasses, somewhere between 60 and 200 years old, mouth curled perpetually downward.

"There's a limit on books," Broom Hilda said, giving me the evil eye.

I needed all of them. I did a mental scramble for a suitable *petite* fib.

"I'm researching a paper for my Women's Sociological History class at Stony Brook." *Excellent, Joan, excellent.* I think my nose started to grow. I smiled. She didn't.

"There is no such class," she said flatly. *Note to self: library ladies know everything.*

"You have a fine," she said. "Forty-six dollars in late fees."

She glared at me over her glasses. I stood condemned as a frivolous book borrower, a flagrant violator of the code of library ethics; an undependable library vagrant who took out books and kept them for six months, until purchasing the book would be cheaper. I didn't have forty-six dollars.

"Societal Mores in Sixteenth-Century Europe."

I raised my voice to show indignation. "I returned that."

"You took it out two years ago and never brought it back."

Damn electives.

"Are you Helen Benjamin's daughter?" she asked, peering at my library card.

Oh no. My mother and her friends of the library activities. All I would hear on Sunday was, "Joanie, you didn't return a book? How could you not return a library book? What if someone wanted to read it?"

"I'm sorry about your fiancé."

Even though her mouth was still curled down, her voice had lost its bite. My eyes began to sting, and I looked away. When I finally glanced back, she was staring at the top of my book pile. *The Woman's Essential Survival Guide: How to Find Romance and Keep Your Self-Respect.*

She grabbed the books and started scanning. Without looking at me, she said, "Just give me five dollars for the fine."

Fifteen minutes later I had the whole pile in the backseat of the car. I had a good cry and then headed home.

Back at the Mole Hole, I scanned, skimmed, speed-read, and bent pages while whipping up a dinner of Hamburger Helper and potato chips, which was as adventurous as I got in the kitchen since the unfortunate chicken incident over a year ago. But I would like it noted Michael was perfectly fine and the scar was barely noticeable. As I munched, I studied the guidelines, the rules, and the suggestions. Finally, in true term paper fashion, I hypothesized in a nutshell, the secret of the male universe. Unless you were in a coma (mental, physical, or emotional), every woman knew this. Except for me, of course.

Men want what they can't have, i.e., the Elusive/Perfect Woman, aka Jennifer. Since men only want what they can't have, then women must catch and keep a man by employing one of two personality types: the Goddess, or the Bitch. I know what everyone would've said. I had my own mental Greek chorus.

Carrie would've said, "They're shits, Joanie, untrustworthy shits. And they don't know what they want."

Louise would've said, "You just need to find a good one— like my Stan."

My mother would've said, "Just be yourself, honey. Be yourself and they will love you for that."

Wasn't that the problem? Nobody wanted the current model. After a lifetime of being Joan, when I tried to be witty or clever I felt like a comic dying in front of a tough crowd. By the time I met Michael I was like a live performance of Mummenschanz. He did most of the talking anyway, oozing relaxed charm as he relayed his college pranks for my nervous giggle. He was also a wicked mimic. Sometimes we'd stop off at a diner after a movie and he'd regale me with dead-on imitations of his parents and their friends until tears of laughter were rolling down my face. Toward the end—I didn't know it was the end at the time—he was somber and quiet; no more impersonations. He had probably grown tired of me. He had me and he knew it. There it was in a nutshell. *He had me. I never had him.*

The question remained: Should I embody the Goddess or the Bitch? I weighed my options against the real McCoy: Jennifer herself.

The Goddess: According to my studies, the Goddess required meticulous cultivation of all personality traits that were coy, fetching, or otherwise adorable. A Goddess is beloved by one and all. His family wants to adopt you and all his friends wish they had you. A natural by-product of this adoration would be a plethora of gifts: jewelry, flowers, gift certificates for pampering, and assorted plush toys. Of course, this aura required excellent verbal communication skills, so that might be an issue.

The Bitch, on the other hand, was a tad tricky. The perks were enormous: top of the line bling due to habitually playing hard to get, hard to get along with, and hard to please. The requirements for conversation were nil (he should be grateful you even showed up). The downside: holidays were high stress as his family and friends hate you. However, everyone would be in agreement on one crucial point: you must be great in bed or why the hell would he put up with you? That was pressure I couldn't take.

So, which one was Jennifer? She was the rarest of all creatures, a combination of both Goddess and Bitch.

Using the laws of statistical probability, I worked it out as follows:

If Goddess + Bitch = Jennifer

Then (Goddess = Jennifer) or (Bitch = Jennifer) = New Joan

Therefore, New Joan = Jennifer

After consideration, it was going to have to be the Goddess. After Michael's parents, being nice *and* having people like me would make a nice change.

Note to self: Spending three years repeating Introduction to Statistics—so worth it.

So I made my decision. Now I needed to acquire a few new skills. There was an entire package to being a Jennifer. It was overwhelming. In order to exhibit charisma, grace, and poise, one must enter a room without the usual Stoogemania performance: tripping, falling, or object breakage. According to the books, sultry eye contact was an essential. What the hell was sultry eye contact? Either you're looking or you're not looking. Somewhere between disinterest and a restraining order was sultry eye contact. I flashed back to Jennifer at her luncheon. She paid close attention to the person speaking, eagerly leaning forward, and then, without warning, leaned back and looked away. She reeled them in with sultry eye contact, then dropped them like a load of coal when they bored her. Everyone else did the work. She had combo moves as well. My research proved it: the smile, nod, speak combo; the turn, smile, turn combo. There were combinations and comments for every conceivable topic. What to say. *Make him think it's a privilege to be part of your world. Let him wonder if you care; he'll keep coming back for more.* How to say it. *Saying thank you is for wimps. Develop an air of entitlement. Make him wonder if he's doing enough to please you.* How had I missed this memo? I had jumped up and down like a bobble-head doll when Michael bought me a gift. The possibilities were endless. Why didn't I know this? Where the hell had I been when all this info was being handed out? Didn't the New York State Educational System realize all girls desperately needed this knowledge rather than the so-called "real" education they provided? The warped priorities of our country's educators were heinous.

There were whole topics I hadn't considered. What about makeup? *Makeup must be applied to appear as if no makeup is worn, leaving a luminous, glowing complexion.* How does one achieve luminous? I preferred to think of my regimen of light foundation and pale lipstick as the fresh, girl next-door look. That's probably why Michael walked off with Jennifer and her luminous, perfectly made-up skin. I would have to figure it out alone. Carrie's color wheel never moved past blue eyeshadow and Louise didn't do makeup. I sighed in relief; at least I could skip clothing. I had clothes, even one of those damn cream-colored pantsuits. The floodgates of knowledge had opened wide to welcome me. I felt a Young Frankenstein moment coming on. *I had created life.*

I bolted upright in bed on Monday morning. I had read everything. Now, could I do it? I needed a trial run before embarking on my great adventure as the new me.

Remember, Joanie, start small. Did da Vinci start with the Mona Lisa*? Was van Gogh's first painting* The Starry Night*? Was Rome built in a day? No, I say! It was not!* A small test module. Un petit combo: eye contact, smile, with a witty comment.

It was 7:15 A.M. I chose a clingy V-neck red dress for my trial run. The makeup application was running smoothly until I smudged my mascara and created a black half moon on my eyelid. I painstakingly removed the mascara only to find my eyelashes welded together every time I blinked. Beauty was a bitch. I was behind schedule and on my way to being late for work. I was working feverishly on repairs with a Q-tip when the phone rang.

"How's it going, beauty school dropout?" Carrie asked.

"Haven't I always supported your projects?" I snapped. "I wasn't there for you when you broke the headlights on Jerry's car?" Carrie always goes for the car. She said it hits them where they live. Jerry and Carrie had attended a wedding. Jerry dumped Carrie for a bridesmaid. He took the bridesmaid to a wedding he had already asked Carrie to. Carrie had already spent money on a dress. Carrie was miffed.

"Joanie, you're making this harder than it is. Trust me. You don't have to change."

"You've been talking to my mother."

"No, but whatever she said, she's right. Screw 'em if they don't like it."

I thought about her statement. Something else I'm not doing.

"Look," I said firmly. "I know what I'm doing."

That was greeted by a moment of silence on the other end.

"Call me later," she said finally.

I stopped in at the deli for my usual buttered roll and coffee with half and half. Usually, the place was a hotbed of construction workers, fertile ground for a test run. Today, there was no one but a gray panther in three-inch heels, her bunions yearning to be free. *Damn.* Then a guy came out from the back. He looked at me. I think I saw his pupils dilate.

"How you doin' today?" he asked, running his hand through his sandy hair.

"Better now," I said, feeling the heat in my cheeks. *Did I just say that?*

My comment took a minute to register; then he smiled. He smiled! "What can I get you?" he asked.

I let him slather a pound of butter on the roll. *Remember, never let on you have doubts about your self-image. You're fine. Everyone else has the problem.*

"Anything else?" he asked.

I felt my inner mute rising up. *Speak, Joanie, speak.* "What do you recommend?" I asked.

He looked me up and down, taking in my clingy red dress.

Smiling, he rang up the total. Grabbing a napkin, he picked up a big chocolate chip cookie and added it to the bag.

"You can afford it. Have a nice day," he said.

"Why, thank you," I purred, flashing a big smile. Compliments and food. *Atta girl, Joan.*

I took my time exiting the deli. Once outside, I allowed myself a brief moment to celebrate my success. Then I looked at my watch. Eight forty-five. Damn.

For the record, I was twenty-two minutes late. During the drive, I pondered which excuse to use. I kept several excuses on regular rotation. Stuck in traffic was good every two weeks, using either the "stalled car" or the "accident" for variation. You had to be careful with this one because there actually had to be an accident. After all, other people used the same expressway. My personal favorite was, "I wasn't feeling well when I got up. I needed a few extra minutes." This was a tidy excuse that immediately elicited sympathy without causing alarm, but it had to be used sparingly lest the boss think he hired a hypochondriac or a chronic sickie that would cost him a fortune in health insurance.

I was like a rat loose in the lab all day; the sales guys in the conference room loved my stewardess bit as I walked around the table handing out the sandwiches (Peanuts? Something to drink? Headsets two dollars.) Two of the guys asked me to stay. Of course I said no. *Always exit the field of play first; leave them wanting more.* The tight ass VPs were not as jovial, but Wells smiled.

Back at my desk the phone rang. My mother.

"How come you never ask if he's here?" I asked.

"Well, is he?"

"No."

"So why would I ask?"

Excellent point. Can't argue with that logic.

"Joanie, Marge's daughter knows a nice young man. . . ."

"Don't even think about it."

"He's a nice boy."

"You don't even know him," I countered.

"I certainly do. He graduated from SUNY Binghamton with a degree in business. He has a lot of hobbies."

"Translation—he has no life."

"You have to give the process a chance, Joanie."

"How's your process going?" I asked.

Dead silence. I decided to change the subject. "I was at the library on Saturday. Eva Braun says hello."

"Don't be fresh, Joanie. Sylvia is a very nice woman. Have you decided when you're going back to school?"

I sighed. "Not yet, Ma. I have typing to do now. I'll figure out the rest of my life over lunch."

"I'm worried about you, Joanie."

"I know, Ma."

* * *

I didn't figure out the rest of my life over lunch, only what I was going to eat for dinner. Occasionally, I drifted into a day-dream of how it was all going to work out. At least now when I thought that, it was based on reality. I was making it happen. Later in the afternoon, Wells emerged from his office and planted himself at my desk. I had begun to suspect he was not highly esteemed by coworkers and underlings alike. He talked a lot when he was with other people but they didn't talk back. He told jokes. No one laughed.

But I liked him. He laughed like a kid. He had lost a little weight, too, and with his thick black hair and dark eyes he looked good. He was always nice to me and patient if I didn't under-stand something.

I looked up at him and the lightbulb went on. The Big Kahuna of experiments. The Successful Businessman. Besides, he was happily married so it was no harm, no foul.

I settled on my strategy of direct eye contact, smile, and a small witticism. If it worked, I might learn the art of small talk, and the world would be a better place.

Okay, Joan, this is it. First, look up. Lean forward, focus, and hold.

"I really enjoy spending three hours with Jenkins working on the forecast," he said.

Okay, Joan, keep your focus. I threw in the extra nod and smile. *Say something. Anything. What would Elizabeth Bennet say? Holly Golightly? Bridget Jones?* I channeled my new inner Jennifer.

"Then you'll love the four-hour follow-up I scheduled for tomorrow," I said.

He smiled. And lingered by the desk.

"Did you order me a sandwich?"

C'mon, Joan, you can do it. What would Jennifer say?

"I thought about it." Pause for effect.

"And?"

"I decided that after the Jenkins thing, you deserved a re-ward, so I did."

He nodded and gave a small laugh. He laughed! Success! I could do this. I was not a social freak who couldn't communi-cate with male human beings. I could be witty, droll, even mildly amusing. I was on my way. Soon enough, I would out-Jennifer Jennifer. I settled back in my chair. This was going to work out after all.

I spent the better part of the week slowly building my combination moves. But I still didn't have a date and no clue where to find one. The situation was desperate. So, desperate measures were taken.

"I'm so happy," my mother crowed. "You won't regret this, Joanie."

I doubted that.

The entire process of date preparation has never been properly clocked. That's because the time varies from female to female. After all, one woman's eyebrow trim was another woman's eyelash curl. I think it's safe to say the mean average time would probably fall somewhere between one to three hours. I went through the Michael era wardrobe and chose the silky black pantsuit with square neck and lacy jacket that hid what needed to be hidden, namely an ever so slight pouch I tamed with light support hose. I recited my rote mental ritual: I should exercise more, I'll start a program next week, followed by, I'll see how I feel. Translation: I won't do anything. An abbreviated Kübler-Ross process, mourning the figure I wouldn't have. Too bad I couldn't get over Michael as quickly.

Carrie never liked the "before the date" part. She said it smelled too much of hopeful anticipation. Louise brought me an arsenal of *Cosmo* magazines, my new Bible. I skimmed as many articles as possible; I could see my Jennifer needed refining. There were entire elements missing. The element of mystery: ("Are You Predictable? 12 Ways to Keep Him Guessing"). The element of surprise: ("10 Ways to Keep the WOW in Your Relationship"). The element of romance: ("20 Ways to Send Him Over the Edge"). When did women have time to work? It was a time management crisis.

I decided to go for a new combo tonight. Mini hair toss,

sideways glance, and witty comment delivered in low, sexy tone. A trifecta.

I racked my brain to craft said comment as Louise scrunched my hair to achieve a faux appearance of volume.

"This could be the one," she said. "This could be your Stan."

"I'll settle for a Tom, Dick, or Harry," I quipped, ignoring the Olympic caliber tumbling routine in my stomach.

"Never settle," she lectured. "I didn't. I got the best guy in the whole world. Someday you're going to meet the right one and then you'll have what Stan and I have."

I'd heard *that* since I was her maid of honor. Right now, my future still looked bright as #1 in the Bridesmaids Hall of Fame.

"Joanie, are you listening?"

"If you were saying Stan called you on his way home from work last night just to tell you he loved you, then yes, I was listening."

After enveloping me in a cloud of hairspray, Louise wished me luck and took off. After she'd gone, I gave myself a final once over in the full-length mirror, and then I broke the cardinal rule of date preparation: never think. A self-imposed mental blackout was essential. All it took was one stray thought for the hell train of free association to take over and wreak havoc. Staring at myself, I realized that Michael never complimented this outfit. Steve never said anything about my clothes. There was a problem with my clothes. They were non-Goddess clothes. Non-Jennifer clothes. Why hadn't I seen this? In seconds, I was in a downhill spiral, ripping my closet apart for an emergency couture alternative and punching in Carrie's number on my cell.

"I have no Jennifer clothes," I cried, on the edge of tears. I blinked madly. My mascara was about to go down in flames.

"What are you wearing?" came the cool reply.

"The black pantsuit with the square top and Michael never said anything about it. It's not a Jennifer outfit. It's boring, it's mundane, it's Joan! I shouldn't be wearing any of the clothes I wore with him. It's bad luck. I should've given them away. No wait! I should've burned them!"

"Stop thinking," she said.

"I started and now I can't stop," I cried. "What if he doesn't like my outfit?"

"He doesn't care about your outfit, Joanie. He cares about getting laid."

"What if I spill something? He'll think I'm a slob."

"He doesn't care if you're a slob, Joanie. He cares about getting laid," she repeated. "Jennifers don't think, they just are."

I considered this as the doorbell rang. "I thought you didn't believe in any of this," I said.

"I didn't want to encourage you. You don't need this shit, Joanie."

The doorbell rang again.

"He's here."

"Call me later."

The quaint Bavarian style inn was full. I admit dating a friend of the family has perks. If it wasn't a first date with a friend of the family, we would've been eating at the diner, a hallmark of Long Island living. They gave us a romantic nook for two by the window. By the time we settled into our seats, I had come to the following conclusions: Brian was cute, able to put two sentences together, and most likely not an ax murderer. This was all I had gleaned before my glass of rosé arrived; things were going fairly well.

I made a very small mess of crumbs with the crispy bread (I waited until he dropped crumbs first). Except for knocking a small portion of the salad onto the table and a minor dressing spill, dinner was event free. I felt extremely proud of myself. We did the routine information exchange, our family trees, how long we had lived on Long Island. Now we were leaning forward, looking interested and sitting in a vacuum of bone-crushing silence. Oh joy. I polished off the wine. He smiled at me. He had a cute smile. He was nice. I was sitting across from a nice, cute guy. I decided it was time to turn up the Jennifer factor.

That was when the first flaw in Project Jennifer reared its ugly head. I was only prepared to respond, not lead. *Not good, Joan. Not good at all.* It was time for verbal volleyball and I was doing a Harpo Marx—without the horn. I was having a lively mental discussion with myself about this dilemma when Brian spoke.

"Where did you go to college?" he asked, smiling shyly.

Here was my opportunity. Reel him in slowly, keep him guessing. A true Jennifer never reveals herself—ensuring he will want more.

I did my combo, smile and slight head toss. "I've been to several. I don't like to be confined."

Excellent, Joan. A nonanswer answer.

He leaned in closer. Beam me up, Scotty; he's coming in for a landing.

"That's cool. A free spirit." His eyes moved over my face. "Are you—you know—with anyone right now?"

Boyish hesitancy. Adorable. I did a sly smile.

"Actually, no one is with me."

Smokin', Joan! Or I should say, Smokin', Jen!

He leaned back. I panicked—I'd lost him. Shit! How did I lose him? Wait—no—he was still with me. He stared at me, his eyes widening. A stare that normally translated into: "You have ranch dressing on your chin." But that didn't happen to Jennifers.

"You're incredible," he said. "I'm glad I met you."

I did a mental tap dance. The waiter arrived and presented two plates of veal. I ate while Brian became a chatty Kathy.

"I feel like it's fate that we met. I mean it is fate. Being friends of friends. Like *Six Degrees of Separation*. I wish I could be like you, you know? Just free like that."

I did a perfect cut of my veal (I kept it on the plate) and answered with a flip, "Well, opposites attract, don't they?"

Brian was approaching catatonia; his pupils were dilating. All he could say was, "Yeah."

I smiled.

He didn't smile back.

Gently he rested his hand on my wrist. "Exactly. And that's good, isn't it?"

I remembered to swallow before answering *(Excellent, Joan. Jennifers don't dribble)* and said, "I think it's perfectly wonderful."

I kept eating (one of my core strengths) while he resumed speaking.

"But what do you do when opposites attract and you think that person is the one but the other person, well, they feel trapped and then you love them but they don't love you. Have you ever been through that?"

Here we go again.

A true Jennifer knew how to handle a date pining for another woman. A true Jennifer would slowly and seductively unleash her natural Goddess and lead her prey away from the other woman all the while singing her rival's praises. As my mother used to say, "Every knock is a boost." And she didn't even take Psychology 101.

Unfortunately for me, I was still a JIT (Jennifer in training) and my radar was completely screwed up by the sight of Brian weeping into our shared tiramisu. I felt myself reverting back to Joan. Damn.

"She said she wanted her freedom," he whined. "And I respect that, I do!"

I was shoveling in the tiramisu solo now but came up for air to hand him a tissue. "Of course you do."

He appealed to me with adorable, imploring teary eyes. "Can't you be in love and still have your freedom?"

"Of course you can." I always did. I was so free I was alone while I was with someone. I was realizing I had been with Michael but Michael had never been with me *while* I was in the relationship.

"Her name is Becky," Brian whimpered. "You're just like her."

The couple at the next table were staring. *What? You think you're the only one whose dinner isn't working out?*

"I'm so glad." At least her name was Becky. It made for a nice change. I polished off the tiramisu with a sigh. There was no use fighting it. I gently placed my arm around Brian's large, muscular shoulder, slipped into my earnest social worker voice, and set to work repairing his relationship with someone else.

"Brian, have you told her how you feel?"

I swear I saw his lower lip quiver. I had never seen a grown man do that.

"I can't," he sniveled.

That's when I realized law school wouldn't have worked for me because you never ask a question you don't already have the answer to. More importantly, never ask a question you don't have the answer to in a crowded restaurant, because then you're an idiot.

"Brian, is it possible that you're afraid if you tell her how you feel, she'll reject you?" While Brian crumbled, I made a mental note to start a piggy bank for my much needed lobotomy.

"Yes!" he sobbed, throwing his head on my shoulder.

The waiter sidled over as if he were entering a quarantined area. I tried to come up with something clever but my inner Jennifer had closed up shop for the night.

"No more tea for us, thanks."

The waiter nodded and slipped the check on the table.

I refused to speak to my mother for the rest of the weekend. She followed her usual ritual, beginning with a series of messages on my answering machine.

BEEP. "Joanie, how was it?"

BEEP. "Joanie, why haven't you called me? I'm getting very concerned."

BEEP. "Joanie, have you fallen down? I'm going to call the police."

BEEP. "All right. Who knew? What can you do? Call me."

I didn't.

She finally caught up with me at the office when I answered my phone.

"Are you trying to kill me?" she asked.

"No, Ma," I answered. "I'm avoiding you."

"How was I supposed to know he was still in love with the other one?"

"You knew his shoe size—how could you not know he was pining for his true love?" I asked, my voice reaching a pitch only dogs could hear.

"Don't dwell."

Another of my mother's expressions that sends my blood pressure skyrocketing.

"What do you mean, 'Don't dwell'? When Michael dumped me, excuse me, when 'Patricia' dumped me, you said 'Don't dwell.' When I got tossed from my apartment, you said, 'Don't dwell'!"

"Joanie, I never said that."

"Well, you've said it so often I assumed you said it."

My first-date Jennifer test drive had been a bust. What now? Why couldn't I get it right? I was so discouraged I was about to ask her if I could come over for dinner. . . . Then I heard it. I strained, listening harder. Yes, music lovers, in the background, the soothing tones of "Bolero" were playing.

"Mother," I said quietly, "is he there? And no, you won't upset me."

"He's coming over this afternoon."

"I have to go, Ma." I didn't want to prolong the conversation. She might actually give me details. If she was getting her hair done in cornrows, I was leaving town.

"Joanie," she said timidly, "are you upset?"

"No, Ma, I'm not upset."

Why should I be upset because my mother was having clandestine sex at two o'clock in the afternoon? I was typing a proposal for long-term disability, fitting for my current romantic state; my mother was having afternoon delight.

I hung up the phone and called Carrie.

"What's wrong?" Carrie asked.

"My mother is having sex and I'm not," I whispered.

A moment of silence.

"Summit meeting at your place, seven o'clock. Get Chinese."

I hung up as Wells came out of the office and presented himself at my desk. I was settling into a routine with him. Every morning I gave him a perky good morning, tidied his desk, made his coffee, and took a discreet whiff of his warm, woodsy aftershave. He replied with a sweet smile. We were developing an easy manner and I was becoming more vocal. To date, it was the best Jennifer testing ground I had. Wells seemed to like it. Plus, I was churning out the daily charts and proposals faster and with fewer mistakes. It wasn't what I had had in mind—actually I had never figured out what I had in mind—but it was steady and dependable. I didn't have to worry. I was going to be here awhile.

As I continued typing he came around behind me, peering over my shoulder.

"Where's the Thomas proposal?" he asked. Without looking, I pointed to the spot where it lay on my desk.

"You'll have to show me," he murmured, close to my ear.

A ripple of panic moved through me. *Relax, Joanie, these are the games grown-ups play.*

Turning, I pointed at the edge of my desk. Our eyes met for a moment; then we broke our gaze and he walked back to the front of the desk. Lizzie and Sheree from Customer Accounts strolled past on their way to their cubes. They gave us an inquisitive look and kept moving, but not before I caught the little smirk on Lizzie's face. Being the office bitch, she'd be a busy bee for the rest of the day.

"Thank you," Wells said with a smile as he picked up the report. "Any exciting plans for the weekend?"

"Dining, dancing, the red-eye to Paris—the usual." It sounded light but suddenly I was in no mood. He stepped closer.

"Is that sarcasm I hear?"

Who told you to know me so well? "My fiancé and I broke up. He married someone else." *NO, JOAN! NO!* Why did I say that? Of all the people to share my thoughts with, why him?

Wells was quiet for a moment.

"I'm sorry to hear that, Joan," he said. He was about to say something else when the phone rang. Businessis interruptus. I picked up.

"Mr. Wells's office, may I help you?" I asked. It was Mrs. Wells. I hadn't met her, but we talked several times a week while we waited for Wells to answer his page. He was hard to find when he was in the building and even harder to find when he wasn't. She was pleasant in a semisnobbish way and chatted about the kids, the house, the vacations. I listened patiently to the tales of a parallel life I should've had. She would ask a few cursory questions about me but never waited for the answers. I put her on hold and looked at Wells.

"Your wife."

His face was blank, unreadable. "Tell her I'm in a meeting." I paused for a split second. This was a first. He'd never asked me to lie outright. It wasn't in my nature to lie; it was too much work trying to remember what I had said. I got back on the line.

"I'm sorry, Linda, he just stepped into a meeting." A few questions answered and a promise to let him know she called and it was done. Easy, no problem.

"Thank you," he said.

"No problem, except now you owe me."

Wells winked at me. Ah, the sign of collusion, the code for "we have a secret." So we did. I returned to my typing. I didn't realize Wells was still standing there. When he spoke, his voice surprised me.

"Joan—"

I looked up at him.

"Your ex is a jerk," he said.

I smiled at him. His face lit up. He did have the sweetest smile. He retreated into his office and closed the door.

The summit meeting had no formal agenda but plenty of comfort food. Scott parked himself on the floor in the living room in front of the television. The Thinker with chips in one hand and a remote in the other. I ingested huge amounts of General Tso's Chicken, soothing my chi into a peaceful state of equilibrium. Carrie fixed a plate of spare ribs for Scott, strolled over to him, handed off the plate, and stroked his hair. He caressed her leg, never taking his eyes off the television.

"I can't believe my mother is having sex and I'm not. This is inherently wrong. I could've been having sex with Brian." *So what if he was screaming, "Yes, Becky, oh yes," the whole time?*

Carrie stepped up and took the lead. "First order of business. Forget Brandon."

"Brian."

"Whatever. Forget about him. It could've been a lot worse. He could've told you all his problems just to get a sympathy screw."

I choked on a piece of broccoli. "What?"

Carrie stared at me, my cue that I had just come dangerously close to the precipice of revealing the scope of my relationship stupidity.

"Oh yeah, right," I countered.

"Louise and I talked it over," Carrie went on. "We're going to brainstorm and come up with the perfect place for you to meet someone."

"Thirty-four percent of women say friends helped them get back in the game," Louise offered.

"Is there a chance I may have sex at the end of all this?" I had my priorities.

Louise took my hand. "Oh, honey, absolutely."

Finally.

"Have you heard from Brian?"

"Thanks for keeping things on track, Louise," Carrie said. Her nostrils were flaring.

"He called. They're engaged—of course. He wanted advice on how to make the marriage work." I didn't bother suppressing a disgusted chuckle. Unbelievable. "I told him to respect her personal space and encourage her inner journey."

"Wow," Louise said, "that's good. *Cosmo?*"

"Social Psych."

"You gave me some of the best advice I've ever gotten," Carrie chimed in.

"When did I do that?"

"When Todd ran off with the shampoo girl from Cut Above and took my CD player, you said be the bigger person because my anger would only destroy me and not him."

"But you broke into their apartment and stole it back," I offered.

"Yes, but if you had given that advice to someone else, it would have been very powerful."

"I think Joan should stop wasting her time," Louise said absently.

Carrie's lips tightened and I wondered why Louise didn't realize that Carrie could take her quite easily.

I dumped the fortune cookies out onto the middle of the table.

"Oh, I didn't tell you!" Louise squealed. "Stan has a coworker whose sister has a friend who knows someone who worked for the caterer who did Michael and Jennifer's latest party!"

Six degrees of separation. Actually seven. Maybe eight. It was all I had to hear. Like a junkie, the monkey was on my back. I needed a fix.

"And they had grilled salmon and three servers—"

"Why do you put yourself through this?" Carrie asked me.

"And a small ice sculpture of a couple kissing," Louise finished.

"Did it melt—did she slip and break her—?"

Carrie glared at me.

"What? I can dream, can't I?" *Well, couldn't I?*

Louise was not to be put off. "So after dinner, in front of the ice sculpture, he presented her with a diamond necklace for her birthday. That's what the party was for—her birthday."

I didn't know what to say. I always thought that when I finally heard something about him, he'd be admitting he'd made the biggest mistake of his life and was leaving her, hoping I would forgive him and take him back. Fantasy number six. I absently started smashing the fortune cookies, sending the slight slips of paper flying across the table. I'll bet they don't have a fortune that says, "You will meet an asshole who will dump you and buy a diamond necklace for someone else."

The sounds of the television, Scott's gnawing, and Attila's little Huns revving up for a pillage party upstairs pulled me back to the moment. It was Carrie who finally stepped in.

"Thank you, Louise. That was more than anyone needed to know. When did you say you were getting a life?"

Louise opened her mouth to answer. I beat her out, choking back the sudden urge to cry.

"Was it just family or were her friends there, too?" I squeaked out.

"Joanie—" Carrie started.

"Well," Louise stumbled, "she said they all seemed close, so I guess it was family and friends."

"I was never close to any of his friends," I mumbled.

"Amazing isn't it," Carrie said flatly, and shot me a look that said, "Enough already."

"Were his parents happy?"

"Joanie!" Carrie cried.

"Okay!" She was right. Enough was enough.

"New topic," Carrie announced. "Sex and how to get some, right?"

"Right," I muttered.

"Okay," Louise began. "What about one of those trips sponsored by the library?"

"The AARP crowd?" I balked. "An older man—great—my wardrobe will appeal to him—"

"There's nothing wrong with your clothes," Carrie jumped in.

"And we'll have long talks," I went on. "I read books from nineteen thirty-six and he was born in nineteen thirty-six. Of course, we can only talk until eight-thirty because that's when he pops his dentures and goes night-night!"

"Approaching hysteria," Carrie warned.

"Hey, maybe I can mix up his glass of Denture Clean! We'll bond."

Scott cranked up the sound on the TV.

"Am I disturbing him?" I asked.

Sitting back, I took a moment to press a blood vessel back into my forehead. Why was this so difficult? Find a man, make sure I'm everything he's ever wanted, whatever that is, and make him fall madly in love with me, end of story. Simple. For everyone else.

"Okay," Carrie said. "Eighty-six the library. How about a seminar on diet and fitness at Borders?" She whipped out a bookstore flyer.

"I don't exercise and I don't eat right."

"Who cares? You look like you do."

"I have nothing to wear," I sulked. A diamond necklace. Where was Jenny-poo going to wear a diamond necklace? What was he going to get her for Christmas? A floor-length fur? A European jaunt? Highly impractical gifts.

"Look on the bright side, Joanie. Whoever he is, he'll be a health nut. You know what that means?" Carrie offered.

I perked up. "A clean blood test?"

"Bingo."

I got up and paced the living room. I was trying to remain optimistic, I really was. But my inner Jennifer was taking a beating and I wasn't getting anywhere.

"Why don't you go back to school?" Louise chirped.

"I'm not going back to school. That's not what I need," I snapped.

"Why not?" Louise pushed. "That's where you met Steve."

Steve was adorable. Not classically handsome but a sweet face you wanted to kiss. I liked kissing him. I should've expressed that more fervently.

"He's probably a neurosurgeon by now and saving lives on a daily basis."

"What if he isn't?" Carrie asked. "What if he's a podiatrist? What would you do then?"

"Have my corns removed at a discount."

I continued wearing out the dingy brown carpet under my feet until I turned to my friends in a fit of frustration.

"Are we saying there isn't one man for me to date on this entire stinking island? No one wants to go out with me?"

"I know someone."

We exchanged surprised glances and turned in unison to gaze down on Scott, eyes still glued to the television, chomping away.

Carrie jumped up from the table and positioned herself between Scott and the TV screen. "Who?" she asked cautiously.

"Marty," Scott said, hitting the remote button.

Carrie stepped aside and turned to me, her eyes lit up like a Christmas tree—or a psychotic. "He's perfect. Joanie, he's a nice guy, hardworking, easy to look at, and he smells good. I'll set it up!"

"Well," Louise said, ignoring Carrie, "I guess I'll head home now that everything's been settled." She gave me a tight smile. "Try to keep me in the loop."

I sighed. I couldn't always keep the delicate balance between the two. In a way, they each represented a different part of my life; Louise for the old, Carrie for the new.

Every momentous undertaking has moments of faltering where the hero (or heroine to be PC) seriously considers giving up, retreating, and going back. Wasn't it possible all of the great women of our time had these moments? Did Chanel falter with the test tube to her nose? Did Grace Kelly have a moment of doubt before saying "I do" and becoming Princess of Monaco? Even without the name, they were Jennifers. As miserable as I was, it would be all too easy to give up and stay Joan. I needed to move ahead. I wanted to be a Jennifer. I needed to be Jennifer. My future happiness depended on it. I was ready to rise to the occasion.

Chapter 8

Someone once said no experience is ever wasted. I don't know who said that, but it sounded wise. My first foray back into the dating game had taught me a valuable lesson—my wardrobe was more Little House than Little Vixen. I wondered if Michael left me for my fashion fizzle.

Mom lent me the extra money for a wardrobe makeover. I was keeping a running tally of the money I owed that she insisted I didn't need to pay back. Pushing back the thought, I entered Macy's and deftly ran the maze of "associates" aiming their perfume spritzers at me. After further research I now knew what I was looking for, the Holy Grail of couture, the little black dress. The whole operation shouldn't be difficult, as long as the dress was shiny, had a hint of spandex, and showed at least a mile of leg. An hour later, there it was in the misses section; it wasn't bigger than a bread box. How could I have come so far in life without realizing the full social and romantic ramifications of the little black dress? Heinous. The top was cut to sit slightly off the shoulder, the rest of it adhered like Saran Wrap before ending at midthigh. I frowned at my image. I had found the dress, but I also found the problem.

I'm tall, five feet seven, and had thought that I carried my weight well. Everything *was* in its place—but there was a little too much of it. I ran my hands down my sides where the dreaded love handles were forming and tried to suck in my jelly belly. Now I knew where the Ring Dings and bagels had gone. This was not a Jennifer waist, these were not Jennifer hips. The dress was Jennifer; I wasn't. I needed a Jennifer body, a lean, mean, sexy machine. I knew what I had to do but first I needed a few casual things. Something classy, sporty, yet seductive. I couldn't wear the little black dress to the Red Lobster, now could I? Three hours, four outfits, and several hundred dollars later, I exited the mall. I had the clothes, the moves, and the attitude, I had even curbed my tendency to klutz out; now I needed the body to go with the package. I stopped at my mother's on the way home.

"Aren't you going to show me what you bought? Why did you need to go shopping? What happened to that nice black pantsuit you had?"

I have never given up hope that not answering these questions will halt the conversation. Silly Joan. I sighed.

"So how many outfits did you get? Four?"

I did a mental scream. How did she do that?

"I'm going to pay you back, Ma!" I cried, but my reply was muffled as I was now knee-deep in my old closet. What happened to the exercise equipment I never used? The step bench, the exercise ball, the thigh master, the toning cords? I had an entire portable gym assembled from Sunday morning infomercials to tame my tummy, tone my thighs, and sculpt and define my chest and arms. My mother's voice was close. She was standing behind me observing my ever-spreading ass pointing skyward as I plunged deeper into the back of the closet.

"Where are my body cords?"

"What?"

"Where are my body cords!" I yelled from the depths of the closet.

"Joanie, I can't hear you."

I extracted myself from the belly of the beast, stood up straight, and smoothed my hair.

I spoke slowly, enunciating each word. "Where is my exercise equipment?"

"You put it all down in the basement," she said, turning

around and strolling out of my room. *My mother, my self.* Except she was having sex.

While schlepping the equipment up the basement steps, I decided that since I had been up and down a dozen times to retrieve all this stuff, I had already exercised. No need to use the step bench today.

"Ma, I'm going to pay you back for everything," I huffed as I hauled up the last components of the brand new me. The wave of guilt was rising.

"Joanie, I'm not worried about the money. Your father was a wonderful provider, Thank God. I'm worried about what you're going to do."

"Ma, I'm fine. I know what I'm doing." I did. Truthfully. Finally, I had things figured out. It was about time.

"Are you staying for dinner?" she asked.

"No den of iniquity tonight?"

My mother blushed. "Joanie, he's a nice man. I want you to meet him."

I gave her a hug and kiss. "I will, Ma. I promise."

All week I flew through my work at the office at top speed as if that would get me to the weekend—and my date with Marty—more quickly.

"Are you on coffee again?" Wells joked.

"Nope," I answered. "No artificial stimulants. I'm high on life."

He laughed. "What's his name?"

"I can only be happy if I'm in a relationship?" I shot back.

His face fell for a moment. "You're not quitting, are you?"

His look of concern made me feel warm all over. It was the first time a man had shown interest in me in months. Wells really was a sweet guy. Other people didn't know him like I did.

"Not to worry," I soothed. "I'm very happy here. And there is no he—yet. I have a date on Friday."

At five o'clock I was grabbing my purse to motor. He stared at me, an amused look on his face.

"I have to prepare."

"You need a week?"

"I would have preferred two." *Men. They don't get it.*

I had started an emergency exercise program. Ten minutes of stepping, ten minutes of upper body, and ten minutes of abs, which really only lasted five minutes.

After work on Friday, I was finishing a two-minute ab blaster when there was a knock at the door. Hauling myself off the floor, I stumbled to the door, my love handles peeking out over the waistband of my shorts. *More abs, I need more abs,* I thought as I threw the door open.

"It's six o'clock, time to stop the insanity, Joanie," Carrie said, checking out my black spandex shorts and sports bra.

"I'm making progress," I wheezed. "Don't you think I'm making progress?"

"Take a shower," she ordered, stepping inside. "Marty called Scott and asked if you could meet him for a drink before dinner. You have to be ready in an hour."

Oh shit.

Thirty minutes later I was seated at the kitchen table, peering at my pores in the magnifying mirror. Louise couldn't make it for the pregame. She had to visit her sick great Uncle Larry who nobody liked. I was packed into the little black dress. Underneath the little black dress were matching black bra and panties—black panties shrouded in support hose.

"I should've exercised more," I lamented.

"You look fine," Carrie said, pushing me into a chair and whipping out the hair gel.

"Do you think black was a good choice?"

Nothing.

"I could have worn the red but black has an air of mystery."

"You're a thirty-year-old secretary who's lived on Long Island her entire life."

"That doesn't matter. I can still have mystery."

I knew she was right. I hated that.

I had pumped her for as many Marty details as possible: height, weight, hair color, arrests, convictions, use of controlled substances. He was not a card carrying member of the Hell's Angels. We weren't going to be busted by narcs during appetizers. He sounded pretty nice. He was thinking of going back to school. Who wasn't? His landscaping business was doing well and he was planning to expand. Ambitious and studious. *Excellent, Joan. This could be a good one.* I would hook up with a man with enough drive to better himself by his own sweat. A stark contrast to my former fiancé, who lived off the fat of his parents, went to school on their dime, and then bought his wife a diamond necklace, which I'm so sure she really needed, and whose idea was it to buy that necklace anyway? He never bought me a necklace, that little—

"Hey, Miss Marple," Carrie said, interrupting my psychopathic free association. "Stop thinking."

Right. Joan, get your inner Jennifer out of the batting cage and up to the plate. It was at that moment that I saw a hair on my chin. I lunged forward, taking the curling iron with me.

"What the hell are you doing!" Carrie yelled. "You're gonna wind up with that bald spot you never wanted!"

"I have a hair—no—two hairs on my chin! I have facial hair!"

"And on the eighth day God created tweezers." With that she slapped them into my hand like a nurse passing a scalpel. How long had I been walking around with the beginnings of a beard?

"I'm Bigfoot," I whined.

"It's all the same in the dark, Joanie."

"Great. Then he'll only feel underarm fat, he won't see it."

Carrie finished the last curl. The hydrofluorocarbon marathon of hair spray followed. If I went outside with a telescope, I'm sure I would've seen another layer of the ozone evaporating before my eyes. *Memo to me: Make generous donation to Greenpeace that I will have to borrow from my mother.*

I surveyed the finished product in the mirror. Not bad. The silky jacket revealed cleavage but hid my less than perfect waistline. Carrie had swept my hair back, leaving wispy curls framing my face and revealing freshwater pearl earrings. My legs, always my best attribute, looked long and lithe. In heels, I was over five ten. Taller is always better. It's slimming. I looked eighty percent Jennifer. Okay, seventy percent. I got up, inhaling deeply—

"By the way, which one did you choose for tonight?" Carrie asked.

I stared blankly.

"The Goddess or the Bitch?" she clarified.

"Oh. The Goddess. Smiling and laughing is easier than snarling and abusing."

She frowned. "That's what they all say."

Entering the dim interior of the bar, I scanned for a blond, blue-eyed guy with a plastic smile of trepidation. We spotted each other at the same moment. He stood up. He was very blond, very cute, and he was smiling. A winner.

"Are you Joan?" he asked hesitantly.

I nodded. *Oh yes, my friend. That would be me.*

We had drinks. We talked. He made jokes. I laughed. We sat down to dinner and by the time the salad arrived I was wondering where we should have the wedding. What is it with women? Is it that whole gatherer/nurturer thing or an unhealthy preoccupation with lace? While we were munching on the fried potato skins, I was mulling over chicken or fish for the reception. His six-foot frame would look good standing next to me in a tux and I suspected six-pack abs were awaiting discovery. I knew I'd love listening to his smooth, silky voice on the other end of the phone.

Immediately, I went to work being charming, coy, and funny. I expunged any mention of nineteenth-century neo-Impressionist painting, the economic impact of the corporate-leveraged buy-outs of the eighties, and the Iran Contra affair. I asked questions and hung on his answers. I made eye contact but not long enough to be seen as aggressive. I allowed our fingers to touch across the table but not to suggest anything more than a platonic first date. I peppered the conversation with just the right amount of awe and praise for his business acumen. As we closed out the evening, I told him, with a smile and a hair flip, just how much I enjoyed myself. I allowed him a chaste kiss on the cheek and a brief brush on the lips. We made a date for the following Saturday night.

I screamed in the car all the way home. Then I screamed while springing like a human pogo stick from the car into the apartment. I screamed into the phone to Carrie.

"He likes me, he really likes me!" I shrieked, doing the Sally Field bit.

"Marty liked Joanie," I heard her say. Mumbling followed.

"What did he say?"

"He said he'll talk to Marty tomorrow," Carrie answered. "Guys don't do recaps on the same night, Joanie."

I didn't know that. Carrie knew that, of course. Undaunted, I dreamed of the flora, plush fauna, and/or chocolates that should be arriving tomorrow. I made Carrie promise to come over the next day.

"You're not dragging me out to exercise."

I ignored her.

I managed to babble a mile a minute as we power-walked around the neighborhood.

"I'm sorry I came over," Carrie huffed. "There is no reason to be doing this."

"Walking is invigorating. Keep moving."

"I can't feel my legs."

I ignored her. "So what else did he say?"

"Joanie, I told you what he said. He had a good time. What else is there?"

"But how did he look when he said it? What was his tone?" Details, I needed details.

"His tone? I don't know what his tone was. It was the tone

of a man who had a good date. Lucky for him he doesn't know it was with a neurotic lunatic. Can we stop walking now?"

"I have to get in shape. I have one week. I should eat better, too."

For the record, I wanted to eat healthier, except most health food didn't taste good; I found that to be a problem.

We turned a corner, approaching a small strip mall.

"Hold it, hold it," Carrie gasped. Ten minutes later, we emerged from the deli. I had a bottle of water and Carrie was working her way through a pint of Ben and Jerry's.

"Don't worry about anything," she said through a mouthful of Cherry Garcia. "Just be yourself."

I stopped short. "That was my problem," I said.

Carrie gave me a sideways glance as she continued to plow through the pint. "Look, Joans, don't read too much into this. Just relax and see where it goes. Even if it doesn't work out—"

"Great, another rejection."

We approached a house with a beat-up beige couch at the curb waiting for garbage pick up. Taking the opportunity for momentary repose, Carrie planted herself.

"I'm not saying don't be positive. Who knows? It might work out. Next Saturday night you could be in the sack before sunrise, but you have to relax. You look at every guy like he's the one and then you're disappointed."

"Carrie, I was practically married. Michael *was* the one."

"Michael was a schmuck."

"Yes, but he was my schmuck."

"You thought Steve was the one."

I did think Steve was the one. And where was he now? A shrink married to a Barbarella type who could bench press twice her weight and had zero body fat? He probably knew, even then, that I was going to be a couch potato; that's why he dumped me. How could he know I would wind up wearing a spandex onesie for the faux appearance of litheness? I looked at Carrie.

"Marty's going to want to have sex with me," I heard myself saying. Carrie gave me a blank look. Somewhere between the spandex onesie and faux litheness, I had come around to sex with Marty. My mind was a frightening place, but it was all I had.

"That's the point. Isn't it?"

"Yes, yes, absolutely." And it was the point. Well, not the whole point, but a considerable part of the point. It was an extremely large part of the point. But I didn't expect it to become an issue so quickly. I was so busy morphing into someone else; I hadn't considered I would have to *be* someone else in bed.

"Joans, just let it ride, everything will work out," she said.

"Don't be so me," I said.

She stared up at me plaintively. "I'm tired."

"You want me to go and get the car, don't you?"

Carrie settled back onto the couch and slipped off her sneakers.

"I'll be back in ten minutes," I said.

The following week I completed a mini Project Jennifer progress report: five pounds gone, new rags, new do, exercise routine down pat, one date with hottie Marty and second date in the wings. That led to thoughts of sex with Marty, which led me back to thoughts of sex with Michael. Rather, thoughts of the missed opportunities for sex with Michael. Against my better judgment I dug out my scrapbook and curled up on the couch. I thumbed through Michael and I at his college roommate's barbecue; Michael smiling on the boardwalk at Jones Beach; Michael and I, hand in hand at a pool party. He was always smiling. I guess that's why I always thought he was happy. I wanted to tear them into little pieces. I knew it would make me feel better. I couldn't bring myself to do it.

I finished the night browsing through snapshots of my father. Why couldn't I find a man like him? Didn't they make that model anymore?

The euphoria of my successful weekend couldn't last forever. Monday, it was back to the routine. Wells asked me to stay late every night but I managed to juggle the high-wire act of working ungodly hours and still exercising. Up at five, quick workout; leave work around six, home for another workout; fall into bed by ten-thirty. And the food issue? Well, since I wouldn't eat anything that tasted bad (read: healthy), I decided to cut down on food altogether—salad in a bag and rice cakes. Mmm-mmm good.

Dinnertime Thursday and I was sitting in Wells's office, a chair pulled up to the desk as we chowed down on Chinese food (the boss wants Chinese—Chinese it is). Realizing that I enjoyed our daily conversations came as a surprise; his war stories about the deals he had brokered and how he'd advanced in the company caught my interest. At that point in my life, he was the smartest guy I'd ever met, and he always said the right thing. Between forkfuls of pork, I managed to recite the list of proposals I'd completed.

"So, this is what happens when you go out on dates—your work ethic improves. You should be out there every night."

"I'll be out this weekend so you're all set for next week," I said.

He smiled. "So, you're going to elope with Mister Wonderful and leave me."

"Hardly." It couldn't be that easy. Could it?

"You think you'd get cold feet?"

"No—well—maybe. I'm not sure I want to get married. After all, I've gone on to bigger and better things."

"Exactly. You're doing the right thing, not crying over spilt milk," he said.

"Absolutely. Tomorrow's a new day."

He went to speak but I held up my hand. We were crossing into Joan territory. "I'm fresh out."

We munched on fried rice for a moment, then he held up his cup. "You're still part of a couple in a way—we make a good team, don't we?"

I raised my cup and we clinked. "Yes, we do."

Our eyes locked. We sat motionless; for the first time we had nothing to say. The quiet was palpable and becoming awkward when the phone rang. Instinctively, I leaned over and picked up the receiver.

"Mr. Wells's office," I said. I listened and handed over the phone. "Your wife."

He rolled his eyes and took the phone from me and said hello. As Wells's voice rose in agitation, that was my cue to pick up the carton of fried rice and leave the office. I settled back at my desk to daydream about Saturday night.

When I left on Friday, Wells grunted a good-bye. Bosses—they're so fickle. Today's typing whiz is tomorrow's flat-leaver. I had given in to the endless roller coaster in my brain. What if Marty did make a move? What if he wanted more than dinner? Could I do it? Of course I could do it. It was like going to the doctor, wasn't it? Open wide and say "Ah"—only in a really good way. I didn't actually know. *Did I just think that?* Too much time with Carrie. I shaved everything in the shower until I was as smooth as a Chihuahua. So Marty wanted to sleep with me. Fine. I was ready. I knew second dates, in some ways, were worse than the first. What were we going to talk about? The purgatory of imagined silences was already scaring the hell out of me. I needed to calm down and get my Jennifer on.

I imagined my inner Jennifer perched on the bathroom tub in a silky black gown, hair cascading strategically over one eye watching me tweeze the hair on my chin. She continued to stare condescendingly as I stood before the mirror and sucked in my stomach, running my palms over my love handles.

"Not too bad," I murmured.

"Don't give up the spandex," she taunted.

I had no time for this. I needed a list of topics to keep the conversation going. School? Books? Current events? Cooking? Some guys like to cook, don't they? My inner Jennifer was now perched atop my night table, flipping through *Cosmo.* *"Why don't you just bring an issue of* National Geographic?*"* I was sunk. This wasn't going to work. How did Jennifers make every man fall in love with them? My inner Jennifer was touching up her lipstick. *"How could they not?"*

I looked myself over. The dress was on, the makeup was on, and the support hose were on. I looked in the mirror and my inner Jennifer stared back at me. *"You're not going to wear that, are you?"* Oh shit.

At the movie theater, we were at Defcon 3.

"Would you like popcorn?"

"Yes, please." *Yes, please?* My inner Jennifer was perched on the counter holding an empty bowl. *"Please, sir, may I have some more?"* *she asked in disgust. Remember: Jennifers don't ask. Everything is yours. How much do you feel like demanding?*

I didn't even watch the movie. My mind was racing to the end of the evening. What if he did want to sleep with me?

By the time we got to Houlihan's my Jennifer skills were draining with alarming speed. Defcon 2. Marty was all smiles—he definitely wanted to sleep with me. What if he wanted to go to his apartment? I didn't bring anything. I didn't even have toothpaste. I should've packed toothpaste. How did women manage with those postage stamp purses that only hold a hairpin and a tissue? Where did they put their toothpaste? What if he wanted to go to my apartment? What if the dog got loose and bit him? We'd have to make a mad dash inside. He'd wake up to the sound of demolition, as Kong had decided to add an extra room onto the house. *Toujours l'amour.* Did I leave underwear in my bed? Why was Wells annoyed with me on Friday? I worked twice as hard as anyone else. What right did he have to be annoyed with me? Did I remember to put deodorant on? Did I trim my toenails? The salad hadn't arrived and I was exhausted. Through it all I still made small talk with Marty about his job and asked about siblings. He mentioned his sister starting college. Before I could padlock my mouth I was off on a tangent about books and classes, offering my tutoring skills, what books did she like, and, "Gosh, I like that, too!"

"You two have a lot in common," he muttered, staring down at his curly fries.

I was asking too many Joan questions, making too many Joan statements. Why didn't I just say, "I can't wait to meet your mother and buy you a sweater for Christmas." My inner Jennifer was choking on a piece of romaine lettuce. *"School books,"* she sputtered, *"what every guy wants to talk about."*

I panicked and mentally examined my options. Six years of schooling didn't provide scintillating storytelling and Michael, Steve, and my employment history were off limits. There wasn't much left. I recited my old standby: The time I set the oven on fire in eighth grade home economics. My inner Jennifer was yawning. Bitch.

I took a deep breath. "Why don't we talk about what you like?" I purred. *Excellent, Joan. Smooth transition.* I leaned forward.

"Football, cars, basketball," he said.

He gave me a shy smile. Ah, we were back on track. A few pointed questions and he was off and running, talking at great length about his car. Apparently, not every kind of car wax was the same. I did not know this. I tried to hang on every word, but my attention kept drifting to the soft curl of his hair falling over his forehead. As he explained the complexities of dual exhaust, I pondered the weighty matter of how it would feel to run my hands through that hair. I decided it would be very nice.

I finally steered the conversation to something we had in common: Carrie's past exploits.

"So you went clubbing with her," he said off the cuff.

"No." I shook my head. "Not my scene."

He leaned back in his chair.

Translation: I didn't go out. I didn't have a life. I didn't know how to have fun. I wouldn't be flying off for a weekend in Vegas. I was a loser. Defcon 1. *Big mistake, Joan! Big!* I could hear the siren blaring. I summoned my inner Jennifer. She couldn't answer. Gasping for air, she clutched her chest and keeled over onto the floor. She needed a crash cart. I needed damage control, Stat.

"I've never needed to go to clubs," I blurted. "Case in point, I just met this great guy and—you know the rest."

He smiled and paid the bill as I mentally mopped the sweat from my brow. I could do this. I knew exactly what I was doing. So it wasn't my best performance. But he didn't call me a cab, did he? He didn't go to the men's room and not come back, did he? Besides, according to Carrie, they're not paying attention anyway. God, I hoped she was right.

He drove me to my apartment, and came around to open my door and help me out. With an eye out for Cujo, I hurried him up the driveway and down the steps to my door.

We faced each other. He held my hands. This was it. Match point. I could pull it off. I made my boldest Jenny move.

"I had a great time," I said. "Would you like to come in and have a drink?" I congratulated myself on this fabulous move until I remembered I had no liquor.

"I can't tonight," he said. His eyes grew gentle. "You're a nice girl, Joan."

I moved a little closer. "I'm not always nice."

He smiled and gave me a kiss on my cheek.

On my cheek.

He gave me a kiss—on—my—cheek.

"I'll call you," he said quietly.

I nodded because that's what people in shock do. I watched him hustle up the steps and a few moments later I heard the roar of his car engine as he pulled away.

I let myself in, slamming the door shut, and dropped my purse. I sank into a chair. My inner Jennifer was sprawled on the couch hooked up to a heart monitor and an IV. She didn't look like she was going to make it.

"Have you considered a life in the church?" she gurgled.

Shit.

I tried to reach Carrie all day Sunday. Clearly she was ducking the loser chick—or protesting the whole Jennifer concept. Joan—Jennifer—what difference did it make? A rose by any other name was still a loser who couldn't hold a man.

On Monday I raced into the office just under the wire, went

into a momentary panic because I thought I forgot to put a bra on, and then slumped over my desk in relief when I realized it was on.

I'm a nice girl. What a rotten thing to say. Michael used to say that. I guess because we met at church. Going to church was yet another in a long line of my mother's great ideas.

We were sitting in the living room after dinner one evening when she looked over at me and announced, "You should go to church."

I choked on my knish. "Church? I thought we were only into the Father, not the Son."

My mother waved her hand. "It's good to experience other cultures." *And have a larger playing field. My mother was no fool.*

By the third Sunday, I had memorized most of the hymns, had my own Bible, and no one had come anywhere near me. My mother suggested I go to the singles functions. That turned out to be unnecessary because the next Sunday Michael walked right up to me and introduced himself.

My first date with Michael vs. my first date with Marty was as different as night and day. It was so easy with Michael. He took care of everything. He picked me up at my house, chose the restaurant, talked easily throughout dinner. He was in complete control of himself. I admired him for that. For someone like me who was always in a state of flux it was refreshing to be with someone who wasn't. When he asked a question, I answered honestly with the first thing that came to mind. There didn't seem to be any reason not to. He smiled; he listened. He made me feel important. It didn't take me long to fall in love. It wasn't a month before he brought me home to meet his parents, or Adolph and Eva as he sometimes referred to them. I thought his father was more Pattonesque, and his mother, "Patricia," appeared catatonic from the moment I walked in the door.

"Where is your family from, dear?" she asked.

"Brooklyn."

Her eyes glazed over.

"That's a lovely outfit, dear. Where did you get it?"

"JC Penney. They were having a sale." Okay, a massive screwup on my part, I admit. I should have said, "Oh, this old thing? One of our shopping trips to Saks." But isn't honesty, not to mention frugality, something to be admired? Would she have been happier if I said I wanted to use her son like a credit card? So they were champagne and I was wine cooler. I could be champagne.

"Your parents don't like me," I said to him in the car on the way home.

"They don't like anyone."

"Your mother looked like she was in pain."

He gave a little chuckle but never answered me.

At the door he kissed me and asked when he could see me again. "I like you, Joan," he said.

And that's how it began.

I finally got Carrie on the phone Monday afternoon.

"What's up?" she asked.

"A kiss on the cheek," I hissed, not caring that Wells was in his office with the door partially open. "A kiss on the cheek!"

"Marty didn't sleep with Joanie," she said away from the phone.

I drummed my fingers on the desk. My phone calls were now threesomes.

"Well?" I said, feeling my blood pressure shooting up to Mother.

"What?" she asked.

"Why not?!?" I said in a hoarse whisper.

"Why not?" she asked Harpo.

A low muffled voice in response. Then silence. Carrie came back on the line.

"We'll find you someone else."

"What the hell does that mean?" I asked through clenched teeth. "Am I boring? Stupid? Ugly? Is he afraid I'm a closet Yanni fan? What?"

"Not every first or second date works out," Carrie soothed.

She was right, of course. I hated that. "The most important thing is to get you out there. I have the perfect place. I spoke to Louise—"

"When? Where has she been?"

"She's had family stuff but that's over now. Anyway, I spoke to her and it's all set up. Leave a couple of hours early tomorrow afternoon and I'll pick you up at your place."

"You're not going to tell me what he said, are you?"

"Don't worry about it, Joans."

I pouted for the rest of the day. To compound my lousy state of mind, Wells was in a good mood. He talked, he joked with me, and then despite my coy and fetching scowl, he gave me the time off with no problem.

"Another date you need four hours to prepare for?" he teased.

"Yes, they're hauling in the makeup trailer and parking it on my lawn. A mini peel, some Botox, a little lipo, and I'll be good to go."

He gave me a long look. "Don't change a thing," he said, then turned and went into his office.

Chapter 9

The next day Carrie stood behind me as I examined myself in the mirror in a flaming red dress. She held up a hanger with a gray silk dress from the Michael Collection. "Wear this," she said.

"You don't like this? I like this."

"Wear the gray one."

I didn't move. I had my pride.

"It's mysterious," she said.

I gave up and snatched the dress off the hanger.

"What mystery? I thought you said Poirot could phone this in. And I don't understand why we're getting ready in the middle of the day—" I muffled, pulling the dress over my head. So much for my hair.

"Listen to me," she said as I emerged. "When you see someone you like, you have to generate interest. Make them come after you." She began to refluff my hair.

"And?" I said finally.

"Just smile, then look away. Catch his eye again, and then smile. Then wait for him to approach you. Wait for him to say something, and then talk."

Okay, I thought. I can do this. Would a Jennifer do this? Carrie answered my thought.

"This doesn't violate your 'code.' This is totally in line with the plan. Think about what's her name."

"Who?"

"The one Michael married."

Out of loyalty to me, Carrie would never call Jennifer by name, instead using *her*, *she*, or *that one*. Carrie was a true friend.

I flashed back to my unhealthy 007 episode at the restaurant in Port Jefferson. Jennifer smiling at the two guys at the table next to her, then chatting with her own group yet including the others, allowing them the great privilege of being part of her world. The tactic had worked for her. But she didn't need them. She had Michael. My Michael.

"Don't think about her too much," Carrie interrupted, short circuiting the warm feeling of rage welling up inside. "You'll go into this with your lips pursed and that's not an attractive look for you. But she does do the whole smile, smile, talk thing."

Yes, she does. And I'm going to do it, too.

Carrie drove into Sayville, an attractive town on the South Shore. We turned a corner on a tree-lined street to find it congested with parked cars. A party at four o'clock in the afternoon? Who has happening parties in broad daylight? Carrie found a spot, did an admirable parallel park and we were out of the car. Then I noticed the other partygoers. They were all dressed conservatively. All the men wore dark suits; all the women were in black, gray, or navy. A stooped, silver-haired man made his way toward a large two-story house with a circular driveway. He was not going to be getting his freak on anytime soon. I stopped short as the lightbulb came on and turned to Carrie.

"A wake?" I cried.

Carrie remained calm. I hated that. "It's the perfect place."

We started walking again.

"A wake . . ." I mumbled. "I don't believe this."

Carrie stopped, perching her hands on her hips. "Would you rather go bar hopping and search for some—"

"—schmuck to cling to so he can eventually suck the emotional life out of me?" It gets a tad annoying to have someone trying to save you from yourself. I knew what I was doing. "You went to bars," I countered.

"And do you remember Warren?"

I didn't.

"We met at Vanderbilts'. He had just been dumped by that blond-haired bitch."

Wasn't ringing any bells.

"And the next time we were at Vanderbilts', somewhere in the middle of 'Stayin' Alive' on seventies night, he ran back to her and I had to take a cab home."

There didn't seem to be much to say except, "Oh yeah."

"Listen to me. This is the best place to meet men. They have to be nice. It takes at least three dates before the wake aura wears off."

"And what's my opening line?" I asked. "Gee, I'm sorry for your loss, what you need now to ease your pain is a committed relationship?"

Carrie was about to answer when Louise rushed up, face flushed. As things clicked into place, I could feel my face reddening with embarrassment. My friend, my best friend since third grade, lost a relative and I was using the wake as a meat market.

"Oh, Louise," I said, reaching for her hand, "was it Uncle Larry?"

Louise barely nodded, then said breathlessly, "I did a sweep. There are at least three eligibles. Everyone's come out of the woodwork for this one. He never spent a dime when he was alive so they're sure there's money and they want to see who gets it." She smiled at me. "One of them has had two jobs in the last year."

"Forget him, he's a loser," Carrie said.

Scott wandered up and snaked his arm around Carrie, rubbing her back.

"Are we going in?" he asked. "All the food will be gone."

I stared at him. Chaplin speaks. Everyone turned to me. I felt like a colonel in a military operation waiting to give the final go. "*Well, all dressed up . . .*"

"We're going in," I said.

"Great," Carrie said. "I told her, this is the perfect place to meet someone."

Louise looked at me. "Eighty percent of couples who met at funerals said they had at least three dates before the breakup."

"What did I tell you, Joanie?" Carrie said.

I would take what I could get. "I thought the rule was you couldn't break up before a major holiday," I said. Which I guessed was why Michael broke up with me by proxy two weeks into January.

"That too," Carrie said.

"Not every holiday," Louise said, taking my arm and moving the group forward. "Just Valentine's Day or Christmas."

"What about Thanksgiving?" I asked.

"Who gives a shit about Thanksgiving?" Carrie returned. "It's just a dead bird."

I put my arm around Louise as we walked up the driveway.

"Louise, I'm really sorry about Uncle Larry," I said quietly.

She patted my hand. "That's okay, Joanie. Everyone hated him."

We entered the playing field and scoped out the situation. It lacked a certain funereal air, which I guessed had a lot to do with Louise's statement. As I thought about it, Louise's "Uncle Larry stories" came back to me. It's nice to put a face to a name—or an urn. I remembered that Uncle Larry had built a distinguished career performing increasingly greater acts of dishonesty directed against his own family. This was the Uncle Larry who convinced family members to go into a time share; giving their cash was the only sharing going on. The sure-fire pyramid scheme that left only Larry at the top followed. Then there was the jewelry exchange outlet that was supposed to make a fortune but fizzled. Apparently, cubic zirconia is easier to spot than Larry thought. Through it all he cried poverty, gave no birthday or Christmas gifts and never contributed to any shared family expenses. Polonius would have been so proud.

The first person we ran into was Louise's nana. She was old, tiny, volatile, and completely uncontrollable; all the prerequisites of a good nana. The family had been talking about sending Nana to a facility where she would be taken care of, but I doubted she would be taken alive—good for her.

Louise wrapped her arms around the little old lady.

"Hi, Nana," she said, giving her a bear hug. I expected Nana to compress like a tube of toothpaste.

"How are you, sweetheart, and your beautiful babies? You look thin," she added, giving Louise a myopic look. "You need to eat. Doesn't she look thin?"

Suddenly Louise was hemmed in on all sides by geriatric panthers commiserating about her weight.

Then Nana turned her eagle eyes on me. "Who's this?" she demanded, invading my personal space. "Who are you?"

"Joan," I squeaked.

"Did you know Larry?" she interrogated.

I shook my head.

"Good! He should burn in hell," she said. "You're not too thin. You look healthy." *Note to me: Consider emergency stomach stapling.* When anyone over the age of seventy tells you you look healthy, you need Weight Watchers.

Out of the corner of my eye, I caught Carrie and Scott backing away, taking refuge by the staircase. Traitors.

"Nana, she's here for me," Louise soothed, putting her hands on Nana's shoulders. "Nana, we're going to have the service soon."

"The bastard, he should burn in hell!" she repeated in stereo.

I could swear I heard a silent chorus of "Say it, Grandma" go up. Louise nodded at me. I made my getaway while I had the chance.

Safely out of the Nana Zone, I regrouped with Carrie and Scott. We scoped the buffet for any single guys but everyone seemed to be coupled.

Carrie was wearing a worried scowl.

"What's wrong?" I asked.

"We should've gotten here earlier," she said, looking grim.
I began to panic.

"It's easier to get them before they pair off, but don't worry."

Louise appeared at my side, carrying a Dom DeLuise portion of blackout cake. "It was the only way I could get away
from Nana," she said, ditching the plate and pointing out
three guys. "Okay—here's the scoop," she began.

Bachelor #1 was a blond, clean-shaven accountant from
Smithtown who enjoyed numbers crunching, watching the
game with the guys, and romantic weekends in Vegas. "He also
enjoys Rogaine," Carrie added, "soon to be moving to hair
plugs." I chanced a glance; his hairline was heading north.

Bachelor #2 was a dark-haired, bearded electrician originally from Queens. He enjoyed walks on the beach, doing
shots with his buddies, and riding his motorcycle on warm af-
ternoons.

"He's kind of cute," I said.

"He knows that," Carrie said. "He'll be schtupping some
bimbo on the side inside a month."

Bachelor #3 was a slightly disheveled unemployed loser
who enjoyed stretching his budget, meeting new challenges
like paying rent, and occasionally living with his mother. He
was really cute. It was a shame.

"Don't bother," Carrie said.

"Why not?" I protested. "Giving a little sympathy doesn't
hurt."

"Would you like to give it on top or on the bottom? That's
the only sympathy he's looking for. Forget him." Naturally all
three liked fine dining but if I hooked up with Bachelor #3, I'd
be paying for the meal.

Carrie shrugged and patted my shoulder. "If this is all that's
available, do what you can. Remember—smile, smile, talk."

Louise's words of encouragement were, "We have thirty
minutes before the service. It shouldn't take too long. They're
not letting anyone give testimonials."

"Why not?"

"They're afraid someone will smash the urn."

And then they left me.

I mentally explained away why finding a boyfriend at a man's wake was not a mortal sin since a) no one liked the deceased, b) others were encouraging me to do this so it must be okay and c) I was sure I wasn't breaking new ground here. Somewhere in this universe there was a couple telling their children how Mommy and Daddy met at a funeral. Wasn't there?

I had to decide which of the three to start with. Bachelor #1 was probably more stable, but Bachelor #2 was cute so I started with him. *Smile, smile, talk. Easy.* I spotted him by the entrance to the kitchen, talking to some blonde.

When the blonde walked off to the buffet I took my opportunity. Smile, Jenny—smile. I smiled. He smiled. The blonde came back and they began to talk. Okay—well, what did I want? An orchestral overture as he sprinted across the room to me? One smile down, one to go. *Okay—work the room.* Cleverly positioning myself where I could be easily seen, I smiled at an octogenarian who sidled over to explain his bladder dysfunction. I pretended to laugh as if his cystoscopy was hilarious so Bachelor #2 would think I was witty, charming, and nice to the elderly. I caught his eye again, and *Smile!* He grinned and put his arm around the blonde. Five minutes later, he was free of the blonde, I was free of Grandpa, he saw I was available and— he walked back into the kitchen.

I had a vision of a schoolteacher leading her young pupils on a field trip through the house and stopping in front of me. Turning to her students, she asks, *"Boys and girls, what does this recent event tell us?"* A six-year-old blond girl steps forward and pipes up, *"From a sociological perspective, we can conclude that the male has no interest in this particular female because she does not exude qualities of allure or mystery typically found in a female with a Jennifer persona. And she's a nice girl."* I was so screwed.

I sighed. Nothing was happening. I looked around and caught Carrie's eye. She motioned to her left. Bachelor #1, at the buffet table, with the plate. I remembered her tip: *Don't start with the confident ones. Start with someone who's a little self-conscious.* The whole pate problem was an equalizer. Strolling over as if the only thing on my mind was sampling the potato salad, I eased up to him. He was spooning out a heaping portion of macaroni salad. This was the moment. It was now or never with Rogaine Man. *Screw smile, smile, talk.* I put my best Jennifer foot forward and said: "My name is Joan." *Excellent, Joan. Highly original. Why don't you ask him what his sign is?*

"Dennis," he replied.

"Funerals are so hard," I blathered, piling food onto my plate as I moved down the line. "You never know what to do or say and I just find them so difficult, you know? Really, all you can do is eat and say you're sorry. And then be sorry for doing all that eating."

Giving what I thought was a cute chuckle, I looked over, to find Dennis gone. *How long has he been gone?* I thought. How many people were watching the lunatic talk to herself? Immediately I regrouped. Reaching out and grasping the table as I bent low, I went to my old standby. "I've lost my contact lens, can you help me?" I had half a dozen people looking.

Making apologies, I said I had a spare and fled upstairs in tears. I was going to lie down in an empty bedroom the way they always do in the movies but when I opened Door #1 I found Bachelor #3 getting it on with a brunette. It was comforting to see a loser getting laid. It gave me hope.

Finally, I found an empty room. Well, not quite empty. On a table near the fireplace, Uncle Larry rested in his genie bottle urn. Strolling over to the fireplace, I looked at the pictures on the mantel, imagining the lives of these strangers, their marriages, relationships, children—all things I didn't have. That I couldn't seem to have no matter what I did.

I made an abrupt turn away from the fireplace, bumping against the table. Hearing a soft thumping noise, I looked down to find the urn lying on its side and gasped. Uncle Larry was out there, literally, in a pile on the carpet. Someone had forgotten to seal the cap on the urn. I looked at my watch and whimpered. In five minutes, Uncle Larry, in his urn, was supposed to be on display downstairs. And I couldn't think straight because next door, Bachelor #3 was moaning!

I began some strange hand-flapping dance as if trying to conjure Barbara Eden to suck Uncle Larry back up into his bottle. Running to the closet, I threw open the door, scanning for a broom. What if someone walked in? The news would race through the house like wildfire. Maybe I could blame it on the lost contact lens. While pondering the sacrilegious implications of using a broom, I spotted my salvation. Plunging into the closet I came out with—a DustBuster. I stood there looking at it. If a broom was sacrilegious, a DustBuster was a free ride to hell. I looked down at Uncle Larry and up at the clock. I made the sign of the cross and got down to it.

I flipped it on. Dead! I shook it. Nothing. I gave it a whack. Still nothing. For the love of God and all that's holy, why don't people charge their household appliances! Dropping to my knees and praying for enough juice to suck up Larry, I plugged it into the wall socket and hit the button. It gave off a low whir. Thank God, I muttered, and then felt a wave of guilt. This was the sum total of a man's life. I was about to Hoover the dead.

The door opened. With a shriek I jumped up, the Dust-Buster sucking thin air.

Carrie looked from me to the floor.

"Uncle Larry had an accident," I cried.

"No shit," Carrie said. Shuffling over, she stood next to me, looking down on the essence that was Larry.

Louise ran in. "What's everyone doing up here?" she asked, following our gaze. "Oh."

"Louise, I'm so sorry," I said above the whine of the Dust-Buster.

"Oh, honey, don't worry, we just have to get the rest of him off the floor."

And into an urn with a neck as thin as a straw.

Scott wandered in, munching on a sandwich. "What are we looking at?" he asked.

"Uncle Larry," Carrie replied.

"No shit," he said. They were made for each other.

We stood around the pile. New waves of guttural moans came through the wall.

"What the hell—?" Carrie said.

"Bachelor Number Three," I whimpered. "And I'm going to hell."

"Try it again," Carrie said.

Scott backed toward the door.

I looked to Louise.

"It's not like it's really him, Joanie," she said.

"If this doesn't work, we'll sweep him under the rug," Carrie said. "Let 'er rip."

I got down to it and Uncle Larry began to disappear. As I clicked it off, I could feel my eyes widen.

"Now what?" Carrie asked.

"I didn't clean out the dirt cup first."

We looked into the dirt cup; a cigarette butt rested among the ashes. . . . Oh, the humanity.

Carrie removed the dirt cup and a small puff of Larry escaped into the air. Next door everything was quiet. Bachelor #3 must be smoking a cigarette. We had only minutes to get Uncle Larry back into his resting place.

My hands were shaking as I tried to ease the ashes into the narrow spout of the urn. "We need a funnel," I muttered.

"Give it to me," Carrie said, tapping the DustBuster and sending ashes flying everywhere. I'd like to think a small amount of Larry returned to his resting place but as the cigarette butt tumbled into the urn, I had my doubts.

Suddenly, we heard footsteps coming up the stairs. We froze. Carrie grabbed an ashtray.

"No, no," I cried, tugging it away from her.

"It's good enough," she said, holding it out. I dumped the remainder of the cup into the ashtray.

"He always did like a good smoke," Louise said.

I put the cap on the urn.

"What the hell are you doing in here?" Nana's voice bellowed in the hallway. "What the hell's the matter with you?" Scampering footsteps followed. Bachelor #3 had been busted.

Nana would be making the rounds. We were next. There was no escaping the wrath of Nana.

Carrie put the urn back on the table and threw the DustBuster back into the closet.

There was a rustling noise behind us. We turned as a unit. Scott had abandoned his post; Nana stood in the doorway. Louise rushed over to her.

"Hi, Nana, are you okay? We were just bringing Uncle Larry down."

"He should burn in hell," she said, patting Louise's cheek. I looked at Nana. She looked at me and at the urn. Did she know? Only Nana knew for sure and she wasn't saying. That was one cool Nana.

We straggled downstairs into the den, Louise reverently carrying Uncle Larry. The urn stood on a small table. The minister said a few words. No one cried. Lots of people smoked. Someone brought down an extra ashtray from upstairs. *Uncle Larry, come on down!*

Somewhere between the minister eulogizing Uncle Larry as "frugal" and then "cautious," the ashtray was passed around, someone took a drag on a cigarette and tapped fresh ash onto Uncle Larry. My heart sank like a stone. I had disturbed a man's spirit, his aura, his eternal rest. Oh yeah, I was so gonna burn.

I caught Carrie's eye. She shrugged.

What kind of person am I? I thought miserably as Nana came up next to me and patted my cheek. "Don't worry, honey. It's about time someone blew a little smoke up his ass. You're a nice girl." Such was the final judgment of Nana. Amen.

As the service broke up, I saw him. Medium height, sandy brown hair, goatee, slim. I smiled. He smiled back. *Here we go again.* I collected my coat, and as the crowd parted, saw him again. What the hell. I smiled. He smiled back.

As we filtered toward the front door, we found ourselves next to each other. "Not a popular man, Uncle Larry," I commented.

"No," he agreed. "You can't choose your family." The comment was without bitterness.

"Spoken like a friend of the family, rather than a member," I said.

He smiled. "I'm a friend of one of the nephews. What's your name?"

My spiritual name is Jennifer but my friends call me Klutzy Joan. "Joan," I replied, beating back my inner rant.

"Ed," he returned; then he was pulled away by a nephew.

Carrie sidled up beside me. "So?"

"Bachelor Number Four," I said.

"Call me," she said, going out the door with Scott.

I got the breakdown from Louise. Thirty-two, single, unattached. Last girlfriend moved for a job change. Not ready for marriage. Friend of Cousin Peter. Generally known as a nice guy. Engineering degree. I was expecting blood type but she didn't offer that.

It was an unexpected end to a full day of disturbing the dead when Ed asked me to grab a cup of coffee. I fought back the faint voice of my inner me, the little voice asking, "Joanie, what are you doing?" At the end of the day I had my answer. Going out on a date with Ed next Saturday night.

Chapter 10

Saturday night didn't turn into Sunday morning but the next three Saturday nights. One night, he had to stop back at his place, and I did a fast inspection. There were no foul smells emanating from his basement, the backyard had not recently been dug up, and there weren't any obvious penchants for whips, chains, or on the flip side, ladies undergarments. I reported my findings to Carrie one afternoon as she lazed on my couch reading *Vanity Fair.*

"I think he's normal," I announced. That was a bold statement to make to Carrie.

"None of them are normal," she said. "They only appear normal."

That comment always upset me. It conjured up visions of my father, a nice, gentle man in a suit and tie. Was he wearing panty hose underneath?

"Some men are normal," I defended.

Carrie flipped a page without looking up. "No they aren't," she said matter-of-factly. "If we knew half of what they were thinking, we'd never go near them. They're all perverts."

"Does that include Houdini?" My new nickname for Scott after his disappearing act at Uncle Larry's wake.

Carrie looked up at me quizzically. I found it amazing that the entire debacle had gone right over her head. For every rotten thing a guy did to her, something was broken. A window, a nose, or various household electronics or appliances. Carrie was nondiscriminatory in her destruction. Personally, I liked her equal opportunity thinking. I directed her down memory lane.

"Scott. The wake?"

She shrugged. "He was hungry."

Love, this is Carrie. Carrie say hello to Love. Love has a fabulous pair of rose-colored glasses for you to try on today.

My friends reacted differently to Ed than to Michael. Carrie actually spoke to him. She even suggested we double date for dinner and a movie. The few times she met Michael she barely grunted. Louise said she was happy for me followed by a warning that forty-six percent of all potential relationships die by the third date. I watched for signs of demise. On our third date he suggested we share dessert and I experienced momentary panic, thinking he was hinting that I needed to lose more weight. I considered bulimia but my mother raised me to never waste food.

I began to panic. Was I missing some sign, a clue that something was wrong? I pressed Louise on the subject over lunch.

"You think he's okay? You think we're okay?"

Louise took my hand. "Oh, honey, yes. He's wonderful. Remember, Joanie, Ed is the lucky one."

Yes, I needed to remember that. I must practice my Jennifer exercises—expectation, entitlement, and effortless grace.

"You'll forget all about Michael," she said, and then proceeded to give me a full update.

"Now they have this house in Great Neck and Jennifer works for some fashion designer in New York City. My friend Mary is the receptionist at Jennifer's salon. I can get you updates all the time."

Super.

"You know Jennifer completed her four-year degree at FIT with honors. Did I tell you that? Mary said Jennifer was wearing a fantastic outfit when she came in for her highlights and lowlights. Mary said it was gorgeous."

I smiled through clenched teeth and wondered what would happen if I shoved Louise's face into the potato salad and put out a contract on Mary.

"But who cares about clothes, Joanie—she doesn't have half your talent."

Yes, Joan, no one files quite the way you do. No one types with as much panache. What did she do besides ooze perfection, carry herself beautifully, and make a stunning appearance? "She's not a nice person," my mother would say. Yes, but her posture was incredible. I wondered if she took ballet. As a child, I took ballet. I did a plié and sank like a stone.

"Anyway, Michael is working for his father now and—"

"Louise, would you mind if we talked about something else?" I said, stifling the sudden urge to cry. It still happened sometimes even though Michael had been out of my life for months. It shouldn't have bothered me anymore but it did. What would Freud say about that? That secretly I still wanted to have sex with Michael, that I had a good old-fashioned case of penis envy? He'd be right. I did have penis envy, because Michael's penis was parking itself inside Jennifer.

I struggled to recover as Louise launched into the exploits of her two adorable children baking a cake and how adorable Stan had done the most romantic thing. I watched the guy behind the counter slicing open a hero roll. *Pardon me, may I borrow your knife? I need to open a vein.*

"So, have you met his parents?"

"No."

"Has he introduced you to his friends?"

"No."

Louise stopped asking questions. I was not prepared for the quiz portion of the lunch. She gave my hand a pat. "Don't worry about it, honey," she said, with a chirp in her voice, "he's just being cautious. You know how men are."

That night I was still thinking about me and Ed and Jennifer and Michael. I didn't have Ed the way Jennifer had Michael or else I would've met the parents, the friends, family pets, and so on. So what exactly were Ed and I? We were past the first-date stage and not officially a couple. I thought Project Jennifer had been progressing nicely. I had de-klutzed after the funeral. There had been no embarrassing silverware gymnastics, no hunks of food hanging from my teeth. I managed to navigate each date without any embarrassing incidents and my hair didn't have that unruly cowlick I loved so much. He said he was glad he met me. I agreed. It took him two hours on the first date to say he'd like to see me again. On the fourth date he said he liked this arrangement. I said I was glad because for the moment I had decided to keep him. He laughed. In between my Jennifer performances (Saturdays at seven P.M.—on demand the other six days), we engaged in lengthy conversations. We had read some of the same books, liked the same movies. I remained cool, calm, collected. I never mentioned my weight, obsessed over my thighs, or commented on my waistline. Everything was fine. I knew exactly what I was doing. Until the fifth date—when everything changed.

We stood at the bottom of the stairs outside my door. Kong's demolition crew had gone for the day and for once, everything was quiet. He ran his fingers through my hair. I looked up at him; we were kissing. I didn't remember the moment between the looking and the kissing, I was just glad I hadn't accidentally hit his teeth or his nose. Then he did the combo kiss/lower body press. Every nerve ending below my waist woke up and said "Hi." I suavely channeled my reaction by freezing in a mind-numbing panic and smiling like an idiot. My inner Jennifer was calling for a lifeboat. *"We're going down,"* she gasped, *throwing me a look of dismay.*

"How about a quiet dinner next Saturday?" he asked. *Okay, clearly laying the presex groundwork. This is it, Joan. This is not a Mummenschanz moment. Answering him might be good.* I looked up at him.

"Are you sure dinner has to be quiet? I think we can make a little noise, don't you?" My inner Jennifer climbed out of the lifeboat, smoothed her dress and waved my temporary membership card at me.

The next morning I navigated the murky waters of a reality

check. I remembered what I said. I remembered what he said. I didn't need a translator. *A nice quiet dinner, means a nice evening with sex. What's the big deal?* It was about time. So, Ed and I would have sex—fine—great—I was ready.

It's not that I didn't want to have sex with Ed. I did. He was cute, polite, well groomed, and the goatee was a turn-on. So there was absolutely no problem with taking Jennifer to the next level. I mean, this was what the Project was all about, wasn't it? Deciding who I wanted and making sure he wanted me. Then making sure he continued to want me. Only now, he wouldn't leave me for his ideal woman because I was his ideal woman. It made for a nice change, even though the whole concept occasionally gave me a migraine.

On Tuesday, I was sitting in a meeting counting how many people were nodding off when I had an epiphany. I had a drawer full of Hanes Her Way. Translation: I had no lingerie. Nil. Nada. Zip. I stared at a Boston cream doughnut, my heart pounding. *Not a good time to go postal.* I controlled my urge to bolt and rush to the nearest Victoria's Secret.

Later I was back at my desk still staring into space, imagining a romantic threesome of Ed, me, and my white cotton band-leg panties, when Wells came out of his office.

"Are you still with us?" he asked.

I snapped to. "Elvis has not left the building."

"Wise men say only fools give quotes for life insurance when health insurance rates were requested," he quipped, handing me back two reports from the morning.

Shit.

I snatched the reports out of his hand. "Sorry, my fault."

"Yes it is. I didn't type them. Everything okay? Is your mom well?"

Are you kidding? She's lost five pounds, bought new clothes, and she glows.

"Yes, she's fine. I'm just feeling very Monday, that's all."

"Well, see, there's your problem. It's Tuesday."

"I'll have them done in a few minutes."

"You'd let me know if something was wrong?"

"I'll call you if I go critical," I assured him. He patted my shoulder, lingered for a moment, then left.

He was sweet, he really was. I knew two nice men. Lucky me.

My credit card was burning a hole in my wallet but I needed another shopping spree. And there was something else; one vital component was missing and I needed help.

I had asked Carrie and Louise to come over for an emergency summit meeting. I needed answers. Hopefully I would get them without too much discussion.

How do you tell your best friends your most intimate secret? What if they looked down on me? Carrie especially. As Scott filed in behind Carrie, I felt myself go light-headed. Why is he here? Was he invited? Was he ever invited? There was nothing I could do now.

"What's up?" Carrie asked, curling up on the couch.

Scott parked himself in his usual spot, rooted to the floor, propped up against the couch, eyes glued to the television, submarine sandwich in hand. Someday we would find out that Scott had reached enlightenment long ago. While we were running around like idiots, his chakras had aligned through a regimen of sandwiches and football.

I paced the floor. "It's been—a while," I stammered. "Really. It feels almost like . . . forever."

Carrie stroked Scott's hair as she talked. "So you're out of practice. New lingerie, a bottle of wine, condoms, some melted chocolate, and you're all set."

I sank onto a chair; I was having problems swallowing. I looked to Louise for help, but she was staring at Carrie as if she had just disembarked from the mother ship.

"What?" Carrie asked.

Louise turned to me. "Let everything happen naturally. You should be enjoying the end of your dry period." I waited for the statistics. I wasn't disappointed. "Forty-seven percent of women say they go through a dry period after coming out of a relationship."

Carrie wandered over to the table where I sat wringing my hands and grabbed a handful of chips. Her hair was now flame red. It used to be black; before that it was blond. Carrie was an amazing example of reinvention. And she did it so easily. Why was I finding it so difficult?

"Hey, are you listening?" she asked, rousing me from my internal panic attack. "Stop thinking. Just settle in and enjoy. But not too much. You need to be on your guard—"

I knew there was a catch.

"—because after you sleep with him he'll probably turn into a shit and then you'll have to dump him before he dumps you."

My underwear wasn't off yet and already this was too complicated for me. I could feel the frustration mounting. *I have questions! I need answers, people! Joanie doesn't like this. Joanie needs to know what to do when the underwear comes off!*

"I'm a little concerned," I began, choosing my words carefully, "that what I do will make him—'happy.'"

Carrie snorted. "Joanie, who gives a shit about his happiness?" I always looked at Scott following Carrie's candid comments. Nothing. Not a look, not a head turn, not an eyebrow raise. How could that not bother him? I think he needed to go back to the lab. "Look, men have two states of being," she went on. "They're either shits or they're not. Do you remember Al?"

I didn't.

"He gave me a soup tureen for my birthday."

My interest was piqued but Louise got there first.

"Why a soup tureen?"

"Because everyone gets a soup tureen as a wedding gift and he said it was a symbol of our future together. What a putz."

"I wanted a soup tureen as a wedding gift," I said. From soup tureens, to weddings, to Michael. I was depressed again. I needed to get back on the subject.

"Okay—what I really need to know—"

Carrie ignored me. "Then he broke up with me, took the soup tureen back, regifted it for Ken and Debbie's wedding, which he was supposed to take me to, but he took that bitch, who gave him herpes, which is what he deserved."

"You have bad luck with weddings," Louise noted.

"You will never catch me getting married," Carrie announced. I glanced over at Scott. In the wake of that piece of news, he took another bite of his sandwich.

Though fascinating, this did not solve my immediate, looming problem. And I still hadn't fessed up. Carrie threw herself back on the couch.

"Joanie, don't worry about it. Just do whatever you did with Michael."

"Look," I said testily, "not all guys like the same things."

"How much can you do down there?" Carrie asked.

C'mon, Joanie. Just admit it. Look at your friends and say, "I have never"— My mouth was open to speak. I looked at Scott and my mouth went dry and I went into a coughing fit. Louise gave a few hearty smacks on my back as I hacked up a lung.

"Hey," Carrie said, "what happened to all the lingerie you had when you were with Michael? Don't tell me it's so sacred you can't use it."

I stared at the floor, wishing it would open up and swallow me whole.

"Joanie?" Carrie said, moving to stand over me.

I couldn't look at her. "What if Michael and I—didn't?"

"Didn't what?" Carrie asked.

I couldn't stand it anymore. I turned on them, my hands flailing wildly. "Didn't. Did not have physical contact. Did not engage in the procreative act. Did not get 'jiggy' with it. Jump each other's bones. Go to his room for boom boom! Okay? WE DID NOT HAVE SEX!"

Carrie stared at me, her eyes widening.

Louise's chin dropped and she made a beeline for the table. Scott polished off his sandwich.

Carrie recovered first. "Oh—hey—that's okay," she said, her voice sounding strained. She looked to Louise for support. "Isn't it, Louise?"

"I think it's beautiful," Louise fawned. "I wish Stan and I had waited—really."

"Forget about it, Joanie," Carrie went on. "He's a shit. You had a great time with Steve. Remember how that was."

Steve. My wonderful relationship with Steve that I bragged about—how he was shy and wanted us to spend time alone together. I told Louise we had been together for six months because six was a nice round number; actually it had been four. I couldn't admit it had just petered out. Why did it peter out? Because he became bored with kind words, helpful phrases, sure I'll do your term paper, nice girl Joan, that's why. I wasn't exciting, mysterious, or alluring. Because he didn't want to explore the Age of Restoration comedy unless it was located in his pants. Since I was busy pontificating on how hedge funds contribute to an unstable economy, odds are I would never get around to looking there. I answered Carrie by sniveling.

"You didn't sleep with Steve either, did you?" she asked.

And then she did the math. No sex with Michael. No sex with Steve. There were only two, so that meant . . .

"Oh—hey—that's okay!" Carrie said, recovering quickly.

I cried. The truth was out. I knew how they felt in the leper colony. Call *Guinness World Records*. Call News 12. Call Ringling Brothers, see the world's only living thirty-year-old virgin (not counting nuns). It had never happened for me. The nice girl who was supposed to meet a nice guy. But the nice guys didn't want me.

"Michael said it would be more romantic if we waited," I whimpered.

"Well, at least he had the decency," was all Carrie said. What the hell did that mean?

"I'm a freak," I cried.

"No, you're not!" cried my Musketeers, gathering around to comfort the pathetic virgin. I should check Craig's List. Maybe someone was looking for a sacrifice to appease the gods.

Suddenly I realized I was Jerry Springer material: Hairy Bigfoot Virgin Women and the Men Who Don't Want Them. My mother and her boyfriend would be guests.

"I don't know how she ended up this way," my mother would blubber, and then regale everyone with tales of her wild sex life.

I inhaled a deep breath. Now I had my chance to undo all of this. As Jennifer, Ed noticed me and he'd stay with me for as long as I wanted—if I could do this right. But how could I catch up on everything I didn't know in three days?

"Guys love innocent girls. Really," Carrie offered as encouragement.

I spiraled into panic. "I can't tell him!"

Scott hauled himself off the floor and wandered to the table. He stared at me for a long moment.

"A virgin," he said. "Cool."

Carrie looked at me in triumph. "We're going to get you ready," she said.

The words of Thoreau sounded in my head to "Go boldly in the direction of my dreams," which I imagined would be more pertinent if I was trying to become a nuclear physicist rather than procure a lover. I decided I would have sex with Ed and he would fall madly in love with me. Reality set in as I stood in front of the mirror surveying my look in a pink demibra and matching thong panties. I had also bought three pairs of stockings for the matching garter belt. It took twenty minutes to get them hooked up, I had twisted a vertebrae, not to mention the mega wedgie from the thong from hell. I didn't want to know what my ass looked like hanging out of the panties that weren't.

"Don't they make little silky things to wear over these?" I asked.

Carrie responded by tossing me something pink the size of a Kleenex.

I ran my fingers under the filmy material. "Don't they come in a floor length? In a solid?"

"You look good," she said. "Besides, he won't care. It's all the same in the dark."

Desperate to find a suitable resting place for the thong, I began to fidget. My formative years (okay, all of my years) were spent in Hanes Her Way; I was finding it difficult to adjust.

"What are you doing?" Carrie asked.

"I'm trying to get comfortable," I whined.

"Stop it."

I returned to the mirror. "I have fat hanging over the hose," I said morosely.

"No you don't, now knock it off."

This from a woman who ate everything in sight and never gained an ounce. There was no God.

"My thighs look like two pork loins! I have belly fat!" I moaned, moving into full meltdown. Too bad my thighs were not. I was about to get naked in front of another human being. Loss of virginity should always take place when you're young and stupid. When you're seventeen everyone looks like a dork so who cares?

"You're standing the wrong way," she replied, throwing up her arms. Moving to my side, she did a three-quarter turn. My mouth fell open. Somewhere between studying Shakespearean comedies and conversational Spanish, I missed the all important skill of the hip swivel and turn.

The angle made her tummy look flat and one thigh in front of the other gave vital coverage to the inner thigh. Newton's apple? Einstein's e=mc²? Child's play compared to this monumental discovery. She knew *everything.*

"You try it," she said.

I swiveled. Stomach pouch concealed? Check. I turned my leg. Inner thighs concealed? Check.

Then I had a moment of clarity. "I can't walk across a room like this, I'll fall on my face."

"He'll come to you," she snapped, tossing lingerie items on the bed.

"Is everything okay?" I asked, always a loaded question with Carrie.

She shrugged and took out another outfit. "Scott's being a pain in the ass."

"How can you tell?"

Carrie threw me a black look.

"I'm sorry, Carrie. Maybe he's working too hard."

Carrie grunted, her sign that she didn't want to talk about it anymore. I turned back to the mirror.

"If I had bigger breasts, my hips would look smaller," I lamented.

"You should have bought the push-up bra," she said behind me.

"I don't do false advertising," I retorted. How could I let him think he was getting the full size and once I undid the hooks, the junior size fell out? Someone had to take a stand. My humble contribution to raging against the machine.

"They don't care, Joanie," she said.

"That's your answer to everything," I snapped. That couldn't be it. Could it?

"That's right. That is the answer. Screw Project Jennifer. 'I've never done this before' should be the first words out of your mouth. Then you'll get the 'take it easy, baby, just relax' treatment."

I stared, spellbound.

"How long do you think this is going to take? He'll get out the pillows, play 'Bolero,' spray Binaca, and ten minutes later strut around flexing his dick because he bagged a virgin."

"And this is what I've been waiting for," I said.

She answered by tossing a black studded bra at me. "Pretty much."

I turned back to the mirror. I'd have to dim the lights before we got started.

While my personal life was falling into place, my living conditions were heading south. Kong and his wrecking crew were demolishing the upstairs interior. I noticed a small drip had developed on my bedroom ceiling and I placed a bucket between the bed and the closet, a definite decor enhancement. I reminded myself to mention it to him on Sunday morning.

On Thursday, Kong's posse called it a night by seven, but my evening hadn't started yet and I was getting antsy. Carrie and Scott were settled on the couch. Louise called to say she was still waiting for the sitter. I was exercising like a lunatic and no one had heard from the woman who was coming to solve the remainder of my problems.

"When will she be here?" I panted.

"Soon," Carrie said through a mouthful of Big Mac.

"I want to finish my routine before she gets here," I huffed, hopping on and off the step bench. "What time did she say?"

"In a little while," she answered. "Stop that."

"My thighs rub together when I walk."

"Hello? Support hose," she retorted.

I now said anything on my mind in front of Scott. He was the second living male who knew I was a virgin. Fat thighs were small potatoes.

I remembered the first time Michael and I had been alone in my new apartment. We were nestling on the couch and his kisses were making my lips tingle. Soon he was doing more than kissing me and I began shaking like a terrier with a nervous condition.

"You okay?" he whispered.

"Yes, I'm fine," I said.

"You've never done this before, have you?" he soothed, smoothing my hair back from my face.

In the good old days, my rapier wit provided no end of snappy comebacks. I was at the top of my game.

"No," I said. "But I'm okay."

"Shh," he said, taking manly control. "Don't worry about it." He looked at me for a long minute. I would have given big bucks for his thoughts. I waited for the kiss off but instead got a kiss.

"I can wait," he said.

I was sure I'd never hear from him again but he kept coming back.

I tripped on the step bench, forcing myself from my daydream.

"You're going to look great with that missing front tooth," Carrie said, starting on the jumbo fries.

In response I launched into a series of upper body gyrations designed to tone and trim the arms, shoulders, and God willing, breasts.

"You look ridiculous," Carrie stated.

"The bra is going to come off," I sputtered. "I want good breasts."

"Any breast is a good breast."

"So right, babe," Scott murmured.

"Stop doing that!" Carrie yelled. I ignored her.

"I have one more exercise." I was losing all sense of feeling in my body. Perhaps because all of the blood had rushed to my head.

"It's good for the back of the thighs," I huffed. "You get down on your knees, lift one leg out straight behind and raise it up and down."

Carrie took a slurp of soda. "If I'm on my knees, I'm going to enjoy myself."

I remember tripping over the bench and hitting the floor, and the euphoria of discovering I still had all my teeth. As I gingerly rolled over, a Devil Dog dangled before my eyes.

"Here," Carrie said. "You deserve it."

She was so right.

At nine o'clock we were in go mode. The kitchen table was cleared. I paced while I waited. Scott was glued to the television, scarfing down the remainder of my snack food. I did a quick calculation of how much of a personal loan I would need to replace it. Carrie and Louise read magazines. A woman was coming to tell me, in a brief two hours, everything I needed to know to become an expert lover. Carrie found her through another hairdresser. I was concerned because the cost for receiving this invaluable information was fifty bucks a piece (not including gratuity) but how can you put a price on knowledge? I expected a tall, willowy, soft-spoken, Jenniferesque woman with the aura of someone who knew the deepest secrets of erotica. When I opened the door, I found a short, chubby, dark-haired woman in her early fifties struggling with three tattered shopping bags.

Carrie peered out from behind me. "Hiya, Roxie," she said. "Come on in."

Carrie, Louise, and I sat around the kitchen table. In front of each of us, a shoe box. Apparently, Roxie was keen on low overhead. While I waited for my lesson in love, Roxie unceremoniously dumped various tubes and lotions from a small carton onto the middle of the table. Carrie gave me the "give it a chance" eyebrow arch, so I waited.

"Thanks for coming on such short notice, Roxie," Carrie said. "We appreciate it."

"No problem," Roxie breezed. "I usually do bachelorette parties. They know more than I do." *I borrowed more money from my mother for this?*

"Okay," she said. "Let's get started. I'll go over the creams quickly and then we'll break open the boxes."

I looked over at Louise. Her hands were clenched and she was wearing a catatonic joker's smile.

"Okay," Roxie continued, regurgitating a memorized spiel as she picked up and slapped down each tube. "You have your mood cream. Vanilla, cherry, or chocolate flavors. Makes the skin hot. A word to the wise. Don't confuse this with K-Y warming jelly. I had a client who did that and she had an intimate evening with a tray of ice cubes. Not that her boyfriend minded—they're all pervs anyway."

"I've heard that," I mumbled.

Roxie stifled a yawn and started chowing down on the potato chips I'd put out for the occasion. I guessed just talking about sex could make you hungry. What did I know?

"Okay. Open your boxes." She patted my shoulder with a greasy hand. "Don't worry, honey, all you need for a successful evening is in this kit."

Louise roused herself from her coma and found her voice.

"What if you're already married?" she asked.

Roxie was now shoving in chips three at a time. "How long? How many kids?" She wiped her hand on her pants.

"Ten years, two kids."

Roxie tapped the last of the chips from the bag into her mouth, crumpled the empty bag and tossed it in the general direction of the garbage, missing by at least a foot. She looked around for more while rolling her tongue around to dig out chip residue stuck behind her molars. I wondered if it was too late for me to become a nun. I love wearing black. It's slimming.

"Let's see, you do it once, maybe twice a week after the kids are in bed. It takes about fifteen minutes and he can still catch the news. Foreplay usually consists of, 'Dinner was great, honey,' or the old standby, 'You're not tired, are you?' "

Louise sat frozen, her mouth hanging open. Roxie moved in for the kill.

"You don't need a kit, honey," she said nonchalantly, "you need a life."

Louise paled and then turned red, her lips pinching together; I thought I could see her blood bubbling to a boil. Someone once said nothing causes such rage as truth and if they didn't they should have. It had never occurred to me that the idyllic life Louise described wasn't. Carrie said nothing even though she could have. Louise wouldn't meet my eyes as we sat in a long moment of awkward silence.

"Okay, let's get this over with," Roxie said with a heavy sigh. "We don't have all night."

"Will I approach sex with the same excitement?" I asked as I lifted the lid.

"Just about," she replied.

We opened the boxes. They each contained one item. That was it. We each took our one item out of our boxes, and the table became a Who's Who of penises on parade. I wasn't stunned. It wasn't like I had never seen the male body. Okay, so I hadn't seen it up close but what teenage babysitter hasn't cruised the television after the kids were asleep and found out Mommy and Daddy indulged in adult viewing? Those experi-

ences only confirmed my worst fear: the world was full of un-
attractive men. Now here it was, up close and personal.

Carrie whipped out a measuring tape. "Is that for accuracy
or reference?" I whispered.

Louise stared, transfixed. Apparently her extensive knowledge of raw statistical data had not prepared her for this.

"Is this considered average or jumbo?" she squeaked. I
sensed an approaching marital crisis.

Roxie leaned over to me. "Honey, it's okay. It can't hurt
you. No matter what they like to think."

"What'd I tell you, Joanie?" Carrie piped up.

Roxie rooted around in a bag and pulled out her master
phallus, as it were, sort of a mini statue of liberty. *Give me your
tired, your poor, your sexually ignorant yearning to be deflowered.*

"We'll start with the washing machine method. Put as
much in your mouth as you can fit. The movement is all in the
tongue. A word of advice girls, breathe through your nose."

Carrie and Louise prepared to dive. I was transfixed. I couldn't
move. Did Jennifer do this? She must. She'd have to, wouldn't
she? She was probably an oral sex champion. And she didn't
learn from a woman tossing up chips and trying to catch them
in her mouth.

"Joanie, you can do it," Louise piped up.

"I can't," I said.

Roxie unwrapped a Tootsie Roll Pop and held it out to me.
"You want to practice with this first?"

I shook my head. She shrugged and popped it in her mouth,
slurping away.

"Honey, you want to take a test drive first. Don't leave it to
chance."

I couldn't look at Carrie. I could feel her eyes boring into
me.

"I can't do it," I reiterated. "Maybe Jennifer doesn't do
this."

"She got a diamond necklace for her birthday," Carrie said.
Oh yeah, she does this.

"Now, why can't you?" Carrie asked through clenched teeth.

"It's looking at me," I said.

Carrie stomped around the table. She leaned over my shoulder to have a look. It was hypnotic. My phallus had two eyes, a nose, and the ridge had a little upturned mouth peeking out. He also had a tie.

"Ignore it," Carrie said flatly.

Louise scampered around to have a look. "It's cute," she cooed. "Like a little old man."

"Honey, never use the word little," Roxie corrected.

"All it needs is a cap," I murmured.

"Ignore it!" Carrie cried. "You need to practice. You need confidence!"

"By fellating Mr. Magoo?" I said miserably.

"I loved that show," Louise said.

Roxie tossed the Tootsie Roll stick, missing the garbage again, and came to take a look. Clucking her tongue, she whipped a bottle of Formula 409 out of the shopping bag and with a paper towel started a vigorous scrubbing motion on my little Magoo.

"Sorry, honey," she said. "My daughter got into the kits. She's on a kick about how I'm encouraging female subservience to men, blah, blah, blah—the penis is the symbol of male control—yada, yada, yada." She examined the results. "Shit, I hope she didn't use permanent marker."

I was impressed by her technique. Now I understood why this woman was in demand. I could swear Magoo was growing before my eyes.

"You must be very successful with men," I finally managed.

"Oh, honey, I'm a lesbian," she said. "I just do this for the money." She walked over to the sink and rinsed little Magoo. It must've been cold water because he was smaller when she gave him back to me. Sayonara, Magoo.

"Okay, girls," she announced. "Let's get down to it."

Well, there was nothing else to do, except take the plunge. If Jennifer could do it, so could I. So I did. We all did. Sensing movement in the room, I looked up. Scott was standing by the table, holding an empty bag of chips, a smile of pure bliss on his lips. Carrie was right. They're all perverts.

* * *

Friday afternoon, five o'clock. The official start of the weekend. The rest of Roxie's class had been uneventful. Her party gifts were a bottle of chocolate sauce and a can of Reddi Wip. I wasn't sure if I was preparing to have sex or starting my own dessert bar. All this fun and calories, too.

"Joan!" Wells's familiar voice broke my thoughts.

Trotting over, I leaned in the doorway. "You bellowed?" I asked.

"You didn't give me the Kinney file," he said, almost pouting.

"It's on your desk."

"No, it isn't. I don't have it," he said, his tone peevish.

Marching over, I stood next to him and lifted the folder out from underneath the pile and handed it over. He leaned back in his chair and looked up at me, penitent.

"Oh, I didn't see it there."

"Did you ask me where it was?" I countered.

"No, no I didn't."

"You don't ask, you don't get," I said flatly.

He stared at me and smiled. It was a very nice smile. I had a job for life.

"Do you like working here?" he asked.

Okay, maybe I didn't. "You can be quite trying, but yes I do."

He rocked in his chair slightly, nodding his head. "We make a good team, don't we?"

"Yes, we do," I agreed. "Now, if you could only find your files, we'd be a well-oiled machine."

He smiled, looked at the clock, then past me out into the hall.

"I guess everybody's leaving," he said casually.

"I'm on my way out, too."

He sat up. "You're leaving me?" he asked, making it sound like I was committing a crime against humanity.

"Can you manage to get along without me until Monday?"

Throwing the file down, he slapped the folder open. "I

guess I'll have to, won't I?" he snapped, screwing up his face like a five-year-old who wasn't able to play with his favorite truck. Unbelievable.

"Well, good night," I said.

"Good night," he replied stiffly.

Bosses. I didn't get them.

Saturday at seven: T minus thirty and counting. I had made every auxiliary preparation possible. To avoid any culinary catastrophes, I went with cold shrimp and pasta salad. Carrie brought a chocolate cake from Muller's bakery. I called my mother to complain of exhaustion. She gave me a twenty minute lecture on the health risks of sleep deprivation and insisted I go to bed; she wouldn't be calling. I now had two buckets strategically placed for my bedroom waterfalls. One near the closet door, the second about a foot from my bed. Luckily nothing was dripping directly over the bed. I couldn't imagine losing my virginity during the Chinese water torture.

My outfit of choice was classic black lace bikini panties, matching push-up bra and garter belt. I wrangled with the garters until I got them closed properly, making sure they were snapped on nice and tight. Slipping into the stilettos, I took a few steps. My knees buckled as my toes screamed in protest. No wonder foot binding never caught on, I thought as I tugged them off. My inner Jennifer lounged in an aromatherapy bath as I applied the finishing touches of mascara and blush in front of the bathroom mirror. I stepped back for a last look. A sexy new Jennifer looked back at me. *"Where are the stilettos?"* she asked. Witch. Total prep time: two hours, twenty-two minutes. *Important statistic: all accumulated date prep time equals time needed to earn bachelor's and master's degrees combined. Note: Do not mention that fact to my mother. Ever.*

The phone rang. "Are you ready?" Carrie asked.

I had one ear glued to the telephone and one straining for a knock at the door.

"Absolutely ready," I snapped back. My self-confidence had perked along with my cleavage. I had emptied my mind. I was not thinking at all. My brain was a blank canvas, a clean slate, a ceaseless void.

"What about faking?" she asked.

"What?" I replied.

"Faking—faking orgasm," she explained. "It doesn't always happen the first time. Do you know what you're going to do?"

Mental paralysis struck; I lost the power of speech.

"I'm sorry I said anything," she said.

Me, too.

"Forget it, don't worry about it." Famous last words. "When he comes, just moan a lot, scream once, and scratch his back."

"In that order?"

"It doesn't matter," she replied. "He won't be thinking about you anyway. Call me tomorrow."

I said good-bye to my friend, the Tony Robbins of healthy sexual relationships. Just the suggestion of faking an orgasm made me nervous. I had never been any good at lying, although I had become adept at telling Wells's wife he was gone when he wasn't. He's a good guy, I thought, with a rush of sympathy. He seems so unhappy with her.

Important marketing principle: a message must be presented at least half a dozen times before it has the intended effect. With sex, the sell curve needed to be shorter—much shorter. As always, Carrie was right; an excitement ratio on a par with watching golf would not keep Ed coming back. What would a Jennifer do? She'd have an amazing orgasm. Heavy moaning was the way to go. I sighed. He wasn't here yet and already I'd sold out. I was part of the hypocrisy.

He arrived at eight, wearing tight blue jeans and a crisp white shirt. His eyes traveled up and down as he took me in, his mouth slightly parted. I had rendered a man speechless! Excellent. Leaning against the doorway, I gave him a warm smile.

"Would you like to come in?" I asked.

He shut the door and slid his arm around me. Pulling me close, he gave me a steamy kiss.

As my lips parted under his, I could hear the delicate plinking of the water into the buckets. I thought it was a nice touch; our own life-sized serenity fountain.

"Hungry?" I whispered.

"M-m-m," he murmered, his lips moving down to my neck. "Very." A feeling of warmth rippled through me.

"So, you want dessert first," I said.

Chuckling, he made his way south, but a sudden crash overhead made him jerk upright. Shrieking and screaming followed. The nightly WWF SmackDown was right on schedule. Bastards.

"What was that?" he asked, straightening up.

Pressing against him, I stroked his cheek. "Not to worry," I whispered. "They're a fun family. Happens all the time."

He returned to nuzzling my neck while the circus raged above our heads.

"Let's go into the bedroom," I purred. In the soft glow of the candles, I hoped he wouldn't notice the mini Niagra Falls.

I nibbled his ear as we sank onto the bed.

"What's with the buckets?"

Damn.

"Never mind," I whispered, unbuttoning his shirt and moving to his belt.

"Whatever you say." Sliding his hand along my leg, he began working on the garter. "Let's get this off."

It wouldn't open.

Moving in for a closer look, he began tugging at it. Nothing. Muttering under his breath, he gave it a twist; it snapped open, ricocheting into his eye.

With a yelp he fell backward, clapping his hand over his face.

"Oh my God!" I cried, hustling him into the bathroom for a better look. The eye was swelling nicely. After a cool soak, he said his vision was clearing. At that moment, pounding began over our heads. Unbelievable! Kong was pulling a Bob Vila on a Saturday night. Carrie was right. Men were schmucks and the überschmuck was doing demolition right over our heads.

Ed looked at me out of his good eye. I knew he was beginning to wonder if he should be somewhere else. I took his face in my hands.

"Why don't we go back to bed," I coaxed. Squinting, he nodded.

"I have something for you," I cooed in his ear. Rolling over, I snatched the tube of mood cream from the night table, waving it at him. "A little something to heat things up."

His smile broadened. Teasing him with kisses, I began to unscrew the cap. It wouldn't budge. *Damn!* Tightening my grip, I squeezed and turned. The cap flew off and the mood cream shot out—into Ed's good eye.

Shit!

Grabbing his eye, he threw his face into the pillow, muffling his moans.

"Oh my God," I cried. "Are you okay?"

He whimpered in response. Gently I pried his hand away. The eye was blowing up like a balloon.

"It's burning," he gasped, struggling to get out of bed. "I need to wash it out."

I moved to follow him.

"No, no, I can do it."

He stumbled down the hall, thudding against the wall; I heard the water running.

This can't be happening, I thought, falling back onto the bed. If I don't get a handle on this my quiet evening of passionate sex will end up in the emergency room.

I lay there, focusing on the slow, persistent dripping of water into the buckets, juxtaposed against the sound of running water from the bathroom. After a few moments, the bathroom faucet shut off. I heard a strange noise. Rushing water? Shooting out of bed, I raced to the bathroom, to find Ed peering into the cabinet under the sink. At that moment, a jet stream of water exploded into his face, rocketing him back into the tub, where he lay like a rag doll.

"Oh . . . my . . . God," I said, staring at his inert figure, imagining the News 12 headline: VIRGIN'S SUITOR KNOCKED UNCONSCIOUS IN FREAK BATHROOM TSUNAMI. *Rescue workers found the victim floating in the bathtub wearing nothing but boxer shorts. He sustained a mild concussion but needed extensive ocular treatment due to an incident involving warming gel and a faulty garter belt.*

Bending over the tub with the water rising above my ankles, I grabbed his wrist. "He has a pulse," I muttered. Thank God. Then I heard a cracking noise and I looked up. The bathroom ceiling was solid. Leaving Ed soaking in the tub, I sloshed back to the bedroom. I looked up at the ceiling. The two drips, my herald of disaster, had morphed into a waterfall. With a cracking sound, a chunk of the ceiling gave way, landing on my bed. Walking into the room, I peered up through the gaping hole. The four-year-old was looking down at me.

She waved.

I waved back.

It took ten minutes for Kong to shut the water off. The master builder came down muttering about how "they" must've hit a pipe. I sat on the couch, dressed in sweat clothes with Ed's head in my lap, ice packs on both his eyes. In between smothered chuckles, the paramedic assured me he'd be fine. Bastard. The final humiliation was calling Carrie to bring over some of Scott's clothes. Ed's clothes were on the floor next to the bed, under a pile of wet plasterboard.

I drove Ed home. Carrie followed in his car.

"Are you sure you're going to be okay?" I asked, helping him to the door. He looked like Rocky after Apollo Creed got done with him.

"Uh-hunh," he mumbled.

"Maybe I should take you to a doctor," I offered.

He held up his hands, shielding himself from the evil virgin.

After letting him struggle for a minute, I finally took his key away and opened the door for him.

"I'll call you tomorrow," I said.

He nodded and shut the door.

* * *

"**I** ruined your evening with Scott," I said to Carrie. We were in her apartment. She was making up the couch.

"He wasn't here," she said shortly.

We sat up for a while, ate nachos, and watched movies. Trying to make me feel better, she brought out my favorites, a little Clooney, a dash of Bond (Connery and Craig). I found it ironic that I was attracted to men with a debonair style while I was the Lucille Ball of dating, leaving a path of injured men behind me, shaken and stirred.

What nugget of wisdom did I cull from this experience? That I couldn't do this. I couldn't pull it off. I said as much to Carrie.

"I should have known something like this would happen," I lamented. "I almost killed Michael."

"Don't be dramatic. That was nothing."

I was not to be put off. "Excuse me, four hours in the emergency room after a teriyaki chicken incident."

Carrie sniffed. "He should've told you he was allergic to ginger. He needs a medic alert bracelet."

I threw up my hands. Unbelievable. How could she not see a pattern? I was the typhoid Mary of relationships.

"Joans, your only problem is you're trying too hard." I looked at her. She was staring at the television.

"Can you clarify, please?" I asked, trying not to sound annoyed.

Carrie turned to me. "Joanie, you're one of the nicest people I know and that's saying a lot. When it happens for you"— she held up her hand as I was about to interrupt—"it's going to be forever. With whoever that is. You look great and if you want to keep the clothes and makeup, good. But I think Ed would've been very happy with Joan, just Joan. I really do."

I sat forward, until I couldn't hold it in any longer. "But I had him. For one brief shining moment, I was a Jennifer."

Silence hung between us.

"Did you get the shoes on?" she asked.

"Just for a minute."

"I'm impressed."

*   *   *

I held a debriefing the next day with Kong. I would be sleeping in the living room for a few days until the ceiling was repaired and my bed replaced. The bathroom pipe could be fixed but more extensive work involving reconstructive plumbing that I didn't understand might have to be done. So entered a "friend" of Kong's, Mike the plumber. He was large, unpleasant looking, and had a scent I didn't care for. We detested each other on sight. Thankfully, "Mike" was able to fix the pipe in three days and then disappeared. With any luck there wouldn't be any "reconstructive plumbing" because Kong was too busy destroying the upstairs and Mike wouldn't be back anytime soon.

Two weeks later I was sitting at my desk on a Friday ruminating over my situation. I still stood behind my theory of Project Jennifer. The reason I knew my hypothesis was correct was evidenced by the fact that I could not achieve my goal. If I came to any other conclusion that would mean that some of us were simply born to be Jennifers, and some of us . . . were not. And I refused to accept that. But it was more than a little troubling that my intense study and effort had yielded nothing, save a large wardrobe, uncomfortable panties, and debilitating bodily injury. I called Carrie for sympathy.

"If you were talking to Louise, I'm sure she'd give you a fast fact as to why this happened."

"I'm sure. Is there a factoid stating that twenty-five percent of all virgins experience difficulty losing their virginity due to faulty plumbing? This is why Marty never called me again, isn't it?" I probed. "He's afraid 'Joan Lovin' will lead to serious hospital time."

"Forget about Marty," Carrie breezed.

"You're never going to tell me, are you?"

"It's not important," she said with finality.

"That's why Steve never hung around. He's probably a marriage counselor now. He could tell even then I had all the earmarks of disaster. He's probably commiserating with other fools who didn't have the good sense to escape."

I was greeted with silence. I was a sexual, romantic, and relationship loser.

"Are you finished?" Carrie asked.

"Yes, I think so, thank you."

"Good. Now—did you talk to Ed?" she asked.

"I called him. He wasn't as angry as I thought he would be. He suggested we take a break. Big surprise."

"Give him a week or two, he'll change his mind."

"I'll call him after his eye treatments are finished. You know, I may have something here," I said, "reverse prostitution. Men could pay me to not sleep with them!"

"You're overreacting," she sniffed.

"No, I'm not," I shot back. "Freaks and weirdos are highly sensitive to their condition."

Wells came out of his office.

"I have to go," I whispered into the phone, and hung up. I thought I detected a faint smile on his face as he sidled up to my desk. I looked up at him. With the hair falling over his forehead, he had that little boy look. It always caught me off guard. I must admit, I had moments when I wanted to run my fingers through that hair.

"How goes the continuing adventures of Joan?" he asked.

"Strange and exciting."

"I'm sorry to pressure you but I need these reports ASAP." He held them out like a child apologizing for writing on the walls.

I smiled and snatched the papers away. "I'll see what I can do," I said.

At seven P.M. I finished the last report. Everyone was long gone. Shoes off, I padded into his office and placed the reports on his desk. as I came in he eyed me and ended his phone call.

"Thank you," he said.

"You're very welcome," I answered.

He got up and walked over to me. A moment of silence passed between us. And at that moment, I saw it. I didn't know where I'd been but all of a sudden, I got it. It all fell into place. Every glance, every exchange, every touch, his standing too close to me. The entire sequence of events came full circle, bringing us to the moment where we stood now.

"So, what do we do now?" he asked softly, looking into my eyes.

My pulse quickened. *What I've been preparing to do.*

As he tipped my chin up and kissed me, I felt a tingle run the length of my body.

"My place?" I said.

"I'll follow you," he whispered.

I arrived at my apartment a few minutes ahead of him. I turned the key in the lock, leaving the door unlatched for him. I didn't rush to the door when I heard it open. I waited and then I turned. He winked at me and with a little smile we headed into the bedroom. Throwing his jacket on the chair, he settled on the bed.

Standing in front of him, I undid the buttons on my dress, watching him watch me. I let the dress fall open, allowing a glimpse, then a full view of my red satin bra and panties.

Eyes darkening, he sat up and reached for me.

I laughed as he pulled me down next to him.

For the first time in my life, the stars were aligned, the earth was spinning perfectly on its axis and all was right with the world. I finally knew what it felt like to make love and be made love to. There was no self-consciousness, no worrying, and no embarrassment. Finally it all worked and worked Jennifer perfect.

At eight-thirty, we said good-bye by the front door.

"I can't stay, I'm sorry," he whispered.

"I know," I said.

"I'll have to do something about that," he said, giving me

another deep kiss. Closing the door behind him, I went back to bed, reliving every moment. I mentally retraced the last months, right up to the present, happy, completely unexpected conclusion. All was perfect and right. Finally, all I had learned had paid off. I had succeeded. Jennifer had arrived.

BEING JENNIFER

Chapter 11

The morning after. In Victorian terminology, I had been de-flowered. In scientific terms, one man had gone where no man had gone before, the hymenal frontier. Everything was different. For starters, I was walking around the apartment like a penguin, but a hot bath and some ibuprofen would fix that. I considered how right Darwin had been. In my case, I had fully evolved.

The phone rang.

"Hi," came the gravelly voice on the other end. My pulse quickened. It was him, calling me the *day after.*

"Hi there," I purred.

"Just calling to see if you're all right." He was checking on me. I had him—he loved me—case closed—dismiss the jury. Thank you all for coming.

"I'm perfect," I answered.

"That was your first time, wasn't it?"

What difference did that make? Can't I get past that? Virginity was so yesterday. *Literally.* "Maybe," I teased.

I heard his low chuckle on the other end. "Well, partner, I'm honored," he said.

Wow, what a cool thing to say.

"I'll see you Monday?" he asked.

"I'll be there."

He was fantastic. And he knew what to do. Okay, I had no

frame of reference. But I did have excellent instincts. And it felt really good. And faking? Moot point.

I lounged in bed, reflecting on how I had made the Jennifer evolution, the look, the moves, the walk, and the talk. Now I needed to think about Jennifer maintenance. How to keep the elements working like a well-oiled machine. I decided to celebrate the momentous occasion with a trip to the bookstore. *Memo to me: Remember to pick up a copy of* Origin of the Species.

I pulled into the strip mall off Sunrise Highway and stepped into Borders. I cruised through the packed shelves with last night replaying in my head.

"I've been waiting for this moment," he whispered.

He was desperately unhappy with his wife.

I decided to peruse the self-help section, even though my self didn't need any help, which was obvious from last night.

"You and me, babe, we're the dream team," he murmured, nibbling on my ear.

They argued constantly. Even out at my desk, I could hear the anger in his voice, the receiver slamming down.

"You're amazing," he breathed, wrapping me in his arms. *"I have plans for us."*

A dozen books later I was tottering over to the café for the requisite bagel and flavored coffee. Everyone knows knowledge cannot be pursued on an empty stomach.

The finishing touches on Jennifer were simple. Since Jennifers are completely relaxed, polished, and in control, I needed only to cultivate more of the same. And why were Jennifers relaxed? Because they lived in complete balance and harmony that could only be achieved from the inside out. My life was not completely balanced and harmonious. If one's surroundings were indicative of their mental state, then my mental state was slightly to the left of anarchy. I needed to create a healthy, controlled mind, which would lead to a healthy body, which would in turn create a total, in-control, powerhouse Jennifer package, the self-actualized woman. Too bad this self-actualization didn't come in a vitamin power-pack or a handy twenty-minute program you study three times a week. There was always a catch. I scoured my stack of books until I came up with the definitive three-phase program to keep my Jennifer aura in tip-top shape:

Phase I
Detox: 8 glasses of water daily. Exercise 30 minutes per day. Lose 10 more pounds with healthy meals (boil-in-bags of vegetables are acceptable). 8 hours of sleep per night. Mega skin care regimen.

Phase II
Continue Phase I and add Lifestyle Adjustment. Create Zenlike atmosphere by purging apartment and purse of clutter.

Phase III
Continue Phases I and II and add the Inner Woman. Daily Meditation. Positive Thinking.

Phase IV
Putting it all together. All phases properly joined to make one fabulous, healthy, positive, well-rested, self-actualized package.

I perused my list. This was it. The finishing touch for Project Jennifer. I thought again about that day in Port Jeff, watching Jennifer hold court at the restaurant. She knew the secret. She took care of herself first. While the world swirled around her, she maintained complete calm. Every woman wanted what she had; and men just wanted her. Now they wanted me. Well, one did. I said a silent adieu to my last bagel and finished it off in one mournful bite. I thought I heard the sound of taps.

I needed to tell Carrie and Louise. I knew Wells would want this to be low key for now, but that didn't mean I couldn't share with my two best friends. I knew they would be happy for me. I knew exactly what I was doing. Wells's marriage was already over. When we were married, Wells and I would probably see a lot of Louise and Stan, dinners together, parties at our house. Realizing my heart was pounding, I took a deep breath to re-Zen. Jennifers were always Zen.

I checked my watch. Three o'clock. I had time to get to the grocery store and still do a mega housecleaning. The rest of my list would have to wait until tomorrow. By Monday, everything would be in place.

I have never been a fan of the meal planning/food shopping experience. I prefer foods prepared with microwave assistance, or products with the word *Helper* in the title. That was over now. Cruising through fruits and vegetables, I bought anything green. Green was good. Green was healthy. I even bought the requisite solid block of tofu. If it didn't work out, I'd use it as a sponge. I bought all things low fat, no fat, low sodium, low carb, and low taste. I spent $175; I hadn't bought one item I would enjoy eating. The coup de gras: paying for it all with a credit card. In winter I would be paying interest on the asparagus I bought in the fall.

By nightfall, the apartment was a shambles; paper bags bulging with Devil Dogs, peanut butter cups, pasta, and cheese; chips and Cheese Doodles lined the kitchen counter. All to make way for trail mix, dried fruit, and rice cakes. In the living room textbooks teetered in piles including my dog-eared copy of Michael's favorite book, *Don Quixote*. After finding out I liked it, too, he had started calling me Sancho. I should throw it out, I thought. It's so Joan. But when it came down to it, I couldn't. I wasn't ready. Wimp. But it couldn't stay in the apartment. I went to Plan B: store everything in the car until Monday and drop it all at Mom's after work. Mom's stud boyfriend could schlep it down to the basement after their daily routine of wild debauchery. I grinned. She wasn't alone.

What *would* I tell my mother? She would know something was different. Not that I couldn't tell her everything. I had nothing to be ashamed of. I wasn't breaking up a marriage. It was already over, but as soon as I said "married" she would go postal and give me the third degree. "What are you doing?" "What about his wife?" "Does he have children?" I couldn't take the thought of spending hours defending his honor (that didn't need defending) and feeling like I needed to defend mine. There's no reason to feel defensive, I thought. I know what I'm doing. Plenty of couples had rocky beginnings, enduring opposition and lack of acceptance by society. At the moment I couldn't think of a single one of those couples, but I was sure they were out there. And they knew what they were doing as well. The important thing—Project Jennifer was a rousing success.

I was congratulating myself on working everything out when there was a knock at my door.

Shit! *Maybe it's him.*

I started hopping around the room, stubbed my toe and then hopped on one leg, cursing like a sailor. *Hello, very un-Jennifer, n'est-ce pas?* I took a deep breath. Zen out Joan. Jennifers can handle any situation, anyone or anything. I hobbled to the door, did the hip thigh move and opened the door.

It was Carrie. She took a long look at me but said nothing. I moved aside to let her in.

She couldn't tell. Could she?

She gave the room a once over, then scrutinized me.

"Spring cleaning," I piped up.

"It's fall," she answered.

I began shuffling books from pile to pile. *C'mon, Joan, spill it. She'll be happy for you.*

Carrie threw herself on the couch and heaved a sigh. "You're walking like a penguin," she said, matter-of-factly.

"Yes, I am," I answered, sounding like a little kid with a new toy. She picked up a magazine and flipped through it.

"Details," she snapped.

For a moment, I considered a coy "What?" or the übercoy

"There's nothing to tell," just to milk the moment. Carrie's eagle eyes bored into mine. I gave up on both. As I announced my devirginization, her lip began curling. She was having a snit fit. This was not how I pictured the big unveiling.

"Where did you meet him?" she probed.

"W-e-l-l, I—actually know him."

For a second Carrie looked almost feline, ready to spring. Then she calmed down. "Wells?" she asked, her voice mirroring her disbelief.

That's the sad thing about being the Sister Maria of women; it's not hard to do the math. I don't know that many men.

"The married boss?"

"He's practically divorced," I countered. *Well, he was.*

"That's what I said. He's married."

Feeling my face grow hot, I pretended to immerse myself in sorting through the mound of books, tossing them into piles.

"You dated Dave," I attacked. "Didn't you?"

When I looked up she was sitting cross-legged, yoga style.

"Oh yeah, I dated Dave," she said with a wave of her hand. "See Dave. See Dave's wife. See the life Dave has with his wife while I sit around like a schmuck waiting for Dave to sneak out to see me—"

"It won't be like that!" I sputtered. I didn't appreciate the comparison. "And by the way, my first time having sex was great; he was world class, a gymnast!"

"What's your frame of reference?"

I tossed another book on the floor, *Communication through the Ages, A Sociological Study.* It landed dangerously close to the couch.

"Joanie, did you or did you not provide moral support during my ten weeks of post-Dave therapy?"

I did. I nodded. She went on.

"Did you or did you not tell me the therapist was absolutely correct when she said a relationship with a married man will never work because—" She paused. "—That man will never be capable of loyalty because he's being disloyal by being with me—you—whatever."

Okay, yes, I did agree with that, but my case was different. Sure I was disappointed that my first post-sexual experience wasn't filled with chocolates and flowers from him, and group hugs, and giggling girl talk with my friends. But we were going to be together. That more than made up for it.

"This is different," I said.

Carrie laughed. Now I was really pissed. She glanced down at the coffee table and something caught her eye. My shopping list.

Snatching it up, she scanned it, then pushed past me into the kitchen. I heard cabinet doors open and close. A moment later, she reappeared.

"There's no food in there," she said. I understood how she felt. I'd experienced a profound sense of loss ever since I got rid of the Yodels.

"Where's Scott?" *Good, Joan. Subtle change of subject. Excellent.*

Her face darkened as her expression soured, a one-two punch. "Obviously he's not here," she snapped.

"What did he do?" I asked.

"What's with the interrogation?" she said, her hands moving to her hips. "You think it's my fault he's not around, don't you?"

Her eyes were clouding, a new look for her. I'd never seen that. She wiped the floor with men, demolished their personal belongings, but she never cried over them.

"No, no, I didn't say that," I rushed on, not knowing what to say. I was pissed because I'd always been there for her through her many lousy boyfriends, and now was it too much for her to be a little happy for me? "I'm sure he's just working." *Or your pissing and moaning drove him away.*

Carrie's face resembled a thundercloud; her jaw clenched, her lips pursed. She looked down at the list. "Didn't you tell me you read a story where the character made all kinds of self-improvement lists?"

Oh shit, I thought. Gatsby. And look how well everything worked out for him. "I don't remember," I mumbled.

She handed off the list to me and scooped up her bag and

keys. Then she gave me a long look. "If you're happy, I'm happy," she said in the most cheerless voice I'd ever heard. "My congratulations to Jennifer."

She picked up one of my new books and read the title, *"Your Happiness, Your Way."* She lobbed it back onto the couch. "I'll tell you the same thing you told me; one day you're going to have the alcoholic's moment of clarity about all this. If Louise was here, she'd tell you statistically when that will happen." With that, she walked out, slamming the door behind her.

What did she know? I thought, feeling my postcoital glow whooshing down the toilet. The woman had a revolving door of relationships dating back to her teens. Her big accomplishment at this moment was dating a sphinx. What right did she have to comment on my relationship? At that moment my inner Jennifer strolled in from the kitchen and began looking around. *What—no flowers? Where's the jewelry?* There was no need to hit the panic button. I was sure the Godiva/Chanel/Tiffany train would be pulling into the station in no time. My post-Jennifer tweaks would take care of everything.

The only area where I had not taken complete control? In bed. No more Joan hesitation. The first time was fine, but I was determined to do better. Sex was the final Jennifer frontier. Only one more day to wait before I saw him again. Sunday couldn't pass fast enough.

The ringing phone pulled me out of sleep. I picked up the receiver.

"Are you trying to worry me to death?"

"Didn't Grandma teach you to announce yourself?" I countered.

"How are you feeling?"

"I'm fine, Ma." *C'mon, Joan, don't you have something to tell your mother?*

"What have you been doing?"

It was a simple question. A simple answer would suffice: Cleaning my apartment. Organizing my life. Watching television. Losing my virginity. I took a deep breath. Talking to your mother about such a major event was an all or nothing deal— you either spit it out immediately or hid it for four years until you finally talked about it because it didn't matter anymore. I wanted to talk to her. I wanted to tell her everything. When it was settled, I would tell her. I consoled myself that it wasn't going to take four years.

"Nothing. Watching television." That was it then. Losing my virginity was now officially a secret.

"Are you sure you're all right?" she probed.

The reality of the question was that parents didn't actually know everything—but they figured if they continued to poke around, eventually the child would crack and spill their guts. I was wise to this because I'd fallen for it so many times.

"I'm fine," I said evenly. The trick is not to get annoyed because then they *know* there is a problem. On the whole, parents are a crafty bunch. You have to watch them.

"So are you coming over tomorrow night?"

That reminded me. "Yeah. Actually, I need to store some stuff in the basement. Is that okay?"

"What time will you be here?" she asked.

"Why, what's up?"

"Nothing. I just want to see you. I can't see my daughter?"

"What's up, Ma?"

Reverse psychology met with dead silence.

"Mom?" I prodded. "Are you sick?" My heart sank while waiting for an answer.

"Don't be ridiculous."

"Are you out of money?"

She made a clucking sound. "Of course not. Your father was a wonderful provider, thank God. And it's our money, Joanie. I just—want to ask you something, that's all. And I don't want to go into it on the telephone."

I realized the old "Tell Me!" game would be useless. We said good-bye and I was left with an entire day to wonder about her question. Lately a lot of people hadn't been giving me answers and it was more than a little frustrating. I still hadn't forgotten or forgiven Carrie for refusing to spill on Marty's critique of me. What could he have said? I spent forty-five minutes removing all signs of body hair and this was the treatment I got. Heinous. I decided it was high time to do some belated celebrating. I called Louise and got ready to go out.

I drove down Louise's block, passing the Hondas and minivans parked in the driveways, and the cars on the street, belonging to basement apartment renters who couldn't afford an apartment complex and homeowners who couldn't afford their mortgage payments. Leaves covered the lawns, swirling in the light breeze. I pulled in behind Stan's Altima, got out and rang the bell. Stan answered the door. I'd known Stan since the ninth grade. About five feet ten with sandy hair and a medium build, he was losing his hair and getting a gut. Bob Dylan was right; the times they are a changin'. For Louise's sake, I hoped he wouldn't resort to the "comb-over."

Louise met Stan in Mr. Kimmel's ninth grade science class. Kimmel had armpit stains and a bad attitude. It's hard to believe romance could flourish under such circumstances. One day, Louise mixed the wrong chem formula and set the lab on fire. Jumping up, Stan grabbed the fire extinguisher and saved the lab, covering Louise with foam. A couple was born. All through high school, it was Louise, Stan, and me, the proverbial third wheel. Having lunch together, sitting in the bleachers watching other kids exercise, and going to school dances. Louise never seemed to mind. When I tried to pull back and stay away she insisted I come along. We used to hang out at her house (her older brother was cute, also not interested in me). When I was sixteen, Louise lost her virginity to Stan in her bedroom while I sat in her living room, watching *Raiders of the Lost Ark* with her eleven-year-old brother. Later, I was the maid of honor at Louise's wedding. That was ten years, and in Stan's case, a handful of hair ago. Now he was the head custodian at one of the elementary schools and Louise's parents helped them buy the house. I didn't see Stan much anymore.

He gave me a kiss on the cheek and said Louise was in the den. He settled back on the couch and resumed watching sports.

I found Louise tossing toys into a bin and spouting useless threats to the kids about no television. Obviously, she had received her manual. I greeted her with an ear to ear grin and entered the den doing a little dance. Letting out a shriek and a giggle, she ran over and crushed me in a bear hug.

"Tell me all about it!" she said breathlessly as the kids rushed over to greet Aunt Joan, who made Mommy so happy she'd probably forget all about the TV ban.

The children were shooed away to their own private Disney world, aka their rooms, and Louise chattered at me a mile a minute while making coffee.

"That is so wonderful! Fantastic! I am thrilled for you!"

It was wonderful, wasn't it? I giggled like a kid. I couldn't help it.

"So what did he say?" Louise leaned in.

"He has plans for us," I said, barely containing myself.

"And?"

Finally, I was the one relating an experience; I had someone giving me all their attention. I paused as I doled out all the good details while Louise oohed and aaahed.

"Do you know thirty-five percent of women say they met their future husband while he was involved in another relationship?"

I knew it. I wasn't hanging out there all alone. We had a long discussion about my situation. Technically speaking, according to Louise, you could say Wells and I were always meant to be together, therefore, he was never meant to be with his wife. Exactly what I thought.

"So you think it's okay?" I asked.

Louise took my hand. "Oh—absolutely."

"Well," I said, "it's nice to know other people have gone through the same situation I have and it all worked out."

"Honey," Louise said, "all that matters is that you've found the right one."

"Yeah, it's amazing how things happen," I blathered.

"Sixty percent of women say they found romance when they least expected it."

A few seconds passed.

"Of course, I don't know how I'd deal with it if my husband ran around with another woman," she mused. And that's when I caught it. The raised eyebrow. I knew Louise's raised eyebrow. She picked up the habit from her mother and her mother used it whenever she disapproved of someone or something.

My face felt warm. Wells wasn't running around. He was with a woman he loved—me.

"Stan would never cheat on me."

"No, never," I said through clenched teeth. "You two are meant to be together."

Louise took a sip of her coffee. "He has a great sense of loyalty."

I nodded. It was best if I didn't say anything else. I wasn't sure what would come out.

She smiled and grabbed my hand. "I'm so happy for you," she said.

And then the eyebrow went up again.

Chapter 12

My eyes flew open after two hours of sleep. Jumping out of bed, I began my routine. One full glass of water, twenty minutes of high impact aerobics, fifteen minutes of weight training, one glass of milk, half of a whole wheat muffin, one orange, and one cooked egg white. Matching black panties and bra under black silk blouse and form-fitting black skirt. Black hose and new pumps. I completed the look with a smart new purse, which I'd purchased in order to avoid cleaning out the old one. Now all I had to do was squeeze in seven more glasses of milk and water, find time to meditate, and I would be all set. One and a half hours later, I left the house tired and starving, but ready to conquer the world.

The Long Island Expressway was a parking lot. Forty minutes and two fender bender delays later, I glided into the office trying to appear nonchalant, but my bladder was about to implode. *Note to self: Start water/milk regimen after morning commute.* I forced myself to stroll to the bathroom.

Emergency averted, I strutted back to my desk and got to work. Part of me wanted to say good morning to Wells, but hey—Jennifers don't grovel. My pen paused over my work as a thought hit me. Would other people know? Would they be able to tell? *No, of course not*, I chided myself. A ludicrous idea. How could they? I was wearing my Jennifer armor. My stomach began to rumble; I glanced at the clock. Two and a half hours to a celery stick and an apple. *There is no God.*

"Good morning," the gravelly voice broke my concentration.

I looked up. He was wearing a dark gray suit with a white shirt and a black tie. He looked yummy.

Easy, Joan. "Good morning back," I said.

"Nice weekend?" he asked casually.

"Excellent," I answered.

"I'm glad to hear that." He grinned. "Can you have these done for me by noon?"

I nodded, he said thanks, and disappeared into his office. That was it. Not a wink, nothing. I could feel my afterglow draining.

As I gulped down another glass of water, I struggled to get my bearings. The old me would have been panicking but I was a Jennifer now and as a Jennifer, I understood. I still had him, but this was business. I finished the reports, transcribed his letters, returned all phone messages, ordered his lunch, Hoovered my celery and apple, brushed, flossed, Listerined, and went to the bathroom four more times before knocking on his door at 11:30 A.M.

"Come in." I entered and closed the door behind me. I sauntered over and dropped the paperwork on his desk.

"That was quick," he said, leaning back in his chair.

"Will there be anything else, Mr. Wells?" I asked.

"Yes, there will, Miss Benjamin."

I slid in front of his chair and perched on his desk. He chuckled and stood up.

"So—you enjoyed Friday night," he whispered, sliding his hands over my hips.

"As much as you did," I answered. His hands were moving under my skirt when the phone rang. I snapped back to reality and slid off the desk. His hand caught mine and, pulling me back, he slid his arm around my shoulder and kissed me.

"I can stop by around seven, how about that?"

"I'll be waiting," I purred.

Now, a true dyed in the wool Jennifer would not have caved so easily. She might have made him wait several days, possibly even a week. Although I was a Jennifer in every sense of the word, let's face it, most Jennifers had a helluva lot of sex. I hadn't and I wanted to.

He smiled and I was out the door.

Okay, I thought as I recapped the rest of my daily schedule over a lunch of mixed salad greens and balsamic vinaigrette. I would have to bolt at five, get to Mom's by five-thirty, unload, get the chitchat done ASAP and be out by six, home by six-thirty, catch a quick shower, and be in Jennifer Love Machine mode by seven. Perfect! I looked down. My bowl was empty. Damn.

By five-thirty my stomach was composing its own symphony as I screeched the car to a halt in my mother's driveway and slammed into park. As my mother opened the door, I heaved a box over the threshold.

"Joanie, slow down," she cried. By that time I had thrown open the door to the basement and begun my descent. I tripped on the second step, my body twisting as my legs went flying out from under me. I let go of the box and grabbed the banister, sending the contents cascading down the stairs. I landed on a hip. My dismount sucked but other than that, a perfect ten. Stifling a moan, I looked up to find my mother standing over me.

"Joanie, my God," she yelped, "are you all right?" I forced myself up the stairs and hobbled to the living room.

"I'm fine, I'm fine," I gasped as pain shot up through my right leg.

I walked it off as I brought in two more boxes and a load of laundry, minus the sheets. My eyes zeroed in on the clock. Ten minutes to six.

"Joanie, take off your coat—sit down."

Head her off at the pass. "Ma, I can't. I have to go. Really. I have to go. I'll do my wash when I come back."

"Nonsense, I'll do it for you."

Before I could say, "Please don't touch my laundry," the bag was open.

"Where are your sheets? Don't you have any sheets?"

Shit.

"I spilled milk on them. I was eating cereal." *Wrong answer, Joan.*

"Joanie, you shouldn't be eating in bed. It's not healthy to eat when you're not sitting up straight."

According to my mother, my life had been in peril since puberty. I had to sit up straight while eating to stave off the evils of a poor digestive tract, read in strobe lighting to protect eye health, drink copious amounts of liquid to preserve bladder and kidney function, not to mention more vitamins, exercise, fruits and vegetables, dressing in layers in winter, higher UV rated sunglasses, bras with more support, and shoes with lower heels. I never understood how I found the time to go to school, let alone work.

"I won't do it again, Ma, I promise," I said, speeding past her.

"Joanie."

I stopped short and turned. I had almost forgotten the question. I took a good look at my mother. She looked fabulous. Rosy cheeks. She had gained weight. Sex was making her fat. Something else for me to worry about.

"Joanie, I need to ask you something." She was wringing her hands. I held my breath. Was my mother getting married—before I did?

"About Randall . . ."

Randall. His name was Randall. She had never mentioned his name. Reverse psychology. If he had no name, he had no credibility, thereby not upsetting me. Now I knew where I got it from. *Memo to me: At first opportunity, read* My Mother My Self.

With that name, I wondered how old Randall was. I had visions of a wizened old man leaning on a cane but my mother was much too happy for that.

"Randall," she started again. "Well—it has been a while—and—well—I would like you to meet Randall."

I would've preferred her running off with Randall, a rash elopement followed by a quickie divorce from Randall, even a wild Club Med vacation with Randall complete with strip shuffleboard. Wanting me to meet Randall implied she wanted me to like Randall, which meant Randall was about to become semi, if not fully, permanent. This shouldn't have bothered me. My mother's happiness was the only thing that mattered. After all, my father had been gone for over twenty years. Still, it was always Mom, me, and the memory of my father, Mark "he was always a good provider, thank God," Benjamin. I guess I never thought someone would ever be in his place. I looked at the clock. Ten minutes after six. I was running out of time. I had a vision of Wells lying on the ground, with Cujo snarling at him, a shred of pant leg hanging from his bared teeth. I had to get home. At this rate my mother would be getting married before me. *Très amusante*. I looked at her and my heart squeezed.

"Of course, I'll meet him, Ma," I said, throwing my arms around her and giving her a quick kiss. "But I have to go now. I'll call you."

Her expression immediately relaxed. She grabbed me and squeezed. My stomach let out a groan. Before she could stuff a muffin in my mouth, I made my escape.

"Joanie, eat something. You look thin," she called after me.

Finally, I was doing something right.

I ran three red lights, burned an inch of rubber off my tires, then slowed to a crawl when I thought I saw a cop out of the corner of my eye. I still made it home in ten minutes. No time for a shower. Off with the office outfit, on with the sexy red bustier. As a knock sounded at the door, I saw a black and blue mosaic spreading across my right thigh. *Memo to me: Love hurts.*

Opening the door with a devil-may-care flair, I found Wells leaning on the door frame.

"Well—hello," I murmured.

"Hello yourself," he answered, slipping inside.

I slid my arms around him, while he tugged lightly at the belt on my overpriced faux silk robe. He pulled me close for a deep kiss that left me breathless. *Okay, Jennifer, let's stay alert.* I had a new secret weapon; I had completely changed my reading material. Forget *Cosmo*—so yesterday. *Mademoiselle* was child's play. I had graduated to *New Woman*, *New American Woman*, and *Total Woman*. In those hallowed pages was every sexual feat I needed. To pull them off, I would need a cornucopia of fat laden desserts, which was a shame because I was counting calories, a jumbo ice cube tray, and the flexibility and athletic prowess of an Olympic gymnast. I hadn't finished reading about the reverse Kneeling Queen maneuver when I realized that little number would probably sprain my back, dislocate my neck, and cripple my knees.

He steered me into the bedroom while undoing the bustier. His kisses made their way south into my Fun Zone, and five minutes later, my crowd went wild. Rolling over onto his back, he caressed my hair and waited. *Jennifer, paging Jennifer, you're on.* And what was my inner Jennifer doing? Fanning herself, eating grapes, and sucking on an ice cube. The ice cube! Bouncing off the bed, I ran into the kitchen and threw open the freezer door. I slapped the tray on the sink, sending two cubes flying. The hell with it, I thought, I am not bending over naked to get an ice cube off the floor. I dug another out from the tray. Rushing toward the hallway, I stepped on one of the cubes, sending my feet flying out from under me. Arms flailing, I went down on my rear, letting out an involuntary squeak. I hobbled back into the bedroom holding the remaining ice cube.

"Everything okay?" he asked.

"Fine," I said through clenched teeth. It was sort of an Oral Olympics if you will. Suck on an ice cube for a minute and then let your tongue do the walking. Needless to say it was not a perfect ten due to some heavy coughing and an occasional gag reflex, but it was a perfectly respectable seven for technical merit, and since I had already lost three pounds, an eight for presentation. I also discovered I had a cavity coming in on the bottom left. Pulling me back up, he rolled over on top of me. Afterward, we lay there quietly for about five minutes. Then he checked his watch, gave me a quick kiss, and got up.

"I have to get going," he said, grabbing his clothes and heading for the bathroom.

Stunned into silence, I stared after him as he left the room. I had expected—something else. I waited for him outside the bathroom door. He came out straightening his tie.

"I'm sorry I can't stay longer," he said, rubbing my shoulders. "We'll have more time next visit, I promise."

He bent and kissed me. "I promise," he murmured. I nodded. I could feel my doubts floating away.

I watched him scoot up the steps and a few seconds later heard the familiar snap of the gate closing. I went back to bed and crawled under the covers. This was good, I decided. Sex was very good. I forgot my bruised thigh and aching hip. I was too exhausted to meditate. Tomorrow was another day.

The shriek of the alarm shocked me awake at five. I had a choice, meditate or have my fabulous breakfast of egg white and half of a grapefruit. Meditation it was. So, how exactly does one meditate? By steady concentration one enters a peaceful state where the mind is clear regardless of outer circumstances. My outer circumstances now consisted of Kong working on the new family room with renewed vigor from sunup to sundown. I cursed his name and refocused, trying to empty my mind.

Ohm.

Was Wells like my father? Would my father have liked Wells?

Ohm.

What would my father have said about my seeing Wells?

Ohm.

It didn't matter. Wells didn't love his wife anymore. These things happen.

Ohm.

"Tell me more about your day at work," Michael had said. We were at that party. He had me snuggled away in a corner. I was facing him, he was facing the party.

Ohm.

"C'mon, Sancho, what did you do today?" he pressed as he kept looking behind me. His eyes would rest on my face for a moment but always return to whatever had captured his attention.

"The big letter A," I teased. He laughed and gave me a kiss.

Ohm.

Finally, I turned around, to find his mother staring at us, Jennifer hovering behind her.

Ohm.

Who cares? Wells loves me.

Ohm.

His wife will probably be happy when he moves out, even relieved.

Ohm.

My father would've been fine with it.

Ohm.

I have no feeling in my left leg.

Ohm.

I wonder whatever happened to Steve?

Ohm.

Oddly enough, I didn't find meditation relaxing but I continued to work at it daily. Wells and I had also settled into a routine. He came to see me two mornings a week, usually Tuesday and Thursday. I forced myself to get up at five to get ready for the Oh My! rather than the Ohm. His evening visits were not as scheduled. It didn't matter because as the winter cold blew in, I made sure I was always home.

I tried meditating over the Thanksgiving holiday but concentration was impossible. I was always wondering where Wells was, was he telling his wife about us, what was he doing with his wife and why didn't he call me? Surely, he could sneak away to call me. When we were together, he kept telling me how much he missed me, how he thought about me all the time. I consoled myself. My Jennifer Goddess remained calm, cool, and charming. Wells would be coming through shortly. As soon as the holidays were over. I was sure.

Things were good all around. Well, not all around. I hadn't spoken to Carrie in weeks. Wells was keeping me pretty busy; finally I actually had a life. She called once or twice. I wanted to talk to her but Wells might be calling so I couldn't stay on. I spoke to Louise; she seemed to perk up every time I mentioned Wells hadn't left his wife yet.

Ruminating on the state of my friendships while lying in bed one Saturday morning, I gave serious thought to taking another crack at meditation. It should be easy, my life was settled. I dozed off but rapping at the door pulled me back to consciousness. I shuffled out of the bedroom, opened the front door and there stood Kong and Mike the Plumber.

"Yeah, Joan, how are you," my landlord said. *That depends on what you're going to say, Oh Great Ape.*

"Mike's gonna start work on your bathroom. It's a big job. All the pipes and tub tile has to be redone. He's got other jobs so he'll be back and forth. He'll try to tell you when he's comin'. This could take a while. We'll have to shut off the water some of the time, too. You got your mother's house for getting your showers and all that, right?"

Shit.

Chapter 13

I had a brief lapse of mental function as "Mikey" explained the entire process of destroying—refurbishing—my bathroom. While he babbled I calculated my ability to bathe in the kitchen sink rather than running back and forth to my mother's house, which would be a bitch. By the time Mikey finished his recitation, I decided it was more than dislike; I hated him. And the feeling was mutual. We stood there glaring at each other. He looked me up and down, and then I swear, he curled his lip. I turned my attention back to the primate as he finished the rundown.

"Yeah, Mike comes highly recommended, Joan."

Translation: *He's a personal friend or even better, a relative.*

"I know it's not the best time there, Joan, but I'd like to get it done for you as soon as possible."

Translation: *Mikey owes me a favor and it's convenient for me to call it in now.*

"He should be able to have this finished before Christmas."

Translation: *If you can flush your toilet by Easter, you'll be lucky.*

I wasn't really listening. My next thought after hygiene was Wells. What the hell was I supposed to do now?

I pressed the master plumber. "So what will your schedule be?"

He managed a few syllables. "I'll come when I can."

My mind flitted wildly. I couldn't have this moron banging pipes while I had Wells's pants down, now could I?

"Can't you tell me what days you'll be here?" I asked, my voice rising an octave.

"When I know, you'll know. You expecting company?" he asked, smirking at me. I realized I was wearing Tweety Bird pajamas and fuzzy Snoopy slippers. Funny how one didn't notice these things at a more optimal time, like before letting strangers through the front door.

"I have a life," I snapped.

He made a noise.

"Okay, calm down there, Joan," Kong droned. "We'll take care of things for you."

I slammed the door after them. What now?

After oversleeping on Monday morning, I clicked into fast forward. First, a mega kickboxing workout fueled by visions of giving Mikey the Wonder Plumber a few choice shots to the groin. At least it kept my mind off food: Oh, for a bacon, egg, and cheese on a roll, I thought as I choked down my breakfast of tea and a no-fat bran muffin. I was exhausted but I was ten pounds thinner. Another five pounds and I would be Jennifer perfect.

I chugged a pint of water for that faux full feeling and made it in to work in record time. Dumping my purse on my desk, I flew into the ladies' room—my morning routine. I might have a kidney malfunction, but my skin looked flawless.

I settled at my desk as Wells peered out from his office. He smiled and strolled back inside. Grabbing my pad and pencil, I sauntered after him, closing the door behind me. He sat down in his chair and assumed his regular position.

"Nice weekend?" he asked casually.

"Fabulous," I shot back, waiting for him to ask for details. He didn't.

I slid onto the desk, slipped off my shoes and ran my foot up his leg. My inner Jennifer was flipping through a Victoria's Secret catalogue while getting a pedicure. "*It's about time,*" she said.

"And what did you do this weekend?" I purred.

"The same as always," he replied. "Did you think about me?" He got up and began pushing between my legs.

I could feel my body temperature rising but managed to control myself. Jennifers were in command of their emotions. I took a deep breath. "I did. Would you like me to tell you what I was thinking?"

He cackled. "Was it naughty?" he asked, nibbling on my ear. My head began to spin.

"What about tonight?" he whispered. *Yes, Joan, what about tonight? Maybe Mikey can have a drink with us before we get started.* I pulled back. I'd gone over my situation a hundred times looking for the up side until I found it.

"We have a small problem," I said, forcing my voice to remain even. After all, one always wants what's not readily available, doesn't one?

He pulled back. "What's that?" he asked cautiously.

"My landlord is renovating my bathroom. The work schedule is a tad erratic."

"Oh," he said, "that is a problem." His features relaxed again. "What do you think we should do about this?"

"Well, I just don't know," I teased. My inner Jennifer was getting a massage. She gave a heavy sigh. *"I'm thinking suite at the Hilton. They have a lovely indoor pool and spa tubs."* We were so on the same page. "We'll go to a hotel. I'll make the reservation."

"You're not going to make me wait, are you?" His lips caught mine. "You know I can't do without you," he murmured.

He glanced around the office, taking in the locked door, the closed blinds. I followed his gaze. He looked at me and smirked. I got his message. Here? Now? I had never dreamed of doing *that*—here. You made love in the privacy of your own home, in a bed, in a suite at the Hilton. I hesitated. He must've read the look of doubt on my face because he cupped his hand around my neck and pulled me close. Well, we could, couldn't we? Jennifers could be sexy and wonderful anywhere—couldn't they?

"Hey, you know I'm working on everything for us, but it's tough. You know how it is." He pulled me closer. "I need you, you know that."

He kissed me again, once, twice, three times, until my objections evaporated. He pulled back, his eyes meeting mine.

"Do you trust me?" he asked in a gentle voice.

Did I? I didn't answer him. He said he needed me. The next thing I knew I was flat on my back on the desk, my legs wrapped around his waist and Wells was whistling while he worked. I opened my eyes. His morning bagel slathered with cream cheese was resting next to my head. I hate to admit it but for a moment, I was sorry I couldn't do both.

For the record, it is extremely difficult to look like you haven't had sex when you actually have had sex. It was the tousled hair, the rosy cheeks, the glow. I strolled out of the bathroom stall, trying to appear as if the most exciting thing I'd done all morning was make photocopies. Lizzie from Customer Accounts wandered in, looked at me out of the corner of her eye and sidled up to the sink next to me.

"Busy morning?" she asked casually, her eyes moving over me.

"Yeah. Lots of reports—a ton." *Good, Joan. Excellent. Excellent answer.*

"You were in there with him a long time today," she probed.

So people were watching. *Easy, Joan. If you snap over it, she'll know.* Then everyone will know.

"You know how he likes to talk. He had a lot to say." The buzz was most people thought he was a jerk, but I knew he wasn't. He was a good guy and had a great sense of humor. They didn't know him like I did.

Lizzie kept staring at me. Finally, she smiled a knowing smile, said "uh-huh" and walked out. I looked in the mirror. That damn glow. I should've camped out in the stall.

I worked hard all day, taking lunch at my desk—if you can call a bed of lettuce with sliced carrots lunch. Wells wandered back and forth from his meetings, laughing and talking with colleagues. He stopped at my desk, handed off reports, collected others. We exchanged smiles. He winked at me. I was relaxed, charming, effortlessly Jenniferesque. Now I knew all about the excitement and romance surrounding clandestine meetings, stolen moments, and various carnal activities with your beloved. We talked as if nothing was going on between us. It was our secret. Jennifers everywhere rose up and applauded. I could absolutely do this for a while. We would just snatch time in the office until we would be together, out in the open, as man and wife.

At five o'clock, he came out of his office, briefcase in hand, and stopped by my desk.

"I've got an appointment at six," he said.

I nodded.

"I'll see you first thing in the morning?"

"Absolutely," I said.

He gave me the happy little boy grin, a wink, and was gone.

I sat at my desk. The office was empty and silent; I was alone. I squared my shoulders and started to clean up for the night.

I was fine with everything. Really. I couldn't be happier.

I sat vibrating in the Spa Lux 1000 massage chair in the window display of the Sharper Image in the mall, feeling restless and uneasy. My mother had insisted I go with her. She was speaking but I wasn't listening. My mind was miles away. There was a life-size Superman display next to me and I had a sudden urge to give him a swift kick. The Man of Steel had done nothing to deserve my wrath.

I didn't want to admit it but despite my cool and collected Jennifer persona, Wells was annoying me. Parading back and forth, talking to me like there was nothing between us. Not that I was expecting an interoffice memo to go out. But I thought that after a while, there would be some recognition, some acknowledgment of the change in our relationship. It was my personal opinion that screwing in the office fell outside the normal realm of day to day business activities.

"Joanie, which one do you think is better?" My mother was holding up two different ultra-comfort, ultra-soft hygienic pillows for Randall.

"Whatever, Mom, I'm sure they're both fine."

"But they're not the same—"

"It's a pillow, Ma! A stinking pillow, what difference does it make?"

My mother was staring at me looking hurt, along with the other shoppers. They didn't look hurt. I was in no mood. She dropped the subject. The Spa Lux 1000 was giving me a headache.

Every day I came home and checked out the bathroom, hoping for a change in the pile of rubble, some sign that Mikey the Wonder Plumber had made an appearance. I stood in the bathroom doorway and surveyed the mess—the same mess. Shit! Another no show. I was washing in shifts, my bathroom was a shambles and I was having sex at seven o'clock in the morning instead of ten in the evening, which should've made me very happy because it's a known fact that everyone looks better after sex. I sighed. There was nothing to be done except deal with it until "Mikey" was done. I flopped on the couch in disgust. Tomorrow was already planned. I would have to be up at five to be in the office by seven for my morning "meeting" with Wells. Naps should definitely be penciled into the work-day agenda. I went into the bedroom and caught a look at the new me in the mirror. My reasonably thin thighs were now unmistakably thin and the jiggle had vanished. My stomach had a slight concave dip. *If Michael could see me now, he'd be sorry he left me*, I thought. I knew he would. He would know I really was good enough for him, good enough for his family. I knew what Carrie would say. "He's a shit, forget him, you're wasting your time." I frowned at the thought. She wasn't always right. I was in a crappy mood just thinking about her. I wondered how she was but if I called it would only end in an argument. I realized now that Wells had been easy, I had him conquered from the start. But Michael would be the true test. I could out-Jennifer Jennifer. With Louise's connections, this was a real possibility, and she might be able to provide the opportunity for one of those classic reunions, running into the one who let you get away. I could have Michael now if I wanted him. I didn't. I just wanted him to see I wasn't Sancho. I was Dulcinea, the object of his affection. I wanted to show him what he'd missed. Only this time, I would be the one walking away.

Chapter 14

December was flying by. I was in every morning at seven and I left at six or later every night. I read Wells's signals like an expert in Morse code. My bag of tricks was growing and I was an expert performer. But every time I thought he was about to commit, he would cool down for a few days. I worried, I fretted, and I began to show my annoyance.

"What's the matter?" he asked innocently one morning as I dropped a pile of reports on his desk.

"Nothing," I sulked.

"You sure?" he asked.

"Yup. You have a ten and a two o'clock today."

"What would I do without you?" he asked, running a hand over my hip.

I looked down at him. "You'd be in a lot of trouble."

"You sure everything's okay?"

"Perfect."

He returned to his presentation. "I'll let it go then."

Let it go? Let it go? *Listen to me, you moron, don't you know everything is not okay?* What schmuck didn't realize he had to pursue the conversation! I could hear Carrie's voice in my head: "They don't give a shit, Joanie." I sulked all day until deciding it was time to teach Mr. Wells a lesson. I was going home at five. He could whistle "Dixie" while his pants were zipped up. He called me in at ten to five.

"Are you going to start talking to me?" he asked.

"I wasn't aware I wasn't. I must've missed the memo," I shot back.

"You're beautiful, do you know that?" He leaned back in his chair.

"Are you trying to make friends with me?"

"I thought we were friends."

Drawn like a magnet, I came closer. He sat up in his chair, sliding his hands over my hips, and then under my skirt and up my thighs.

"Is everything okay?" I asked, attempting to start a real conversation, with real dialogue. "Lately, you seem preoccupied."

"Everything's fine," he said easily. "You are incredible." His hands slid higher. "Let's wait until everyone leaves," he murmured.

"I think someone is taking a lot for granted here," I said, my voice coming out as a whisper. "How do you know I'm interested?"

He grinned.

Everyone was gone by six. I straddled him in his office chair.

I leaned against him. "Wouldn't you rather be doing this lying down in a king-size bed, in a comfy hotel suite, with champagne, room service, and a DO NOT DISTURB sign on the door?"

He chuckled.

"It would be so much easier to see all of me," I whispered. "If you're good, Santa may give that to you for Christmas."

He pulled me closer. "You don't have to do that."

Not the answer I was looking for.

"And where else would you like to make love?"

Ah, now we were getting somewhere. Well, Jennifer, where do you want to go? A hotel room is small potatoes.

I paused, feigning deep thought. "What about a cruise? Some place exotic."

He braced his hands around my waist. "Fiji? Do you think you've been a good girl this year?"

"M-m-m," I said, running my fingers through his hair. "And I deserve something sparkly, too."

He chuckled. "I'll see what I can do."

I was thinking something in three or four carats. He would move out, come in with the bling, plus the cruise. I hoped Jennifer wasn't congratulating herself too hard for wrapping things up with Michael in six months. I would come in well under that time. My inner Jennifer was looking at me with respect and awe. *"You've come a long way, Jenny,"* she said.

Christmas was fast approaching. My pursuit of self-actualization into a woman of strength and harmony was going well. I had tamed every area of my life with two exceptions: sleep and meditation. The former I couldn't get nearly enough of and I couldn't seem to do the latter. Either exercise led back to the same place: my father.

The dream I had was always the same. He was picking me up from school on my first day of kindergarten. He looked at me with his kind face and rosy cheeks wearing the same jovial smile I knew from his pictures. He held my hand as we walked to the car. "What did you learn today?" he asked. I was chattering to him, but he kept asking that same question. And suddenly I was an adult and he was standing before me. He still smiled but his eyes were sad. "What did you learn today?" he asked. And then my eyes flew open.

I had been avoiding my mother since the mall incident. I dropped off and picked up my laundry when I knew she'd be out with her friends. I was hiding the new, improved, super slim me. As a Jewish mother, she'd see my weight loss and call the paramedics. We had been communicating by answering machine.

BEEP. "Joanie, I never see you anymore."

BEEP. "Joanie, are you feeling all right?"

BEEP. "Joanie, I'm worried about you."

BEEP. "Joanie, Marge knows a nice young man who's studying to be a doctor."

BEEP. "Joanie, don't forget Randall is coming for dinner Christmas day. He's very excited to meet you."

I had forgotten about this. There was no avoiding it. I would have to go. This would require buying Randall a Christmas present.

When I was a child, we celebrated Hanukkah, so I was told. As I grew up, I met Louise, who celebrated Christmas, and so did my mother's new friends on the island. My mother took to the new holiday with ease. I think it was all part of the post-father-dying recovery plan She wanted me to be happy and it was a second gift opportunity. But gift-giving meant gift-buying and I was still facing a severe cash flow problem after financing my transformation. I also had to get something for Wells.

What to do? I admit guys get a raw deal. Entire jewelry stores are filled with bling for women. Guys get one little case in a corner, with cuff links, tie tacs, and money clips. Other than that, the entire male race has been relegated to ties, jeans, and sweaters, all either blue, brown, or black. A wardrobe for the Amish. I had crawled through every store in the mall several times and found one nice pair of mother-of-pearl links—four hundred dollars worth of nice. I realized my previous gift-giving had been on a par with a gift certificate for a root canal. Yet another area where I'd gone wrong with Michael, the "we've been married for decades" Christmas gifts: sweaters, socks, and CDs. My version of a threesome? Old Spice after-shave, cologne, and soap on a rope. The better to strangle our relationship with, my dear.

Jennifers get reservations for two at a luxury hotel and spend the night in the hot tub, drinking champagne, eating chocolate-covered strawberries, and making love until dawn. But Wells didn't want that. I sighed. So, even though the cuff links were not my Jennifer choice, they were going to have to do. I consoled myself, they would fit in with his country club, summer house in the Hamptons lifestyle—a lifestyle soon to be mine as well.

After crawling the mall, I crept into the house, my stomach howling. The aromas of the food court had made me realize I'd been hungry since October. I contemplated going to the store to buy something that could be classified as food rather than a horticultural experiment. I tossed my purse down on the table and saw my assortment of bras and panties that I had hand washed that morning lying on a kitchen chair. I had left them hanging on the shower rod. So who the hell put them there? Then I heard clanging coming from the bathroom. Grabbing my lingerie, I threw them on the bed. This was the icing on the cake. Mikey had been fondling my tiger print thong. I parked myself in the bathroom doorway, arms folded across my chest.

"I'm thinking of getting a steel tub like the ones they had in the Old West," I said. "I can put it in the kitchen."

Mikey continued to swing his instrument of destruction at my tub tiles without missing a beat.

"Nice undies," he said.

I stiffened. "Worry about your own Fruit of the Looms—not mine," I shot back.

"Where's loverboy?" he asked.

"None of your damn business," I answered. *Good, Joan. Snappy comeback soon to be followed by nah-nah-nah-nah-nah.*

"At home with the little woman, huh?" he continued.

I was stunned silent.

I'm being judged by my plumber? My plumber is giving me a morality check?

There was a persistent rapping at the door.

"Stick your nose back in your pipes. It's where you belong." *Excellent, Joan. The perfect combo of guilt and lameness wrapped in cruelty.*

"Will do," he said without looking at me.

I sulked my way to the door and opened it to find Carrie standing there, looking pretty sulky herself. I moved aside to let her enter.

"So, how's it going, Heidi?" she asked, strolling past me into the apartment.

I trailed after her into the living room and found her staring at the bare bookcase. "Since when are you into the illiterate look?"

"I read the books," I snapped. "I didn't need them anymore. Where's Scott?"

She mumbled something about working and followed the yellow brick road of dirt and dust to the bathroom.

"Hey," she said, peeking her head in the doorway.

Mikey turned around. "Hey back," he said.

"You have a name?" she asked.

"Mike."

"Ooh—bad choice. You might want to change that."

"I don't care what his name is," I said defensively.

"What's wrong with Mike? Is that the married one's name?" he added.

"I don't appreciate this discussion of my personal life," I said.

"No, Mike is the bastard ex-fiancé," Carrie informed him, as if I wasn't even there.

"Oh, rebounding, huh?"

"I am not rebounding!" I snapped.

Mikey took a closer look at Carrie. "Don't I know you?"

Carrie shrugged.

"Someone else whose property you've wrecked?" I inquired.

The lightbulb went on. "Yeah, now I remember. You used to date Johnny. You guys hung out at the Lucky Tavern."

"Yeah," she acknowledged. "He broke up with me, so I went down there and threw a Coors in his face."

"Which landed on me," Mikey said.

"That was you!"

They laughed merrily. It was old home week in my bathroom.

"And then I punched him."

"And he fell on me."

"So how are you?" Carrie asked enthusiastically.

"I'm doin' okay." He smiled. "You're better off. He was a schmuck." And then he gave her a warm smile. Sure, for her, he smiles. It's my bathroom and I'm persona non grata.

"We're strolling down memory lane now?" I said. "I'd like to shower before New Year's."

He ignored me. "Are you really friends with her?"

"Do you mind?" I yelled. I walked away from the both of them. I heard Carrie say, "She wasn't always like this." That's right. I used to let people walk all over me and tolerated everyone's shit without as much as a word. Those days were over.

I raged around the bedroom, clearing away the lingerie and the dry cleaning. I was stuffing my lingerie in a drawer when the door creaked and Carrie walked in. She fingered a Donna Karan dress lying on the bed.

"Since when can you afford this?" she asked, sounding concerned.

"I'm doing just fine," I lied, snatching it out of her hand.

"He's too cheap to give you a raise."

I didn't answer.

"You look like shit, you know. Don't you eat?"

"I'm fine."

She eyed the men's catalogues spread out on my bed. "Don't tell me you're buying him a Christmas gift."

I plucked them up and threw them in the closet.

"Well, great," she said. "You should get him some chia pet spread. If he puts it in his pants, maybe he'll grow balls and leave his wife."

"Maybe you should get some for Scott. He might actually commit, if you haven't frightened him away yet."

Carrie's mouth dropped open. I knew what I said, but I wasn't taking it back. That was the old Joan. The new Joan wasn't going to take her sarcastic shit. I turned and continued putting my clothes away.

"How about breaking his windows or destroying something in his apartment? I'm sure he'd change his mind and run out and buy that ring you've been waiting for."

Carrie said nothing. Her eyes filled. I could've kept going. Part of me wanted to but I forced myself to stop.

"I appreciate you coming over to explain my life to me but I have it all under control."

"I didn't come over to explain your life to you," she said.

I gave up struggling to put a little black dress on a hanger and threw it on the bed. "Then why are you here?" I demanded. She shrugged.

"Well, you can go, because I'm just fine. Wells is fine. *We're* fine. Everything is going to work out."

"Don't forget to send me an invitation to the wedding." She walked out. I heard the door slam and then a loud crash in the bathroom.

I ran to the bathroom to find Mikey staring at a rotting pipe in the middle of the gaping hole in the bathroom wall.

"This is going to take longer than I thought," he said.

Shit.

The art of money management is an intricate affair. Debits, credits, deposits, withdrawals. I have never been one for money management. I had checks, therefore I had money. My previous Michael-approved pseudo-employment had provided me with an ample amount of income. I never discussed money with Wells. The Jennifer Persona left no room for financial woes; it was assumed Jennifers had money. Appearing desperate was out of the question. But as I'd spent the last three months charging like a stampeding bull for my brand new sophisticated wardrobe and lifestyle, "desperate" was certainly the appropriate term.

A few days later, as I handed my credit card over for Wells's cuff links, I mentally figured my plan of attack. I would apply for new cards with zero percent APR, and then transfer all my balances, which would take approximately two to three weeks. In the meantime, I'd continue to pay the minimum due, which in total amounted to about $600 a month. I didn't have $600 a month, but since I didn't eat, my food budget could go toward credit card debt. Once the balances were transferred, I could reduce the minimum amount due. With my earning power, I figured I would be able to pay off my debts in time for retirement. I would think about it later. For now, I had it under control. I knew what I was doing. Once Wells and I were together, out in the open, things would be different.

* * *

I showed up at my mother's house the afternoon of Christmas Eve. After the assorted gasps at my skeletal appearance—an absolute exaggeration—I settled on the couch. I was sure Louise's nana would've called an ambulance by now.

"Joanie, you have to eat something. You're so thin."

"I'm eating better now than I ever have before. I even eat tofu. I feel great." *Liar, liar, pants on fire.*

"Be careful with strange foods. You could get an upset stomach."

The pressure of remaining calm weighed on me like a boulder. I tried to pretend nothing was wrong, but something *was* wrong, very wrong. Wells was not here with me. There had been no presents. No gifts exchanged. And he wasn't home packing his bags, preparing to move out. He had already packed his bags to go on a cruise—*with her*. He had waited until yesterday to tell me. While everyone was joking and laughing in the holiday spirit, he had called me into his office.

"Hey." He traced the line of my jaw with his finger. "It's a family vacation with the kids. I have to go. Do you think I'm going to be happy away from my girl?"

He kissed me and then whispered in my ear, "I just need to find the right moment to tell her." He kissed me again. "We'll have our own special Christmas when I get back. I already have your present. We'll celebrate."

But that didn't stop the anger from rising in my throat. I should've been happy that the waiting would soon be over. But I couldn't sleep. I kept seeing them together, wondering where he was, what he was doing, did he tell her yet?

I woke up on Christmas morning with my mother standing over me wearing a Santa hat and a nightgown that said, "I brake for reindeer."

"Joanie, come open your presents. I'm making breakfast." The thought of real food was revolting. Maybe if she put green food coloring on everything, my stomach would think it was a salad. Exhausted, I forced myself out of bed. Under the tree, a panacea of packages in brightly colored wrapping, ribbons, and bows awaited. The smell of pancakes was in the air. We'd moved from post-Daddy to pre-Randall.

I plowed through my gifts. Sweaters, perfume, gift certificates. I didn't have as much for her but I did shop. What the hell. I was up to my ass in debt anyway. What's a few hundred more?

"Oh, Joanie, you shouldn't have," she said as she put on the gold hoop earrings. "Thank you!" She threw her arms around me.

"Mom, why isn't Randall here?"

"He's coming in a little while."

"No, Mom, why didn't he stay over?"

"Well . . ." She blushed. "Joanie, I didn't think it was right."

"Mom, I'm thirty."

She got up off the couch and went to check the pancakes. "You're still my daughter and I wanted you to meet him first."

She put a hungry man plate of pancakes on the dining room table and then scooted down the hall. I was at the table having a little pancake with my syrup when she reappeared and placed a college brochure next to my plate.

"I thought you might want to have a look," she said.

"Can I have my breakfast first?"

She sat down and took my hand. I sensed the manual was out of the drawer. "Joanie, I just want you to be settled. I want you to know what you're doing with your life." *I'm having an affair with a married man who's going to leave his wife and marry me.*

There was a knock at the door.

"I know what I'm doing. I'm answering the door." I crossed the living room, into the hallway, opened the door, and standing in front of me was Randall. He was tall and sturdy, with a full head of salt and pepper hair and a kind face. He resembled my father.

He brought me gifts and sat like an expectant father as I opened them. Cartier perfume and a sparkly pink sweater with long sleeves from Macy's. Ten extra points if he picked it out himself. This was new territory for me—what was proper etiquette with Mother's new boyfriend?

"Thank you very much," I said. "This was very thoughtful of you."

"You're very welcome."

That was easy enough. We got up to finish breakfast. He took my hand and gave it a squeeze. At that moment, I knew my mom had found a good one.

Throughout dinner that evening, I listened while they talked. What did they talk about? Everything. Their friends, the movie they saw, the books they were reading, their plans for New Year's Eve and the weekend after that. They chatted easily; I felt like an eavesdropper on their life together. A life I didn't have with Wells. I could feel my agitation rising; I dealt with it by shoving in more turkey, a low fat, low carb, heart smart food. Randall roused me from my thoughts.

"Joan, your mother mentioned your apartment is not really working out."

"That's not quite true," I said, giving my mother a dagger of death stare. She was unmoved.

"You have no bathroom, Joanie. You can't even wash your hands. You could get an infection."

"It's temporary—and I wash my hands in the kitchen."

"I wanted to let you know that I have some friends who have an empty apartment in their home. I could introduce you if you'd like."

This was a smooth "your mother has been telling me how crappy your life is and I feel I have to do something because I'm sleeping with her." Six months ago I would've jumped at the idea of someone helping me out.

"Thank you," I said. "I'll definitely keep it in mind."

"Joanie's thinking of going back to school," my mother blurted.

I was unaware of this.

"That's wonderful," Randall said. "Best thing for you."

I took another mouthful of peas even though I was fairly certain I was going to heave. And then I smiled.

* * *

The day after Christmas I was going in as Mikey went out.
"I'll be back after New Year's," he said.
"How will I live without you?" I answered.
He ignored me and walked out.

Chapter 15

A week into the New Year, Wells returned, tanned and relaxed. I slid into his office; I stood in front of his desk, waiting. He who talks first—loses.

"How was your holiday?" he asked.

"Wonderful," I said. "Yours?"

"Not what I would've liked."

What does that mean? That doesn't sound like "I told my wife I'm leaving her." That sounds like "I ordered the steak rare and it came well done." It's shit or get off the pot time, mon amour. He got up and came around the desk, sliding his hands around my back. *Not this time,* I thought, floating out of his grip.

"If you'd like to see me—all of me—and receive your present—you will have to come to my place. Tonight. Six-thirty." So what if the bathroom resembled a demilitarized zone? He could pee before he came over.

He smiled but he didn't look happy. Good.

At six-thirty I was pacing the living room floor, dressed in a see-through baby doll slip. At seven the doorbell rang. He came in carrying boxes, one smaller than the other, both wrapped with a huge gold bow.

I presented him with the small shiny box and could barely sit still while he opened it.

He smiled. He said "wow" and "thank you" and kissed me.

Then it was my turn. I forced a smile but before the wrapping was off the larger box I knew it was chocolate. *Joan isn't happy.* "Let's see what else you've brought," I said.

I tried to appear nonchalant as I tugged at the wrapping on the small box. It was perfume, Evening in Paris. Even my mother didn't wear this crap anymore. He bought me perfume and chocolates. This was what I'd been waiting for? And I knew he stopped at the mall on his way over. That's why he was late.

Santa was a little pressed for time, n'est-ce pas? *Did Santa get lost on his way to the jewelry department? Joanie doesn't see a diamond necklace.* I felt a primal scream coming on. I sucked in a deep breath and pushed the feeling down.

"Shh," he soothed. "I haven't been able to get a minute alone but you know how special you are. I wouldn't come empty-handed, would I?"

I gave him a sideways glance and pinched my lips together. "You didn't tell her."

"You're not going to be mad at me now, are you? Don't be mad at me. I'm going to make it up to you. I promise. The kids were there. I couldn't upset them."

He leaned in for a kiss but I held back.

"Before Valentine's Day," I said. "Or you can leave now."

Uh, hello? When did Goddess Jennifer become Bitch Jennifer? "When he showed up with crappy chocolate and perfume. You go, girl," my inner Bitch Jennifer said, pointing at me with perfectly manicured bloodred fingernails. She was right. This was no time for the finesse of a Goddess.

"As soon as I get a chance," he soothed.

"Valentine's Day," I repeated. I ran my hand under the film of the slip. "Or you can stay home. I don't think your wife has one of these, does she?"

His face hardened into a smooth stone, and I watched him take a deep breath. "Valentine's Day," he relented, giving me that little boy look. "Now are you going to stop being mad at me?"

We went to bed. As soon as it was over, he was up and getting dressed. He leaned over, kissed my forehead. "I'm sorry, you know I can't stay."

I threw on my silky robe and sat in a chair at the kitchen table. I could hear the sounds of his rustling in the bathroom. He didn't ask me how I was managing with the plumbing problem.

I wondered what Randall did after he and my mom—well, I didn't want a visual on that. I wondered what Michael did in the aftermath with Jennifer. Did they talk? Go to sleep? Lie close to each other or retreat to their own side of the bed? I even wondered what Steve would have done. What was he doing now? Did he have a wife? A girlfriend? Both? Was he considerate after sex or did he just roll over and mumble good night? I heard the door open and Wells emerged.

"I see they didn't finish yet," he said.

"No," I answered. "Soon." I didn't get up.

He put on his overcoat and leaned over and gave me a quick kiss. "See you tomorrow?"

"Absolutely."

"Well," he said. "Thank you."

With that, he was gone.

"You're welcome," I said into the silence.

Chapter 16

Freud explained the three components of the human psyche, the id, the ego, and the superego. Loosely translated, the id was raw desire, the ego was self-control, and the Superego was the rampaging fear of burning in hell for all eternity if you did something wrong. The id has always been portrayed as something bad; a person must avoid the id, tie it down, lock it in a closet, put it to bed, and if it calls out that it has to go to the bathroom or wants a drink of water, ignore it. I decided that Freud was all wrong about the id. He made it sound like desire was bad. I now saw that the id was simply a vehicle for change. The id inspired you to be something more than what you were. My id had propelled my journey toward Jennifer nirvana and I had reached my goal. I was Jennifer. To paraphrase Gordon Gekko, "Id is good, id works." Gone was the inability to speak up, make a bold statement, return a sharp-tongued retort, or simply take what I wanted. The old Joan had vanished. I would be unrecognizable to Michael or Steve. And I was all the better for it. I stopped agonizing over the age-old questions that had haunted my days and especially my nights in the aftermath of Michael. "Why did this happen?" and my other favorite, "What did I do wrong?" I knew now and I had corrected those failures. I was new and improved. I could live without having to mentally chastise myself over every move I made. My mind was tranquil—there were no great dilemmas to wrap myself around. I lived on instinct—that was all I needed.

I had mastered my life down to my hunger pangs. I had settled at 115 pounds and felt good about my slim figure. I never thought about my food as I ate it—it was a means to an end.

And Wells? After the Christmas cruise debacle, I took steps to bring the situation back in line. There was still time to have this wrapped up before the six-month mark. My Bitch Jennifer was up at the plate ready to bat. There was no reason for me to come in to work while roosters were still crowing. I showed up early some mornings and later on others. After a while he began to ask me, "Will I see you tomorrow morning?" "We'll see," I would say, relishing the look of longing on his face. Despite his promises, he wasn't any closer to leaving his wife. I wracked my brain for a way to move the process forward but it was tricky.

And then the winter's deep freeze moved indoors. He became sullen and irritable, losing his patience and finding fault with my work.

"These charts are wrong." He slapped the presentation folder down on my desk. "Do them over."

"This is what you asked for," I snapped.

"If you can't follow directions, then I suggest you ask. Understand?"

I ignored him and he stalked off into his office. I sat at my desk, shaking. I had to be careful not to push too hard. My bank balance was draining like a bursting dam, and retaking ground by threatening to quit was out of the question. After weeks of sparring, he did a 360-degree turn and asked me to meet him outside the office early one morning. *All hail Bitch Jennifer.* I could use a suite at the Hilton right about now.

When I pulled into the parking lot of a motel on Sunrise Highway, I sucked in a breath. The low one-story building resembled a dingy strip mall only with a dozen doors. My inner Jennifer was holding out a bottle of hand sanitizer. *"This doesn't look like the Hilton, now does it?"*

Ten minutes later, we were in the motel room. Wells was

pawing at the buttons on my dress, telling me how beautiful I was, as if nothing had been wrong. I stole quick glances at the worn bedspread. The room was clean—that was the best I could say about it. He nudged against me.

"Have you been a naughty girl?" he whispered in my ear.

Wells loved role playing. I assumed this was the "naughty secretary" scenario. I wondered if he numbered them. In a split second I had to make a decision. I caught a glimpse of myself in the mirror, the brand new Escada dress and stiletto boots. I had barely made the minimum due on my credit card. I played along.

"No, I've been very bad," I purred.

And then it happened. My inner Joan appeared. She was sitting on the edge of the bed. *What are you doing?"*

I squeezed my eyes shut, pushing her out of my mind.

The days drifted by. His mood reverted to happy-go-lucky replete with a ridiculous grin that showed all of his teeth.

He kept smiling.

I kept waiting.

One morning, I was redoing my garters in Wells's office as he zipped up. The phone rang and instinctively, I picked it up.

"Mr. Wells's office," I said mechanically.

"Hi, Joan—is my husband anywhere?" asked the wife of Mr. Wells.

"He's just outside, talking to someone, Linda," I answered pleasantly.

"How are you, Joan?"

"I'm fine." I was standing in the middle of the office, the buttons on my blouse still undone, one garter unattached. A sudden urge to run and hide came over me.

"Good. I hope you had a nice holiday. Our cruise was fabulous. The weather was gorgeous, and the food was unbelievable. Just fantastic. What have you been up to?"

I've been degrading myself in a shitbag hotel with your husband. "Oh, the same."

My inner Joan was sitting behind the desk, wearing a dark suit, typing. *"She sounds pretty nice. What are you doing?"*

"Well, if you ever get a chance to go on a cruise, you should. They have everything . . ."

She kept talking, her pleasant voice droning. She sounded different, almost friendly. *Please don't speak anymore. I can't stand to hear the sound of your voice.*

I could feel Wells staring at me. I ignored him.

"Here he is now."

"Tim tells me how hard you work. Take care of yourself, Joan," she said.

"I will. You, too."

I handed the phone to Wells.

My fingers flew over the last of my buttons as I tried to ignore the sound of him talking softly to his wife. I walked out of the office and closed the door behind me.

Carrie's voice sounded in my head. *"They're all shits, Joanie. They're all shits who can't be trusted."*

I pushed the thought away. I sat down at my desk, ignoring the knowing looks from people walking past.

And there was my inner Joan rearing her ugly head. She was diligently filing. *"He's been using you, lying to you all these months. I'll stay with my original question—What are you doing?"*

I went into the bathroom and heaved up the remains of my breakfast.

He lied. He's not going to leave her. He never intended to leave her. I stared at my face in the bathroom mirror.

My inner Jennifer stood next to me, touching up her makeup. *"You're making the rest of us look bad,"* she said.

I left at four o'clock with a cursory word about a headache. He put a hand on my shoulder and gave a light squeeze.

"Take care of yourself, okay?" he said.

I shrugged off his hand and left.

I threw my purse onto the seat and got in the car. Just another day at the office. I didn't want to think about anything. There was nothing to think about.

I entered the Mole Hole to find Mikey working feverishly

with a partner. Oh joy. Batman has brought Robin. Just what this job needs, a dynamic duo of stupidity.

"Is this Moe or Curly?" I asked.

"He answers to Richie," Mike said tersely. I didn't apologize. Better to be the spawn from hell than get kicked in the ass and let everyone make a jerk out of you. Which was what Wells had been doing.

"When is this episode of *This Old Bathroom* going to end?" I said to Mikey.

"As soon as fucking possible."

"Do you have any bottled water?" Richie asked.

"Go upstairs," Mike said, before I could open my mouth. Richie pushed past me.

Silence.

"I would've given him water," I said.

"Don't sweat it," he said.

I had never offered Mikey anything, water, juice, soda, nothing. Not even a low carb, no fat, no taste cookie. And why should I? Why did I have to feed the person who was screwing up my entire existence, and making a filthy mess? Only putzy Joan would reward him for disrupting her life on a daily basis. Not anymore.

After several days of moping about Wells, I headed over to Louise's to decompress. Maybe she had some news about Michael. At Louise's I found the usual chaos: toys everywhere, screaming children, screaming Louise, and Stan and his emerging beer belly sprawled in the den watching television.

"Stan, will you see what the hell she's crying about!" Louise bellowed. I heard a litany of muttered obscenities as the recliner slammed down to terra firma and Stan stomped through the kitchen.

I gave him a wave.

"Hey, Joanie," he grunted on his way through.

I listened as Stan yelled at every child in the living room, regardless of whether they belonged to him, and left them all crying.

"Happy now?" he said as he shuffled back through the kitchen. *Atta boy, Stan.*

Louise then yelled at Stan and the kids while I searched the upper cabinets for any sign of aspirin.

"Useless," she muttered on her way back into the kitchen. She plopped herself on a bar stool.

"God, Joanie, you're so thin. What did you cut out?"

Everything.

"Just some carbs," I said.

"Well, you look great. So? How's it going with Wells?"

"He's still got a few details to work out." *Sure he does.*

"Good," she said, with a little smile. "But it's coming along, right?" she asked, composing her face. It was too late. I caught it. She was pleased that it was not going well. I didn't dare mention the holiday debacle. She might release balloons and streamers.

"Yeah."

I suppose I always knew this about Louise. That smug satisfaction when things didn't work out. I remembered when Michael and I were engaged Louise became unusually quiet. She thought I didn't notice. When everything finally went south, she perked up, happy, and content, all while clucking her sympathy. Louise's Zen level rose in direct proportion to my misery; the pressure was enormous.

I decided not to let my good friend get off so easy. I could tell a few white lies and let her twist in the wind. "We talk all the time about where we'll live. He wants me to have a brand new house to decorate."

"Oh, that's great," she answered, but her expression fell and she wouldn't make eye contact. I took a deep breath. My job was done.

Suddenly, she gripped my arm. "I almost forgot to tell you— Michael and Jennifer are going to a dinner party in Port Jefferson next month. A big gala for friends of his parents."

Bingo. I felt a rush of adrenaline and my heart went into overdrive. "Do you need to RSVP to get in?"

"No, it's not a benefit or anything. It's a private party, they have a room reserved."

Perfect. I pushed the thought of my stalled efforts with Wells to the back of my mind. This was it. This was my opportunity, the moment I had been waiting for, a chance to out-Jennifer Jennifer and let Michael eat his heart out. I wanted to see Michael's face when he saw the new me. Let him look long and hard at what he missed.

"Can you get me the exact date and time?"

"I can," she said, squeezing my arm as a true friend should. "And I will. Now are you coming to my Super Bowl party?"

"Yeah, sure."

She got up and brought out another box of cookies.

"You don't think Carrie will come, do you?" she asked.

Louise offered me some Double Stuf Oreo cookies. Even though I was feeling light-headed, I refused.

"Did you invite her?"

"I did, but that was a while ago. You're not friends with her anymore, are you?"

Good question. Was I? I hadn't seen Carrie in over a month, not since our argument. I hadn't called or dropped by—nothing. I wanted to pick up the phone. I wanted to talk to her, find out what happened with Scott, find out what was happening with her. I wanted to say I was sorry.

"We still see each other," I answered.

Louise made a face. "I guess if she comes, she comes," she said.

I walked into my apartment and was greeted with silence. I flopped onto the couch, clutching a pillow to my stomach. I felt horrible. My mind was racing but I didn't want to think. Not about my good friend Louise, or Carrie, or Michael—certainly not about Wells. And I didn't want to think about my life and where it was or wasn't going. I wanted to go out but didn't know where to go; at the same time I wanted to hide in the house. I wanted to call someone, my mother, or Carrie, but I didn't know what to say and damn it, I wanted food. I was starving. I closed my eyes and let sleep take me away. I didn't see my father in my dreams. I hadn't for a long time. I was on my own.

* * *

At the end of the week I walked into the apartment as Mikey
was lugging his tool box out.

"I'll miss you, too," he said.

I stopped in my tracks, my eyes lit up; I could swear I heard
angels singing.

"You're done?" I asked, incredulous. "Totally?"

"Yeah," he said.

So, that was that. "Well," I stumbled, "uhh . . ."

He just looked at me. A flicker of shame and embarrassment clamored at my door but I wouldn't let it in. I straightened and lifted my chin, Jennifer style.

"Well," I said with a smile, "thank you very much."

He grunted and was out the door.

I shrugged. So who was he to me anyway? No one. Did he
have any effect on my life whatsoever? That would be a no. So
was there anything in this life I should be feeling remotely
guilty about? I should say not. I was extremely glad I had this
little chat with myself. I felt better already.

I looked around. I guess it was back to business as usual.

The next day at work, I found myself dropping a subtle hint
to Wells before lunch that my home improvement was completed, followed by his innocent, "Really? How did it turn
out?" and my coy reply, "Come see for yourself."

Why did I do that? *Because Jennifers don't quit. They get what
they want.* But did I even want Wells anymore? I didn't want to
think about it.

He took the bait, nodding his acquiescence.

By six-fifteen I was annoyed, at seven I felt a significant rise
in my blood pressure, and by eight I was paging him and he
was conveniently not answering. Maybe he dropped the pager
into very deep water with himself attached to it. *Wouldn't that
be a shame*, I thought. I went to bed at two A.M. I couldn't sleep.
I got in at eight the next morning. He mentioned nothing.
Not one word. By ten o'clock I had had it. *You should quit. Tell
him you're quitting. That'll fix him.*

I stormed into his office. He was searching his desk.

"I forgot the Boris file last night."

"That's not all you forgot," I said.

My credit card bill reads like the national debt. I can't quit.

He came around the side of the desk, taking my face in his hands. "Hey, you know, I'm sorry. I couldn't get away. I'll bet you looked gorgeous."

"As a matter of fact, I did. Too bad for you," I heard myself say. "Who knows when you'll get another chance?"

"Really," he said. He stood there, his face calm, almost meditative.

We stood staring at each other, almost in the same spots as the first night we came together, only now there was a thick silence in place of the anxious anticipation.

"Well, I'm ready to make it up to you—right now."

He was waiting. And what if I said no? What else was I holding onto him with but that? It was a little late to be pulling an Anne Boleyn. That cat was clearly out of the bag and long gone. I wanted to scream. I felt every muscle in my body constrict, holding me in place until I was almost shaking. If I gave him a hard time I could look forward to another bout of his criticism leading to—what? *Getting someone else to do the typing, while I teetered on the edge of bankruptcy. And failure.* I smiled and nodded.

"That's my girl," he said. And then he did make it up to me. Right then—on the new couch he had put in his office for clients.

Don't think. Don't think of anything. Just do it and don't think about it. And I did. And then it was done.

Watching him cross the room to his private bathroom, I took in the developing bald spot, the paunch peeking over his belt. In an instant, I saw him for what he was: a mundane little man in middle management, who reached his maximum level of incompetence.

"You know how much I love you, right?" he asked. *Whatever.* He promised not to forget Friday night at my apartment. Our usual plan: I leave work first and he followed twenty minutes later. I remembered the French had a phrase for my situation, *cinq à sept*, or *five to seven*, the time when married men and women met their lovers.

He didn't show up. I paced through the apartment thinking about our nonconversations. *"I have something for you,"* I would tease. What was that? What do I have? A ham and swiss? It was like bad *Dynasty* dialogue. That's exactly what it was. That's all it ever was. *He wasn't going to do anything. But what if he was? What if he was on his way over? What if he was going to leave her?* I rearranged my lingerie drawers while I fumed. I decided to put the bras on the left, bustiers in the center, panties on the right. Then I thought no—it should be bras on the left, panties in the middle, bustiers on the right because some bustiers and bras could go with the same panty. *He's not coming, miserable bastard—he's not coming. I know it. Useless shit.* Carrie was right. If she was still speaking to me I would've told her she was right. My red satin bra was missing. I ripped all my drawers apart, then realized I was pulling the drawers out of the dresser onto the floor. I couldn't breathe. Why couldn't I breathe? My face was wet and my eyes were burning and I didn't understand any of this, least of all how I could lose a red bra. How does a flaming red bra disappear? Is there a bra gnome that sneaks in at night when I'm sleeping to remove various pieces of my lingerie? I overturned my laundry hamper, dumping out all my clothes. Nothing. Dammit! I had to find it. Maybe I left it at my mother's. It had to be there. Shit! I had to know if it was there. If I leave and he shows up and I'm not here! *What if he comes?* I ripped a pair of jeans from a hanger and threw them on. *He's not coming. He's not coming.* I pulled my shirt over my head, tossed on my coat, and was out the door. If Randall the love machine was there, he would just have to deal with it.

My mother opened the door and I charged into the house.

"What's the matter?" she cried.

"Nothing."

"Why are you crying?"

"I'm not," I yelled, heading for the laundry room. I dove into a pile of dirty clothes while my mother hovered over me.

"Joanie, what is it? What's the matter? What's happened?"

"Nothing has happened. Nothing's wrong. I'm looking for something," I screamed. I could hear the high pitch of my voice inside my head. My mother was staring at me wide-eyed, her cheeks flushed.

"Joanie, please sit down. Calm down! Stay here tonight."

I stormed into my old room, my mother trailing behind me, and began pawing through the closet.

"Joanie, please, what's the matter with you? You're always at work. You never come over. You don't eat. Tell me, what's wrong?" she pleaded.

I straightened up. My head was throbbing. I sucked in a deep breath, attempting to get under control and stop scaring my mother. "Nothing is wrong," I said with exaggerated calm. "I have a date and I need a certain piece of clothing."

My mother put her hands on my shoulders and then stroked my hair. "Oh, Joanie, clothes don't matter. Men want a well-rounded, attractive, intelligent woman—which you are."

I caught a glint of red at the bottom of a laundry bag.

"A-ha!" I yelled as I dove in. I withdrew the bra, waving it triumphantly, and turned to my mother.

"No, Ma, they don't want an attractive, intelligent woman. They don't want a woman who can tell them about the decisive battles of the Civil War, or how to grammatically dissect a sentence, or discuss the pros and cons of a leveraged buyout. They don't want to know what Betsy Ross said when she finished sewing the American flag. You know what they want?" I whirled the bra around, over my head.

"This—this is what they want!" I proclaimed.

My mother looked as though she'd been struck. "You're dating a transvestite?" she whispered. I have heard of people letting out screams of utter frustration at moments of heightened hysteria in order to release tension and feel better. I tried it. I didn't.

"*I'm* wearing it, Ma!" I stuffed the bra into my purse and flew past her to the door.

"Joanie, what's really going on?"

I didn't answer.

She gripped my arm. "Joanie, Joanie," my mother pleaded, her eyes filling up. "I'm so worried about you. I don't know what to do with you."

"Nothing, Ma. Absolutely nothing."

"What are you doing?" she asked.

I didn't answer.

I had no answer.

I didn't know.

Chapter 17

I did calm down but not before I had raced back to my apartment, flew down the stairs and found no note, no sign he had come and gone. I shoved the key in the door, threw down my purse and broke down. I cried until I finally collapsed into bed and fell asleep.

On Monday morning I showed no signs of Friday night's fiasco when he said his customary, "Good morning, partner." Partner. Teammate. As in "We make a good team, don't we?" I loved those little expressions. One member of the team makes a little more money than the other and has a house in the Hamptons, *n'est-ce pas?*

As I stood next to his desk waiting for him to sign a letter, I leaned over and whispered in his ear, "I'm so sorry."

"For what?" he asked, his eyes wide with panic.

"For what you missed on Friday night," I said, and I walked out of his office.

Deep inside my mind, I heard my inner Joan crying out even as she was overshadowed by my howling stomach and the endless monologue running through my head. I heard her small voice calling: *wrong, wrong, wrong.* I agreed. My life had become a rote exercise—none of it gave me any joy. But my major concern now was financial solvency. Even though the earth no longer moved with Wells, the thought of making a change sent shivers of panic and confusion coursing through me. We said nothing to each other afterward. When had we ever had a meaningful conversation? But I didn't have to sit home alone if I didn't want to. He usually made his way around to an invite at five minutes to five if he was interested.

"What are you doing this evening?"

"I haven't decided yet." *You should've said you had a date.*

"I won't get done until around nine."

Let me get the Vienna Boy's Choir to sing a mournful tune. "I'm sorry to hear that." *Can we get this over with?*

"I guess that would be too late?"

Careful, Joanie, don't antagonize too much. You need this job.

"I didn't say that."

He relaxed and appeared pleased. "Good."

My inner Joan was not a happy camper and the more I ignored her, the more my Joan-ness manifested itself in my organizational skills; my apartment morphed into a black hole. The universe was completely out of order: outfits couldn't be found, socks were lost, paperwork went astray. A misplaced W-2 form spiraled a Saturday morning into disaster in the form of a heap of belongings in the middle of my living room, my own *Close Encounters of the Third Kind.* Too bad I didn't have a match. I was in a pretty incendiary mood. And there didn't seem to be any end in sight.

I started picking through the mess on Sunday morning, hoping to find clean clothes for the Super Bowl party. My mother called.

"Joanie, what's happening over there?" She was attempting to sound relaxed but I knew she was freaking out.

"I'm fine, Mom. No visions, hallucinations. My stuffed animals are not sending me nonverbal messages."

"Joanie, that isn't funny. Randall is having a Super Bowl party. Why don't you come?"

"Mom, it's bad enough I'm going to one of these things at all. I'm not going to one for the Centrum Silver crowd."

Dead silence on the other end. It was out there. I couldn't take it back. I'd insulted my mother. I never did that. I was annoying, exasperating, and a pain in the ass, but not insulting.

Whoever said you only hurt the ones you love knew what he was talking about.

"Joanie, that wasn't very nice."

"I know, Ma, I'm sorry. I don't know why I said that."

"You haven't been very nice for a while, Joanie. It's because you don't like Randall, isn't it?"

Oh shit.

"Yes, Ma. I mean—no—I do like him. I really do. I think he's a nice man."

"I think you're upset that I'm seeing him." She sounded like she was choking up.

"No, Ma, I'm not, not at all!"

On the other end, I could hear my mother sniffling. I couldn't handle it. I could feel my eyes filling up. If I started, I wasn't sure I could stop. My mother crying was always a sensitive area for me. If my mother cried, the world as I knew it stopped turning. I took a deep breath and responded by becoming the ultracaring and dependable Joan she knew and loved.

"Mom, I do like Randall. I think he's wonderful and I'm very happy you're seeing him. I think you should continue to see him. I don't want you breaking up with him. I just have a headache and I don't want to go to this party, that's all." *Oh, and I'm having an affair with a lowlife shit, excuse me a lowlife married shit, that I happen to work for.*

"You're sure?" she gurgled.

"Yes, Mom, I'm sure."

"Joanie, I'm so worried about you. You're so angry, and you're unhappy all the time. What can I do for you?"

Nothing. Absolutely nothing. The only person who can do something is me. "I'm fine, Ma. I'm just tired."

My poor mother. I wasn't supposed to turn out like this. I was supposed to be headed for the Good Ship Lollipop at age twenty; hand in hand with a reincarnated Andy Hardy they were saving in the lab just for me. I was angry and I knew why. Everything was running on Wells's schedule, on his mood swings, on his timetable. Somehow, despite all my planning, I had broken the cardinal rule of the Jennifer code: I had lost control.

I picked out my outfit for Louise's Super Bowl party. Tight blue jeans, black boots, form-hugging black sweater over Victoria's Secret black satin padded Miracle Bra. I was going to make sure this party worked out right. Tonight was my night.

I arrived fashionably late. The place was a zoo, a swarming hive of wives, girlfriends, husbands, boyfriends, and children. Wives and girlfriends huddled in the kitchen, husbands and boyfriends hunkered down in the den in front of the plasma TV complete with surround sound system. Children ran back and forth, annoying each parent at will.

I didn't know these women. Well, I should correct that. I didn't *know* these women but I certainly knew *of* them. This was Louise's other life; her married friends and their husbands and children. The life I was supposed to have when I married Michael. As I met everyone, I recalled the highly personal details I knew about them via Louise. "It's nice to meet you," I said to Debbie. *And don't worry. The odds of your husband finding out you slept with his best friend are statistically low. Really.* I said it was nice to see Maggie again when we realized we had met briefly at a school play for Louise's daughter. *I'm sure Louise doesn't have any hard feelings about that pyramid scheme even though you sucked her in for two grand and she called you a greedy thieving bitch.* I congratulated Maggie on her upcoming marriage to Bob. *Not to worry, most men sow their wild oats right up to the wedding—not with the bride's sister, but hey, what can you do?* How much was true? Who knew? They all seemed pretty nice. It didn't take me long to realize the feeling was not mutual. Around the world from the biggest banquet to the smallest dinner party—a single man is always welcome but a single woman might as well have *pariah* tattooed on her forehead. The law of sociology or the jungle dictates that women size up other women and if that other woman is alone, they circle the wagons and sharpen their claws. The first nail in my coffin was my weight.

"How do you stay so thin?" Maggie asked. I decided to let them have this round.

"Starvation," I said, inviting a chorus of tut-tuts and motherly advice on how that wasn't good for me.

The woman introduced as Mary wrapped an arm around my shoulder. "I know it's been hard for you, but you can't let it affect you this way," she said.

Let what affect me this way? I took a second look at Mary. Oh shit. So this was Mary, Louise's connection at Jennifer's salon.

And what the hell did she mean by that anyway? Don't let Michael dumping you a year ago get to you or you can't let sleeping with a married man who shows no sign of leaving his wife get to you? Until that moment, the fact that Louise's friends might know everything about my dirty laundry, past and present, hadn't really entered my mind. Sex had made me stupid.

"Un-huh," I said blandly.

"He's moved on. Now you have to get over him and move on," Mary continued, giving me the "you're such a pathetic loser" look.

Just what I needed, a mini Michael recap. I came to a Super Bowl party to be reminded of the pain and humiliation of my failed relationship. How delightful.

"You can't let them drive you crazy," Debbie chimed in.

Louise gave me a hug of support. She was way too happy, thus solidifying my theory that she thrived on my misery.

Maggie moved in for a little heart to heart. "This man isn't any good either, honey, he has no loyalty at all, obviously." Oh, here we go, we're in Wells territory. For a moment, things grew fuzzy at the edges. I thought I would pass out. Of course it could have been the smell of the nachos and cheese dip.

I did a quick mental six degrees of separation. Did anyone know him? Maybe their husbands knew him? Maybe they wouldn't tell their husbands. Silly rabbit. Of course they would. Maybe they had met his wife through some strange kismet of two worlds colliding: their children's school, a church outing, a local business association. The possibilities were endless. I was definitely going to pass out.

"Obviously," came a voice behind me. It was Carrie. I turned as she strolled in from the den.

Carrie's face was pale and she had dark circles under her eyes. She looked like crap. Our eyes met. I blinked first and looked away. Not only couldn't I look at her, I couldn't think of a thing to say. Louise gave me a "Can you believe it?" look. I ignored her.

Maggie took my hand as I managed a brilliant comeback: "It's a lot more complicated than that. We're working through it."

Working through what? He's a shit. And he's not leaving her.

"Honey, you don't want to be a woman known for dating married men. You'll find yourself alone."

This coming from a woman whose sister was slowly making her way through the wedding party, including the groom. Maggie had recently been through a second divorce, her boyfriend Bob had been through his first. She was definitely in the running for the Long Island Liz Taylor award. Everyone needed a hobby.

"How long have you been waiting?" she pressed.

I'm sorry, are we friends? And the arm around my shoulder was getting a bit old.

"Not long," I said. *Six months, three days.* I looked down at my empty ring finger.

Maggie threw up her hands. "Oh, honey, if they don't go for a separation before the six month mark, it's not happening."

Carrie was glaring at me. What did Maggie know? I didn't need advice from someone whose fiancé didn't see impending marriage as a reason to stop screwing around.

"We've discussed the future," I said, sounding way too confident—which I thought made me sound a little desperate—which only annoyed me more.

Louise grabbed me by the hand as the men started to get rowdy, shouting about kickoff time. Carrie lagged behind as we moved as a mass to the den.

"Can you believe she came?" Louise whispered.

I shrugged.

"Don't forget Michael in Port Jeff next Saturday night."

As if that was even possible. And she knew it wasn't.

"Eight o'clock. I'll be there."

We gathered in the den, done in rich masculine brown and beige tones. An overstuffed couch and two easy chairs were strategically placed for optimum viewing. The women gathered round their men. Maggie slid in next to Bob on the couch. He was medium height, his black hair slightly receding. He was muscular, but not a muscle-head. She draped her arm over his shoulder and smiled at me. The same smile Jennifer gave me at the party.

Technically, there were two ways this act could be interpreted. One: she's a nice woman who gave me advice out of the goodness of her heart, and her smile is a symbol of encouragement saying, "You could have something wonderful, too." Two: she's a vindictive bitch who's taunting me. If it was a year ago, I would have seriously considered theory one. Silly rabbit. As for theory two, Jennifer would take care of that.

I got up to get more water and fill up on M&M's. According to a new variation in my diet, chocolate was good, as long as you exercised two hours a day and ate nothing else. I looked up to watch the opening kickoff and found Carrie right next to me.

"I'm surprised you came," I said, shoveling in the candy to ease the sick feeling in my stomach that was my constant companion. I leaned on a table for momentary support.

"I didn't come to see Louise," she shot back. "I thought you'd given up on eating."

"Where's Scott?" I asked. It was a low blow, and I knew it. Obviously something was wrong. I was sorry I'd asked but now it was out.

"I don't want to talk about it," she replied.

"Well, I don't want to talk about anything else," I said, and walked back to my chair.

I expected her to leave. Part of me wanted her to leave. It would've made me feel better if she wasn't there.

After the thrill of the kickoff the game settled down into the commercials, commentary, more commercials, and occasionally an actual play. I attempted to ignore Maggie but she made that difficult as she kept steering the conversation back to relationships, highlighting the one I didn't have and her upcoming marriage to Bob. (*How old are you, Joan? Wow, I'm glad it didn't take me that long to get married. No offense, Joan, honey. Oh, none taken, Mags.*) I would've been really upset if it weren't for the law of averages. In real world statistics, the law of averages states: paper covers rock, rock covers scissors, men never stop and ask for directions, dates with a menu of spaghetti and corn on the cob never end well, and most women do not care for football. And Maggie was no exception to the law of averages. The ladies drifted out one by one until all the women had abandoned their posts, except for me and Carrie. Mumbling something about too much beer, Bob took off to the bathroom. I sauntered over to the snack table and refilled my cup, then sat down on the edge of the couch. Next to Bob's spot. I could feel Carrie's eyes on me as I lounged there—waiting. Bob came back in, giving me a smile as he sank down next to me.

"What are we up to?" he asked.

"Second and four." I smiled, holding out my cup of M&M's.

"Thanks," he said, dumping out a handful. "So you're into football," he said. We shared the rest of the M&M's. I asked strategic questions and paid attention as he answered. The conversation wasn't important. It never is. The whole thing was easy. Like a mouse to the cheese. My inner Joan sat down in a chair. She was wearing a pair of jeans and a comfy sweater; she had a cup of popcorn in her hand. *"This is really low, you know that, don't you? How long are you going to do this?"* I chowed down on M&M's and ignored her.

It's amazing how things just happen. It was halftime. I excused myself to go to the bathroom, then I ran into Bob as I was coming out and he was going in. When he came out of the bathroom, I just happened to be in Stan's study looking at the kids' peewee soccer ribbons, a fascinating topic for the unmarried, childless woman.

"These are their awards, huh?" he said, poking his head in. Bob was cute, but not a master of small talk. Actually, he wasn't that cute.

"Do you go to the games?" he asked.

"I used to. I prefer grown-up games now," I said, stepping into his personal space and turning on the Jennifer smile. His eyes had that soft look they all get when they're trying to score. The term *bedroom eyes* is more elegant but who are we kidding.

He laughed. "What kinds of games do you like to play?" he asked softly.

"All kinds," I said. Noise came from the kitchen. He was eyeing the hallway. Could he get away with it? The coast was clear. We leaned in and kissed. I didn't think anything. There was nothing to think.

He was mine for the taking. I listened to his quickened breathing. His hands were heavy as they made their way up my shirt. In the back of my mind floated a thought—*when will this be over?* Footsteps in the hallway put an end to it.

Emerging from the study with Bob on my heels, I ran into Carrie. Skirting past her, I went directly to the kitchen. A commercial was blaring from the TV in the den and the guys were filing in and out, their plates sagging under the weight of heroes and salads.

Something happens when two people have been in flagrante. They give off a vibe, an aura that telegraphs to others. Bob came in a minute later and curled around Maggie like a repentant puppy who just shit on the carpet. She patted his cheek and looked at me. I gave her a sweet smile. She didn't smile back. Bob attempted to look cool but another smirk from me and her radar flew up.

"Where were you?" Maggie quizzed him.

He mumbled a reply.

Louise threw me a strange look. Soon Mags kept asking Bob if he was all right. I would have enjoyed her well-deserved misery but I was too busy repressing the desire to vomit. I couldn't sit still in the second half. And then I knew I was

going to throw up. It was always a problem to heave in someone else's bathroom because of the added weight of making
sure you were neat as you hurled. I emerged from the bathroom twenty minutes later and sidestepped into the kitchen
for a glass of water. The cool water went down, soothing my
raw throat.

"From the Goddess to the Bitch," Carrie said quietly. "That
wasn't so hard, was it?"

I turned to her. She didn't look angry, she looked miserable.
I should've been more concerned about her but I couldn't get
past the pounding in my head, the feeling that I couldn't
breathe. I couldn't help her. I couldn't help myself.

"You're a little late with your observation," I said.

"You picked quite a prize, what with the incoming gut and
the balding head."

"I don't need an intervention."

Carrie grabbed her coat off a chair and threw her purse
over her shoulder. For a minute, I thought she was going to
cry.

"You're right," she said. "I forgot. You know exactly what
you're doing." She strode past me and walked out.

The sounds emanating from the den were not from the
television but Bob and Maggie working successfully toward an
argument. Now I knew why Carrie never smiled when she told
me about her infamous rampages of revenge. There was no joy
or satisfaction, only the moment of triumph, which soon left a
bad taste in your mouth.

I felt that in my own small way, I'd discovered the meaning of
life. At times life simply carries you along. The euphoria or
misery of the unexpected and unexplainable propels people
through their existence. One is left to make decisions and adjustments, and then forge ahead making the best of what life
hands you.

The following Saturday night I made the best of my situation and made my decision. I put on my best Vera Wang and

my black, strappy pumps with the four-inch heels. I did my hair in sexy, upswept ringlets. Slipping into my winter-white coat, I headed out to see Michael.

As I reached the restaurant, my heart began pounding. The plan was simple: plant myself at the bar, tank up on alcohol to steady my nerves, and wait for Michael to come down searching for a restroom. I'd confront him, show him what he missed and then walk out, making him watch as he loses me a second time. End of story. There was one flaw in the plan: I should have eaten something if I was going to load up on alcohol. Damn.

I perched on a bar stool right in front of the stairs to sit and wait. An hour later I was sucking down my third wine spritzer, partly in self-defense. I had been cornered by Donald the dentist, who was regaling me with the fascinating particulars of how to properly fit dentures and his aggressive ten-year plan for moving his practice to the Hamptons so he could retire on the bloated fees he planned on charging for whitening the teeth of the rich and famous. I sat there wearing a numb smile. At the moment, I would have welcomed a root canal. Then his lawyer friend, Stuart, showed up. Great, Dull and Duller. Stuart didn't need to tell me he was a lawyer. He babbled his sanctimonious rhetoric with a bloated air of pseudosuperiority. Shithead. They rotated their spiels between the perils of neglecting to floss and Perry Mason with tales of his billable hours. I considered running screaming from the building but managed to give a fine performance of strategic laughs and hair flip combos. Effortlessly Jenniferesque. I could've had either of them.

"So why is a beautiful woman like you sitting here all alone?" Donald the dentist asked me.

"But I'm not alone." What the hell. Might as well play the game while I wait.

"What do you do for a living?"

"What do you do for fun?"

"How would you describe yourself?"

I'm an assistant in a large commercial insurance firm. I enjoy

*long walks on the beach, travel, and of course, engaging in a ruinous
illicit affair with my married shithead boss. However, the conve-
nience is spectacular.*

What am I doing and where the hell is Michael?

I eased off the bar stool. "If you boys will excuse me for just
a moment."

Dopey and Doc got up. "You will come back?" they asked
in unison.

I gave my sweetest smile. "Count on it," I purred.

I made a beeline for the stairs. When I reached the top, I
scanned the room on the left—a birthday celebration complete with deejay spinning retro Meatloaf on the turntable.
Definitely not a retirement party for Boring, Boring, Redundant,
and Boring Esq. I looked to my right just as the door opened.
An octogenarian holding the arm of a younger man emerged.
Bingo. I ducked inside. People were mingling and chatting while
others sat at their tables drinking. It was déjà vu. I thought my
heart would explode as I scanned the room for any sign of
Michael—or Jennifer. People smiled at me, the smile you give
a stranger. No one remembered me. Finally an older man came
over to me.

"May I help you find your table, dear?"

I scrambled. "Actually, I was downstairs having dinner and
met an old friend who mentioned Michael Weber was here. He's
an acquaintance from college. I thought I would say hello."
You're good ,Joan. It flows off the tongue.

"I'm sorry, dear—but you've missed him. He was here but
his wife wasn't feeling well, so they left shortly after the party
started."

My heart sank.

"Are you sure?" I asked.

"I should know, dear," he said with a laugh. "It's my party."
He touched my arm and lowered his voice. "I've heard it's
been a difficult pregnancy. Hopefully, it will get better."

Pregnancy? Pregnancy. Jennifer is pregnant. I nodded and
walked out.

I don't remember collecting my coat or leaving the building. I found myself shivering outside, staring at the restaurant and the Lincoln Town Cars, BMWs, and Lexuses belonging to the beautiful people inside. I didn't belong with the beautiful people. After months of work and practice to be the new me, not to mention the twenty-two percent interest I was paying on the couture, I was still on the outside looking in. The next thing I knew, I had a handful of stones and I was throwing them one at a time at the Lincoln Town Cars, BMWs and Lexuses belonging to those beautiful people. I came here to see Don Quixote and where was he? Home with his perfect pregnant wife, that's where. The stone made a cracking sound as it hit the pavement: *She's pregnant. She's having his child. He's having a child with her.* Another cracking sound, only louder as the next stone landed closer to a Lexus. *He's at home with his perfect pregnant wife, giving her a back rub or a foot massage during her difficult pregnancy. I was supposed to be his perfect wife. I was supposed to get the back rub and the foot massage.* The next stone just missed the window of a silver Beamer.

"That was close. Should I tell you what you win if you hit one?"

I turned to find the cop from the bush/restaurant incident. My own personal Officer Krupke, who did not exclusively work the day shift. Shit. "No, sir."

"What are you doing?" he asked. Why did they ask questions they knew there was no answer to? I hated that.

"I'm going home. Right now."

"Is there a problem?" he asked.

"No, sir," I answered.

"Does that car belong to the same person you were preoccupied with at the restaurant?" he asked, pointing down the street.

"No, sir," I said.

His eyes narrowed. "How much have you had to drink?"

I could see it all now. Calling my mother at eleven o'clock at night so she could tell Randall to put his pants on and come with her to the station.

"Only two. I was trying to throw a stone in the water but I

have terrible aim." *And I make up terrible lies.* "But I was about to call a taxi and head straight home. Really."

Officer Krupke squinted at me like I was nuts. Perhaps I deserved that for shucking pebbles while wearing a floor-length evening dress and stiletto heels. He advanced a step closer.

"Un-huh," he said. I thought the excuse was fairly original. Poor but original. I didn't think sarcasm was necessary. People were too cynical these days.

"Get the cab now and go straight home, got that? Any more attempted aggravated assault, destruction of private property, disturbing the peace, or practicing for the Olympic long distance throw, and I'm going to arrest you. Understand?"

I stumbled up the street toward the pay phone. Thirty minutes later the taxi pulled into the parking lot where I was still sitting in my car, still processing the latest turn of events.

When I finally flopped fully dressed into my bed it was one A.M. and I let the alcohol haze take me away until I woke up at four A.M. Eyes open, I lay there in the dark.

What am I doing?

I had discovered the meaning of life. Life doesn't simply carry you along. Life offers a continuous series of forks in the road at which you must make concrete decisions. The decisions you make cause the unexpected and unexplainable and it was how you handled the unexpected and unexplainable that made all the difference.

One evening, I was pondering this great truth while looking in the mirror, adjusting the bobby pin holding the nurse's cap on my head. The nurse's cap complemented the nurse's outfit I was wearing. One of Wells's favorites. The top was unbuttoned to the waist, exposing a snow white lace bra with removable fabric cups; white crotchless panties, garters and stockings completed the outfit. The pièce de résistance: four-inch patent leather stiletto heels that were numbing my arches, making it difficult to walk. Two hours of preparation for fifteen minutes of role playing with a balding, boring, middle-aged man who didn't give a damn about me. I wanted to tell him to go to hell but every time I looked at my credit card bill I broke out in a cold sweat. I had less money now than when I started this job.

"How about we play a game when I come over?" he had whispered in my ear. *Sure, why not. Let's play desperate, indebted secretary sleeps with hack middle management stooge because she's not in the mood to play Little Red Riding Hood goes to the unemployment office.* The love nest now had zero aura with the ear-splitting sounds of a melee of musical instruments emanating from upstairs. The new torture. The children had reached the age to begin partaking of the musical arts. Little bastards. Somehow over the din, I heard the knock at the door. *Valentino cometh to tell me how he loveth me, how much I meaneth to him, and how he can only stayeth for twenty minutes.* I sucked back the urge to cry. As I went to the door, my ankle turned, I stumbled, almost sailing into the wall. I muffled my moans as sharp pain shot through my ankles. Taking a deep breath I put on my sexiest smile and opened the door. It was Carrie. She looked me up and down.

"Look on the bright side," she said, waltzing past me. "I could've been your mother."

"How do you know it's okay to come in?"

She tossed down her purse and sank onto the couch. "If it wasn't, you would've slammed the door in my face."

She was right. And where was the five-minute lover? As usual, he didn't even have the decency to call. Self-degradation got no respect.

I turned slowly. No more rapid rudder moves in these shoes. I glanced at the clock. Twenty minutes late. He wasn't coming. The little shit.

I hobbled into the bedroom to get my robe.

"You look like crap—you know that," I called over my shoulder. And then I tripped over a shoe and pitched headlong onto the bed. I lay there face down. I gave a momentary thought to not getting up.

"Do you think I should change my hair?" Carrie was standing in the doorway.

I forced myself to roll over and sit up. "As a hairdresser, aren't you the only one who can answer that question?"

Carrie looked like she was going to cry. She began to pace the bedroom. I felt a pang of guilt. "I don't know if you should change your hair."

"Men like longer hair on women."

"What difference does it make?" I shot back. "They won't notice in the dark."

Carrie stopped pacing and turned to me as I struggled into my fuzzy robe.

"What's your problem? Mister Excitement cancelled so he could stay home and clip his toenails with his wife?"

"What's yours?" I attacked. "Where's Scott? Or maybe a better question, who is he with?"

"At least mine spends his time with unattached consenting adults and I don't have to play Naughty Nurse Nan!"

"Maybe you should have, then he'd still be around—and he *will* be here!"

"He's not coming, Joanie. If he doesn't show up for this— he's not showing up for anything else."

"I decide when I want to see him! It's my choice!"

"Right. You choose to see him, you choose never to see your friends, you choose to have no life!"

"At least I don't drive my boyfriends away!"

Carrie's face grew beet red and her eyes welled up. I was having trouble seeing straight myself. The damn shoes were cutting off the blood flow to my brain.

"You don't have to drive them away," she attacked. "They leave you!"

I jumped up, letting out a string of obscenities as pain shot through my feet.

"Michael's mother made him break up with me!" I railed, getting up in her face.

"No, she didn't, Joanie," she said in a level tone. "He was never going to marry you. He was using you to piss them off. He would've dumped you himself, but he got one over on them by getting his mother to do it!"

"Shut up! Shut up!" I screamed. "That's a lie!" I grabbed a magazine, flinging it at her. "You drove Scott away by bad-mouthing every guy you ever knew!"

"I didn't drive him away. He was stolen. By someone like you!"

She shoved me and I shoved back. We went at it—hair pulling, slapping, the whole nine yards. I had never partici-pated in a girl fight before. In the middle of it all I decided it was too bad Scott wasn't here because being a pervert, he would've enjoyed it. In the scuffle we tripped over my step bench and went sprawling onto the carpet. We lay there inert, gasping, and bruised. All of a sudden Carrie burst into tears, which was a really good thing because if she had been her usual self she would've kicked my ass. And then I cried. She was right about Michael, right about Wells. She was always right.

"I'm sorry," she sniveled.

"Me too." I hiccupped. "Are you sure he's seeing someone else?"

"I wouldn't know?" she asked.

Of course she would know. We lay there, trying to catch our breath. She turned to me. "I know where the girlfriend lives," she said finally. "Will you come with me?"

"Of course I will."

Carrie grabbed my hands, heaving me to my feet, and rushed me toward the door.

"I can't go like this," I protested.

She shoved my coat at me. "I'm on a roll."

Butch and Sundance, together again. I hope it ends better for us than it did for them.

We rounded a corner in a quaint little neighborhood in Port Jefferson. Most of the houses had wraparound porches and a small grassy yard in front, some enclosed by fences. It was a modest, well-kept area.

I didn't mind following Carrie on her latest quest for destruction. I owed her my support. I'd been a bitch. I didn't mind creeping around the side of the house or crawling through the bushes to peek through a window. And I didn't mind crouching on all fours in the dirt when we detected movement inside the house. But I did mind the up draft into my crotchless panties.

"C'mon, let's try the back," Carrie whispered, tugging on my sleeve.

I tried to get to my feet, tripped and fell into a shrub.

"C'mon," she urged hoarsely.

I stumbled after her in the dark and found her trying the screen door. Breaking and entering? Technically—no. It was open. Extremely poor manners—yes. Silently, we crept into the kitchen. At least, it was quiet until my stilettos hit the tiled kitchen floor with a loud *click click click*. Carrie grabbed my arm and squeezed, pulling me down to the floor.

We were the only ones on this level. Crawling to the basement door, Carrie slowly slid it open. The noise of the television wafted up from below. I spied a bag of candy on the kitchen table and dug out a mini Krackel bar. Low to the ground, Carrie edged into the stairwell and began crawling down onto the landing. I winced as she leaned over so far she slid down the first two steps with a soft thump.

There was a rustling of movement in the basement. We froze, then suddenly Carrie backed up and came leapfrogging over to me. I was impressed. I had no idea she could do that.

"I wouldn't be out here semicommando if I was with Steve," I whispered, inhaling a miniature Hershey Dark Chocolate. "I would've been a normal, happy, well-adjusted individual." He was probably an accountant working nine to five, except during tax season of course.

We heard the heavy thump of footsteps on the basement stairs.

"Behind the counter," she snarled, giving me a shove. We dove for cover.

I could see the front page of *Newsday*: "Long Island's Naughty Nurse." My mother would hold an open house for her friends to condole with her and say things like "She used to be such a nice girl" as they watched News 12. A reporter standing outside the house would give the scandalous details: *"The suspect was discovered in the house scantily clad in a nurse's costume. Police have not confirmed what the suspect was doing in the house but they are investigating the possibility that the house is being used for porno filming. Back to you in the studio, Jim."*

A man entered the kitchen. We peered around the counter. His back was to us as he opened a cabinet, grabbed a bag of Fritos, opened the fridge, got a couple of beers, and slammed the door shut. We heard heavy footsteps thudding back down the stairs into the basement.

Bounding up, Carrie threw open the fridge door. I realized my legs were numb. Getting up was going to be tricky.

"A-ha! I knew it!"

"What?" I struggled up, clutching the countertop. I had no sensation in my feet. My shoes would have to be surgically removed. Would my health insurance cover this?

Carrie held out a can of Reddi Wip. Exhibit A.

"I need a gurney," I moaned.

"A-ha!" she said again. Exhibit B was a jar of maraschino cherries.

"We know she has a poor diet?" I gasped, leaning on the counter.

"It's an orgy! That pervert! You know what they do with this, don't you?" she asked. Apparently she had her prima facie case. She didn't wait for my answer.

"Follow me," she ordered, storming off to the basement door.

"I don't think that's possible," I gasped as I took a few halting steps.

"Wait a minute," I called after her. "What do they do with the cherries?" I'd read every sex book and article I could get my hands on and had never seen any reference to maraschino cherries. How come she knew everything? "What do they do with the cherries?" I pressed.

But Carrie was bounding down the stairs anger first, making plenty of racket as she went. When I finally hobbled my way down the stairs I found her standing over Scott and Marty, my nonparamour. They were sprawled on the couch, their mouths open, gaping up at her like two deer in the headlights. Chip bags and beer cans littered the coffee table, and a basketball game was blasting on the plasma screen. We had entered the hallowed haven of the reclusive male.

As an opener, Carrie threw the whipped cream can at Scott.

"So where is she?" Carrie demanded. She was just to the left of sane.

Marty inched up.

"What are you doing, babe?" Scott asked, his voice calm.

Carrie held up the jar of cherries. "Where is she? Were you saving these for your little halftime orgy, you little pervert? I was in love with you! I can't believe I was in love with you! Here, let me help you get in the mood!"

Snapping the lid off the cherries, she dumped them in Scott's lap. I was deeply jealous. If I had done that to Michael, I would've felt so much better about the whole situation.

Springing up, Marty grabbed Carrie, trying to hold her back.

"Hands off, freak!" I yelled, and stumbling forward, got a fistful of his hair.

Everything after that was a blur. I remember Carrie emptying the Reddi Wip can on Scott and pelting him with anything she could lay her hands on. Marty, trying to shake me off, clutched my coat and tore it off.

"Whoa!" he said, his eyes as big as saucers as he took in Nurse Nan.

"Eyes back in your head, pervert!" I said, taking a swing at him. He dodged but I got hold of his shirt. We struggled and fell in a heap on the floor.

At that moment, a girl carrying a pizza box came in, shrieked, and dropped the box.

And then the police came.

*   *   *

Ten minutes later we had all been separated. There were two cops. One was my Officer Krupke.

"Not you again," he said, sounding exasperated. I thought of asking him for his address. We spent so much time together I should at least send him a Christmas card.

The second cop was younger and busy doing the Joe Friday thing. "Neighbors reported two suspicious females creeping around the property. Why did you break in?"

"The door was open," Carrie shot back. She then turned on Scott. "Did Marty introduce you to her?"

"What are you talking about?" Scott replied calmly.

"That's enough," Krupke interrupted. Carrie knew no fear. She ignored him.

"So where the hell have you been? And who the hell is she?" she asked, pointing to the girl cowering behind Marty.

"She's my sister," Marty said, still staring at me.

"So you set them up!" Carrie exploded.

"Hey!" Joe Friday moved toward Carrie. I feared we were getting into choke hold territory. "You want me to cuff her?" he asked Scott.

Scott stepped forward and took Carrie's hand.

"I saw you with her," Carrie snuffled. "And you're never around. You told me you were working." Carrie was crying now.

Both cops rolled their eyes.

Scott turned back to the coffee table, rooting around underneath the snack bags, and brought out a small velvet box.

"I was working, babe. Marty set me up with some night work so I could afford this—I picked it up for you today."

He opened the box. For a man of few words, he came across with the goods. That was a nice ring.

"You got this for me," Carrie blubbered. She had officially left the building.

"I love you, babe," Scott said.

Carrie threw her arms around him and sobbed.

"He loves me," she slobbered to Krupke.

"I'm touched," he answered.

Officer Friday turned his steely gaze on me. "Where does the Happy Hooker fit into this?" he asked.

"Hey!" I said. *Excellent retort, Joan.*

"She went on a blind date with Marty," Carrie sniveled.

"I can't imagine why it didn't work out," Krupke said.

I had to defend myself. "He refused to sleep with me," I protested.

"Why wouldn't you sleep with her?" Friday asked, giving me the once over.

A moment of silence. Well?

Marty sighed with resignation. "She was too pure, man. It would've been like doing my sister."

"You're kidding," Krupke said.

"You didn't know her back then. She's changed." Marty looked at me. "You're not wearing underwear, are you?"

Everyone looked at me.

Okay, now I had definitely discovered the meaning of life. Life was a series of decisions. Most people spent their life making crappy decisions, and screwing up their lives. Life then propelled them into a series of unexpected and unexplainable circumstances, which were basically out of their control. Simply put, we humans spend the majority of our time trying to crawl out of the hole we create and wondering how we got ourselves into the hole to begin with.

Nietzsche who?

Chapter 18

The next morning I got up, got dressed, and drove to work. I sat at my desk staring at the piles of paper. Wells came in with his usual "Hi, partner" and disappeared into his office. He came out of his office ten minutes later and stood in front of me.

"Can you make dinner reservations for seven o'clock tonight for a party of four? Call my wife and she'll tell you where we're going."

My mind was very still.

"You okay?" he asked.

"I'm fine," I said.

"You did a great job on the report. You made me look good, as usual."

I said nothing.

"Are you going out to lunch today?" he fished. "We have a few things to go over—"

"No, we don't," I heard myself say.

Wells just stared at me. "Don't what?" he asked.

I shut off my computer and got up. "We don't have anything to go over and I can't make a reservation for your dinner."

He froze, staring at me with widening eyes. I stood up, took my purse and pulled the strap onto my shoulder.

As if suddenly remembering where we were, his eyes darted around to see if anyone was watching. "Why not?" he asked, as if we were having a routine conversation.

"Because I quit."

His face grew red. "You don't mean that," he said, keeping his voice low. "Would you come inside, please? We have a lot to talk about. There are things I need to tell you," he said.

"We don't talk. We never have. If you want to talk, talk to your wife. Any plans you have don't involve me. I have my own plans."

I turned and strolled down the hall. I never looked back.

My moment of clarity had come.

JENNIFER REVISITED

Chapter 19

The first thing I did was eat. I didn't wolf a quart of ice cream and throw up. It was more like a four-piece chicken meal from Kentucky Fried followed by a double shot, a Twinkie and a Devil Dog, and then I threw up. I called my mother. I told her almost everything, about the debt and the quitting, but not Wells. I couldn't tell her that. There was no way I'd make the rent. She said she would call Randall. He had friends; someone could find me a job, even if it was only temporary.

And then there was the problem of the credit card debt. Five thousand dollars worth. My mother had controlled herself for as long as she could until the uncontrollable urge for one of her "Just tell me" Q&A sessions took over.

"Joanie, just tell me, what did you spend it on?" she asked.

Yes, Joan, explain to your mother about your elegant hooker wardrobe for the discreet discerning male adulterer.

"I don't know, Ma," I sputtered. "I just bought stuff. I was so unhappy, I lived on the Shopping Network. You know how people do that." I'd have to borrow a set of Ginsu knives and a ton of Joan Rivers jewelry from someone to show as an example. I sure as hell couldn't produce a leopard print thong.

"Mom, can I come back for a few months, just until I get straightened out?"

I heard silence from the other end of the phone.

"You don't really want to come back, do you?" she asked.

Okay, Joan. You have no money and your mother won't let you come home.

"Mom, I can't pay the rent. If you could loan me some of the college money—"

"Joanie, you know I'll try to help you." She said Randall would call his friends with the empty apartment. He would make the arrangements about the rent. Whatever it was, it would be less than the overpriced, underwhelming dump I was living in. I was packing up my life in boxes again.

"I want you to be happy. You can get a new job and still go back to school. Joanie, you have to figure out what you want to do." She said not to worry but I could tell she was worried. The money wouldn't last forever.

My mother wasn't angry. She was never angry. Women spend their lives distancing themselves from their mothers but I realized in some ways I used to be a lot like her. And I knew I wasn't like her anymore. I knew that when I was in bed at night thinking, I would always be a little sorry about that.

Louise called. I told her my news.

"You're kidding!" She sounded thrilled, almost chirpy.

"No, I'm not. I got up and walked out."

"Do you know thirty-seven percent of women say they broke up a relationship on the spot? So, what are you going to do? Do you have any money?"

I suppressed the old urge to spill my guts to lap up Louise's support now that I knew Louise wasn't interested in being supportive. Louise's happiness at my misery annoyed me. I decided to be irritating. "Not to worry, it's all worked out. I'm moving to a new place in two weeks. Much nicer."

She waited for details. I didn't give any.

"Well, that's great. I have Brownie meetings or I'd help you pack."

I told her not to worry about it.

Carrie helped me pack. As I piled my clothes on the bed, I saw exactly what I had been doing over the last six months. It didn't matter how many other times Wells had probably done this, I had done it. That's all that mattered. I couldn't take anything back. I had no feelings of love for Wells; now I was sure I never did. Maybe it would've been better if I had. I sank onto the bed, next to the pile of clothing. Carrie patted my shoulder as I had a good cry.

"Don't worry," she said. "You'll never do it again."

Scott came with Marty for the move out. I thought it was good of Marty to help carry out my couch considering I had jumped him just a few weeks earlier. I drove over ahead of them to the apartment I hadn't even seen yet. Randall said it was good and that was good enough for me. There was a flower bed lining the walkway up to the door. The apartment was small but wouldn't cause claustrophobia. The rooms were bright and airy. In the living room a sliding door opened out to a small patio with room for a table and two chairs. I went to sleep that night with the boxes arranged to provide a clear path to the bathroom. Carrie left me with my own words as she said good-bye.

"It's all going to work out, Joanie. You'll see." She had always been right. I hoped her streak was going to hold.

My mother showed up the next day, bagels in one hand and Randall bringing up the rear carrying a large carton.

"Should he be lugging that?" I asked as she kissed me hello.

"He's very healthy, honey, don't worry," she said, her cheeks flushing.

I pictured Randall as Superman and my mother in thigh-highs with a miniskirt playing spunky reporter Lois Lane. Of course there would be a generous application of Bengay (hip flexor muscle) for him, and Crème de la Mer serum for her (wrinkles).

"Don't tell me any more, Ma."

"How do you like it?" Randall huffed as he carried in the last box.

"I like it a lot," I said. I did.

"I'm going to say hello to Dan," he called over his shoulder on his way out the door.

Dan and his wife, Maureen, were a nice middle-aged couple. Maureen was originally from down South somewhere and her genteel manner clung to her in spite of the barrage of Northeastern brusqueness. She probably sounded polite even when she called Dan a schmuck.

My mother settled on a kitchen chair. "Did you clean out the fridge before you put food in?"

"Yes, Ma."

"You didn't, did you?"

"No, Ma, you know I didn't."

She set to work rerinsing the dishes in the drainer.

"Is there a problem?" I asked.

"You look better, Joanie."

A steady diet of carbo-loading and chocolate will do that. Five pounds were already back. She was cleaning my counter.

"Mom, is something bothering you?" *Aside from the fact that my life is a shambles and Daddy just posthumously paid my first month's rent.*

"Joanie, the state college is having their open house—"

"Next week, Ma, I know. I'm going."

She threw her arms around me. "Do you know what you want to take?"

Are you kidding?

"Never mind, you'll figure it out. As long as you go back, that's what's important."

She gave me another hug. I felt her back heave as she controlled herself. She held me at arm's length.

"Are you okay now, Joanie?"

"Yes, Ma. I'm okay."

She went for the closet.

"You're not vacuuming my carpet, Ma."

My stomach had settled into a daily routine of handsprings to the point of nausea from morning until night. I kept thinking about what I would've been doing at the office. I even thought of Wells, where he was and what he was doing—a knee-jerk reaction. He had called my cell phone several times in the first few days, leaving messages of "I don't understand," "Talk to me," and "You mean so much to me." Translation: who's going to type my stuff and unzip my pants? Whether there was any grain of truth to his pleadings, I didn't know. I didn't want to know. Every time he left a message it made me think back to when we first started, when it was new and exciting. But now I saw things for what they were. There was never anything there.

They say the secret to recovery is activity. Mentally, I kept forcing myself out of the past to focus on the here and now. I called the Human Resources Department, told them I had a family emergency and that's why I left. Randall cranked up the Love Network and got me a part-time job at a friend's office. Typing, filing, and phones. Enough for food and gas money. It wouldn't be a problem going on interviews. I needed another job—fast. My mother wouldn't say it, but the money wasn't going to hold out forever.

I oriented myself to college, filled out everything in triplicate and wrote a personal essay on a major goal I wanted to accomplish. I love college applications—they're exercises in overkill, just like job interviews. What's my major goal? What is my heart's desire? To graduate, of course. I did not include any mention of my other goal—to be a person other than myself—which I had failed miserably. Why? I had become the Jennifer I had always dreamed of being and ended up with nothing. After all that, I was back to me again. What now?

I met my college mentor on a bright, crisp Tuesday afternoon. Kevin was a soft-spoken ethereal man in his forties wearing a blue shirt, blue jeans, granny glasses, and sandals. My mentor. The older, wiser soul who would be the guiding force of my educational, not to mention life journey. Poor fool. He glanced over my portfolio, asked a few cursory questions about my responsibilities at Wells's office and perused my essay. After he finished, he gently laid down the paperwork on his desk and leaned back in his chair.

"Okay, Joan, let's talk about you. What would you like to be when you grow up?"

And then I broke down and sobbed.

The metamorphosis that comes over men at the sight of a blubbering woman is fascinating. It begins with shock, which quickly becomes a cross between guilt and bewilderment until settling into full-fledged panic. Next, they look around help-lessly, wondering if they could pass the buck to someone else—someone with emergency provisions like sedatives and chocolate to put an end to the hysteria. Finally resigned to their fate, they uncomfortably wait for the deluge to end. Kevin offered a tissue. I took the box and hugged it to my chest.

"You don't have to decide now," he said.

I'd almost feel sorry for them, if they weren't such shits.

Chapter 20

I cried a lot. When I was driving, when I was watching television. Everything was so screwed up and I didn't understand how it all got to be that way. Okay, I knew how. I had been there. What about my psychological theory? The id was a positive agent of change. The vehicle that spurred people to move out into the unknown and experiment with the possibilities, read: mindless pursuit of something to the exclusion of all else because you felt like having it, with no regard for rhyme, reason, or intelligence. My id was an idiot.

Immanuel Kant explained the two kinds of knowledge, a priori: that which is known, and a posteriori: knowledge gained as a result of experience. One didn't need to learn something solely through a posteriori knowledge, a priori would be fine. Which meant, technically, you wouldn't need to experience something to know the truth of it. For example, you wouldn't need to actually have an affair with a married man to know it was a bad idea. To accept that fact a priori would've been fine, except no one ever does that. Then Kant said that all knowledge comes by way of experience. He understood human nature: no one listens. In layman's terms: I had been a schmuck.

The crying couldn't go on too long. I didn't want Dan and Maureen to get the idea that they had a Sylvia Plath clone living in their house. They'd mention it to Randall and the next thing I knew my mother would have the fire department breaking down the door. Thankfully there was something that spurred me to dry my tears: my bank statement. It was amazing how removal of stupidity from one's life acted as a clarifying agent. Big news flash—I had no cash. And the prospect of money coming in was low as well. I couldn't seem to get interviews lined up.

I had faxed my résumé to every company in the paper looking for a secretary. Nothing. If they didn't call you in the first twenty-four hours, they didn't want you.

Everything I owned was strewn all over my bed. Carrie was dividing my wardrobe between corporate America wear and evening wear while Louise kept folding things away. Louise had insisted on coming over to help. Ending a twenty-year friendship was something I just couldn't deal with at the moment so I didn't object. The gang was all here but they weren't getting along, not even for my sake. Louise spoke only to me. And Carrie spoke only to me. The result was scintillating non-conversation. As Tolkien would've said: Even now the fellowship is breaking.

Louise held up a crotchless panty. "You did not wear this."

"Don't ask," I replied, shoving my bra collection into a bag.

"Well, I must say," I announced, "that things are at their absolute best. No job, my money gone on trashy clothes, and I'm completely in a financial hole." I sank onto the bed. If I had my inner Jennifer here, I'd punch her lights out. Bimbo.

"Joanie, it's going to be fine," Carrie said. Since the engagement, she had risen to a plane of blissful stupidity. Alex from *Fatal Attraction* had morphed into Rebecca of Sunnybrook Farm. But I couldn't fault her for it. She'd been so miserable, she deserved to be happy.

While I was shoving my X-rated lingerie into a trash bag, I found myself thinking about my college economics class. We learned about Adam Smith and the history of commerce, how people once lived by directly exchanging one item for another. Back then I thought maybe it wasn't such an advancement to forsake direct bartering of goods for currency. But Adam Smith saw the future was money. Although I'm sure selling slightly used peek-a-boo bras and matching crotchless panty sets for cash was not what Adam had in mind. And I couldn't even do that. Bummer.

"Joanie, it's a well-known fact that eighty-two percent of women are at their lowest point careerwise before there's a turnaround," Louise offered.

"You made that up." I would've liked to say more but I held my tongue.

Louise squared her shoulders. "I did not!" she protested. "I switched magazines. *Modern Woman* is much more upbeat."

"And so much more accurate," Carrie interjected.

I turned on Louise. "Is this the same magazine that talks about 'Ten Incredible Ways to Drive Him Wild'? Why don't they publish something for men to read, like 'Her G-Spot, We Make It So Simple Even a Fool Could Find It'!"

Carrie was standing there gaping at me. She wasn't sure what to do with the new Joan. "Don't be so me, Joanie," she said.

One of the bra hooks caught on the bag, ripping a whole in the side. I kicked the bag out of the way.

"Joanie, calm down," Louise soothed.

"Why?" I countered. "Look at the useless skills I've acquired. I can't wait until the next high school reunion. What have you done, Susie? I run a small business and I'm a valuable member of the community. And what have you done, Lucy? I'm a teacher, helping children learn critical academic and life skills. And what have you done, Joanie? I can bring a man to orgasm using nothing more than hot fudge sauce while humming 'Start Me Up' but I can't get a lousy job and put my life in order!"

I flopped into a chair and glanced up to find them looking down on me, their mouths hanging open. I get that a lot.

"How do you do that?" Louise asked.

"Don't ask," I replied.

"I didn't know you could do that," Carrie said. "I think you're overdoing your moment of clarity, Joans. Are you reading again?"

I couldn't help it. My mother knew my weakness. Books. And she'd been buying them for me nonstop. I tried to stay away, soaking my brain with mindless television channel surfing, but I couldn't resist. Before I knew it, I was knee deep in my journey to a happier me. Doing what mattered, knowing what mattered, caring about what mattered, loving life and loving myself, which only served to remind me how crappy my life was and that I was basically an idiot. Carrie was reading my mind.

"It's those books your mother gave you, isn't it?"

I tossed one to her from the pile. "Here," I said. "I found out what color my parachute is. You know what color it is? It's black. My parachute is black and it's full of holes!"

"Don't be melodramatic," she said. "It's all going to work out."

Why hadn't someone hit me when I used to say that? They should have. It was annoying.

"The last time I said that, I lost my fiancé, my apartment, and my job. If I get any more optimistic, I'll be homeless, or worse, living in my mother's house listening to her and Randall shake their groove thing in the next room."

Louise came over to me and draped her arm around my shoulder. "You're going to find someone," she reassured me.

What, another gem like Stan? Could there be a second model out there somewhere? I bit my tongue before I said it. I had to remind myself to be nice. *Oh God, please let me be nice.* I didn't answer her. I knew how bad things were for me. Louise was way too happy.

We moved into the living room, where Carrie threw herself on my couch with a bag of Doritos.

"Hey, those have to last the whole week," I protested.

"Relax, I'll buy you another bag."

I sat down at the table and opened *Newsday* to the Help Wanted. Why was this so difficult? I slammed the newspaper shut. "How am I supposed to get a job when no one calls me back?"

"Joanie, just go to an agency. You go in, meet them, and

they get you a job. You'll finish school, rise to a position of power, get a male secretary, and shit all over him. And then you'll meet the perfect man at my wedding."

Uh-oh. The wedding. I had my own variation of Einstein's $e=mc^2$. Wedding=ugly bridesmaid dress*dyed pumps to the exponential power of ridiculous cost or $(UBD)^*(DP)^\$$.

"Carrie, about the wedding—" I began.

"Don't worry, Joans—I'll cover the costs. I really need you there." Carrie was okay—even though she was always right about everything.

God, I hoped she was right this time.

Going to an employment agency was like a dating service, only everyone's financial future depended on it. Since the head-hunter was under enormous pressure to collect a commission, it was hardly a scenario ripe for a relaxed, Zen transaction. When I arrived at the office the first order of business was to pass me around to every desk until I resembled a New York filet. *Do you type? Absolutely. File? Of course. Computer Skills? I'm a whiz. I am multitasking Mensa material.* I told all of this to my headhunter, who looked like she just rolled out of bed, as she downed her third cup of coffee in twenty minutes. Which got me to thinking: how did one get hired to work for an employment agency? What was the criteria? *Can you ask pointed questions that will push nervous people over the edge into hysteria? Can you look at someone's résumé and arch your brow in such a way as to make the person feel they have no skills, no hope, and no future in any industry? Do you feel comfortable administering mind-numbing aptitude tests that will cause someone to freak to the point of losing bladder control? Do you feel strangely at home at cattle calls?* I spent three hours taking the tests. A full physical didn't take this long. *Congratulations, Miss Benjamin, your heart rate is fine, your blood pressure is normal, and your words per minute is seventy-five with one hundred percent accuracy.* I went in at nine expecting to be out in an hour. At noon they were bringing in lunch. I restrained from asking for a ham and swiss. My headhunter looked like she needed a vacation or at least some Timothy Leary strength Xanax. She consulted with her colleagues. They had a job. Could I go over right now? Why not? I was ready to heave from the stress, so I was in the perfect frame of mind. She wished me luck and reminded me to say I'd been with the agency for some time. That was a shame as I had planned to announce to my prospective employer that I had just walked in off the street this morning and they hadn't even checked my references. I sat through the interview for a company not knowing what they did nor did I care. Why did I leave my last job? Excellent question. *Yes, Joan, why did you suddenly leave your last place of employment without securing future employment?* All I could come up with was a "deep desire to search for a new opportunity" and put down the HR Department for a contact number. I wasn't out in the parking lot when the cell phone rang.

"How did it go?" came the breathless voice of my headhunter.

"Almost as well as my last root canal," I said.

"Well, what did they say?" she pressed.

Note to self: living on commission is not the way to go. "They thanked me for coming and they'll be in touch," I replied. Interview speak for "Go back to the Help Wanted, honey. It's not happening today."

"I have something else for you."

"Oh, good," I said. "I haven't been demoralized enough today."

"It's a good company," she pressed. *Are they providing a paycheck? Then I would think so.* "They provide networking solutions for small- to medium-size businesses." *Your point being?* "They need an assistant for three people. It's typing, filing, phones, meeting planning, and Excel spreadsheets." *And a partridge in a pear tree.*

Rent was due in two weeks, which meant another trip to the Bank of Mater. "I'll go," I said.

The office suite was tastefully decorated, the people seemed polite, and the Human Resources person hated me on sight. If I had said I could type one hundred words per minute while pouring coffee and answering the phone, she would have lamented I couldn't pat my head and touch my nose at the same time while doing it. I said ability to anticipate the needs of your boss was crucial. Colonel Klebb disagreed; my potential boss was independent. I said a sense of deportment and calm was essential. Klebb shook her head; a sense of liveliness and energy were practically engraved into the job description. I thanked her for her time and got up and left. I shouldn't have done that but obviously I wasn't going to fit in and I didn't want to.

I made the mistake of answering my cell phone in the parking lot.

"Why did you leave?" My headhunter demanded, her voice cracking.

"It wasn't going well. She didn't care for me."

"You don't know that," she said shrilly. "You don't know that." I was driving my headhunter to a breakdown. She probably had no medical insurance to cover the Xanax.

"My skills were not a match for the company's needs." Who said I didn't understand corporate America speak? I thought I heard weeping from the other end of the line.

"I'm really shocked by this," she whimpered.

"You'll get over it."

I had no offers coming in from the Internet. Now I didn't expect to hear from my headhunter, who needed a new job herself.

Shit.

I had picked the worst time to abandon healthy eating habits, but teetering on the brink of financial ruin went much better with a box of Ring Dings rather than a salad with no-fat dressing. Exercise had become nonexistent and depression is not known for improving muscle tone. I had jumped from a size six to an eight and I saw signs of inching toward a ten. Carrie took it upon herself to try and steer me back on track. Somewhere between Scott's proposal and her first wedding dress fitting, a strange metamorphosis had taken place.

"I should exercise more," she said one day as we lounged outside on my patio.

I gave her a wide-eyed look. "Do you mean that as a general statement as in 'I should work toward world peace more' or you personally should exercise?" The girl would drive across a supermarket parking lot rather than walk.

"No, really, I should be in better shape for the wedding. I want him to be proud of me."

I failed to see the point. "You look fine. He knows what you look like."

"I know, I know. I just wonder what he thinks. Maybe he thinks I'm fat. Do you think I'm fat?"

"No, I don't think you're fat." A snappy answer was crucial. Any hesitation could have devastating effects. It was part of the code of friendship.

"I'm just worried he won't think I'm pretty anymore."

"Keep the lights off. He'll use the Braille method and won't know the difference."

Carrie looked like she was going to cry. I had a brief Odd Couple moment. When did I become Oscar, and she become me?

"What are we taking?" I asked.

"Yoga."

I have nothing against physical exercise. However, I was already at peace with the idea of *not* exercising and my muscles had happily begun to atrophy. Still, I went to yoga class. I breathed, did the upward dog and the downward dog, and nearly had a back spasm that would have put Benji in a brace. I spent most of the time clinging to my center, a nifty arrangement wherein I stood still and didn't have to do anything. Carrie did the poses with no problem; she was the picture of serenity. At least someone was.

We walked out together. She walked. I schlepped.

"That was great," she said. "Don't you think that was great?"

I needed a heating pad. "Very nice," I said.

"You're not breathing deeply enough. You're supposed to be drawing breath from your core."

"My core collapsed."

"Thanks for coming with me," she said.

"No problem."

We stopped by my car, the car my mother was paying the insurance for. I had so much to be proud of.

"It's all going to work out, you know," she said.

"Don't be so me, Carrie," I answered.

"It's weird isn't it?" she said.

Yes, it was.

They say yoga clears the mind, which is true. At home I breathed deeply, clung to my standing posture, and my mind became crystal clear as the phone rang. I hadn't paid the phone bill. I answered the phone and spoke to a Mrs. Howard, whom I didn't know, and she was not from an agency.

"I saw your résumé on the Internet," she said. "I'd like to talk to you about a job."

I was so thankful I only grasped vague details: a computer software company, located close to the Nassau County border, and the president needed an assistant. I was there the next morning. Mrs. Howard was a pleasant woman in her late thirties, with closely cropped blond hair and a brown tweed suit.

I sat pensively as she looked over my résumé. On the inside, I was freaking out. *Oh God, I need this job.*

"You have computer skills?" she asked.

"Mrs. Howard, I am fully versed in Word, Excel, and Power-Point. Whatever is needed." *Easy, Joanie, don't look too eager. Maintain calm.*

"And your greatest strengths are . . . ?"

"Detail oriented, multitasker, excellent communication skills." *Screw maintaining calm. I need this job. I need to pay my phone bill.*

"And your weakness would be . . . ?"

"Perfectionist."

Mrs. Howard sighed. It was then I sensed her lack of interest. She sat back in her chair. "What do you want out of this position?"

Not this one again. "I would like not just a job but a career. I want to build a long, productive, and mutually-rewarding relationship."

"Naturally," she said, staring through me.

This meeting was over. Mentally she had me out of the office and out of the building. I envisioned myself clinging to her leg as she dragged me to the front door.

"*A-One Answers to Interview Questions* by Mullin. Right?" she asked quietly.

"Yes," I sighed.

"*How to Survive the Nightmare of Interviews* is also good."

"I read that," I said. "Yes, it is."

Should I just say thank you and leave or wait for the added humiliation of being dismissed? Decisions, decisions.

"Mrs. Howard . . ." I began.

"This is not your typical position," she said.

Do I have to wear clown shoes and the big nose? Does he want to receive his messages in rhyme? What?

"Mr. Duncan isn't here right now."

Your point being?

"In addition to your responsibilities, you'll have to go to his home, pick up his mail, and walk his dog."

I'm unemployed. If it's necessary, I'll wash the dog.

"There's been a rash of burglaries in the neighborhood lately and it must appear as if someone is home."

"Not a problem."

Mrs. Howard wasn't convinced. "Peter Duncan is a—difficult man."

Not only did I not have the job but now she was trying to convince me I didn't want it. *Is this a new interview technique?* "I understand."

"He's very direct."

Attila the Hun. "I can handle him."

She leaned forward. "Joan, he'll be extremely blunt. He's short tempered."

"Fine."

"You'll hand in work and he'll throw it back at you."

"I understand. He's not in touch with his feminine side."

"He's not in touch with his human side."

At least it wasn't me she objected to.

"Joan, I have to tell you, you'll be the eighth secretary in fourteen months."

Oh shit, I needed this job. What else could I say?

"Mrs. Howard, you know I have the office skills, I know I have the people skills. I can do this job."

She looked over my résumé again. "You've got it. Are you with any employment agencies?"

"Yes."

"Stay in touch with them, Joan. You'll be calling them again soon."

We shook hands and I walked out of the stately office decorated with burnished mahogany furniture, my feet sinking ever so slightly into the luxurious ecru carpeting, past the receptionist sitting at the glass-topped desk and into the bright sunshine. I had a job.

Chapter 21

It was quiet. From the moment I woke up until I went to sleep, it was quiet. My landlords, Dan and Maureen, kept to themselves except when they made lasagna and brought me a tray. The apartment was in perfect condition, no ceiling cascading to the floor, pipe explosions or other random acts of structural collapse. Then I went to work.

On my first day, Mrs. Howard escorted me around and introduced me to everyone. They greeted me with a friendly handshake and an embarrassed look of pity. By lunchtime I was certain a betting pool existed as to how long I was going to last. My desk was large, made of fine cherrywood, and situated in a small, pleasant anteroom. Two double doors to the right led to the general reception area. To my left was another set of double doors leading into the office of The Man Himself. Mrs. Howard showed me his office. Not a paper clip was out of place. She dropped hints that my desk should be neat and orderly. The massive mahogany desk had an executive chair behind it and two chairs for lesser gods in front. A round conference table with four chairs, all done in the style known as expensive, sat in the middle of the room. To the left, a couch, a coffee table, and a private bathroom because no one must ever know he needed to pee. *Note to self: New boss is controlling anal retentive nutcase.* No wonder the salary was better than average. They calculated in hazard pay. Mrs. Howard showed me my workload of typing and filing, which would keep me busy for approximately one and a half hours per day. No one spoke to me or came anywhere near me. I understood. I worked for the boss and they figured there was no point getting friendly; I would be gone soon.

So there I was with time on my hands and nothing to do but think. I needed to figure out how to proceed. I had lived my life in two completely different ways, running the gamut from the best to the worst person I could be. Now I wasn't sure what I wanted, who I wanted to be or how I would get there. I wasn't convinced the original Jennifer goal was even correct. So what was the goal? I came to no conclusion. Another afternoon well spent. I left each night at five o'clock, said good night to Mrs. Howard, asked if there was anything specific for tomorrow, to which she always said no. She would tell me if Duncan called in. I always asked if he had wanted to speak to me in the vain hope that he had some curiosity about his latest assistant. She always said no.

After work I went straight home. I never spoke to Louise unless she called me, my mother was busy with Randall, and Carrie had Scott. I spent my evenings e-mailing completed assignments to my mentor, reading chapters, and writing term papers. I had the vague feeling I was waiting for something but I didn't know what it was. To make matters worse, I was sure I wasn't supposed to be waiting for something but rather doing something. I didn't know what that was either. I had settled on a major, settled on a job, at least temporarily, but *I* wasn't settled. I was drifting and I knew enough to know that. I just didn't know what to do about it.

I sat down on the couch in my mentor's office. He sat in his chair, wearing his standard blue shirt, brown pants, and sneakers, waiting for his herbal tea to steep.

After my initial meltdown in front of him, things had been going okay. He still kept extra Kleenex on hand, just in case.

"So, what have you decided?" he asked.

"Can I ask what you thought of my paper first?"

He smiled, fished through a pile and drew out my report. "You're doing well; however, your English professor had a few comments. He thought your argument that Jane Austen was not a feminist and betrayed women was interesting. But he felt your statement that Mr. Darcy got off too easy after his disgusting and demoralizing treatment of Elizabeth and pronouncing him a sexist bastard lacked scholarly research."

He may have had a point. "I was working out some issues," I said.

"I thought as much," he replied.

The maharishi put my paper down. "Which leads back to my question—what have you decided? What are you going to major in?"

"I told you, business," I said concisely. He didn't respond with an enthusiastic "Oh right" as I hoped.

"I don't want you to take something because it's the simple thing to do." *Heaven forbid. I'd screw up my track record if I did that.* "My job is to help you find the path that will lead to your fulfillment. And remember, Joan, everything that happens in your life affects the way you do business. Your interpersonal skills are just as important as your technical skills."

Thousands of mentors in the Long Island area, and I was paired with the Gandhi of Business Administration. I could've told him—stay off the path. Avoid the path at all costs. My path was so screwed up it made the yellow brick road look benign, flying monkeys and all.

"I want to major in business." Besides, what he said wasn't true. Not everything in your life affects your business life. And then I thought about Wells. As a potential merger, or nonmerger, that was a disaster, ergo I would be lousy in business because I was an idiot. And then my eyes started to tear. The Dalai Lama handed me a box of tissues.

"Perhaps we should work on methods to channel past disappointments into future successes."

I blew my nose and sniveled, "Okay."

"Choose a positive thought and focus on that thought for one minute."

Then he dunked his Oreo cookie into his tea, took a bite, and leaned back in his chair, chewing, with his hands folded and his eyes closed. If he started levitating I was out of there.

Once I'd gotten familiar with the office, it became time to make the pilgrimage to the sacred manse of The Man Himself. There's always mystery surrounding the boss's house. You're expecting gold faucets, velvet carpeting, crystal chandeliers. It wasn't even close. The house was large for only one person—four bedrooms. The property was professionally maintained; Duncan wasn't a mower pushin' man. I hadn't even met him and I knew that.

Mrs. Howard brought me inside so Sherlock the boxer didn't mistake me for a large snack. He approached me lazily and offered his paw. The überwatchdog. If Duncan had taught him to open the door, the burglars could just knock. I guess I have an honest face because she showed me where the bills and the checkbook were kept. The job of running Peter Duncan's house was now mine. The furniture was comfortable and expensive. The great room was a high-tech playground with the required large plasma screen display and surround sound. I investigated the bedroom. A king-size bed but only one dresser. The rest of the room was empty except for a chair. I wandered back to the living room. Sherlock followed. One lamp on one end table, a sofa but no matching loveseat or chair. A peek into the den revealed a couch but no coffee table. Something was wrong with this picture.

"He's separated," Carrie said later that night as she dumped out the last of the shrimp and lobster sauce. Scott was gnawing on a spare rib while watching basketball. The world was spinning on its axis once again.

"No way," I protested, "he's divorced. Carrie, I'm right about this. There's furniture missing from every room in the house. He's living in a million-dollar house and has one couch in his living room."

"He's separated. If he was divorced he would've put it behind him and bought new stuff. It's still an open wound. He doesn't have closure."

Closure? Carrie didn't use the word closure. I gave her a look.

"Marty's sister loaned me some books," she said sheepishly. "It's good to read."

"How's she doing?" I inquired.

"Better. She's still a little compulsive about checking the doors and windows. ADT is coming tomorrow to install the security system."

"Were the floodlights extra or included?"

"Extra."

I looked at Carrie, waiting for more. "I just thought it would be good to expand my horizons," she said. "You know, be a little more interesting."

I looked at Scott staring at the TV like one of the cast in *Dawn of the Dead*. She didn't need to worry. God knows she was the most interesting person I'd ever met.

"Don't change too much," I offered. "You may not be able to change back. Or worse, you may not want to." I glanced around for telltale signs of bridal magazines.

"I thought we were looking at bridesmaid's dresses?" I asked.

"I don't want you to feel like you have to. We don't have to."

"Carrie, it's okay to talk about the wedding. Although I respectfully object to the wearing of anything yellow or peach."

She gave me a hug.

"Any more egg rolls?" Scott piped up.

They were going to be very happy together.

Every morning I arrived at Duncan's house by nine. I let Sherlock out and filled his food and water bowls and then headed to the office, where I typed, filed, and answered the phone. I almost spoke to Duncan once, in written form at least, when he faxed over a report. Except the cover sheet said, "Give to Jane Howard." I deluded myself into thinking he was avoiding me because if he spoke to me he'd really like me and then he'd want me to stay. I amused myself sometimes. Every day I looked for something from him: an e-mail, a letter, a note by carrier pigeon, some shred of confirmation that he knew I existed. Nothing but Mrs. Howard telling me he was going to be away longer than expected. It would be another month. There was a second in command, a Charles something or other. He never remembered my name. One morning he passed me in the hallway and said, "Good Morning, Jennifer." Bastard.

I left every day after lunch and went back to the house to let Sherlock out and sort through the mail. I organized the teetering mail piles into binders, making copies of the checks that I wrote. I even alphabetized the accounts. I needed a life. Sherlock and I would sit out on the front steps watching the parade of police cars cruising up and down the block, casing the neighborhood after the latest burglary. If there wasn't a *Dragnet* convention, we would lounge on the couch, which I'm sure neither of us was allowed to do. What the hell, I was getting fired anyway. Sherlock was keeping me company rather than the other way around. At the moment, he was the only man in my life. He seemed to like me.

I would call Mrs. Howard if I was running late to tell her I was on my way. Sometimes she would say not to worry, why didn't I just go home. *Yes, Joan, why don't you? Do you even work here?*

I walked into my mentor's office during his lunch hour and found the little Buddha reading *The Art of the Deal* while drinking his ginseng tea.

"Does it have a happy ending?" I asked as I sat down.

He closed the book and smiled at me. "Who knows? He's not done yet." Of course, O Enlightened One.

"Joan, you're doing extremely well with your political science course but your professor expressed some concerns. Your essay on Henry VIII was supposed to be about consolidation of power. Referring to him as a 'tiny little man' with a 'tiny little dick' regarding his treatment of his wives doesn't address the paper's theme."

"Well," I said, revving up, "if he can't treat members of his own household with dignity, he can't treat his allies or even his enemies with dignity, and that makes him a poor boss and substandard CEO." *Ha! Take that, Kerouac.*

He sat back, dunking a Keebler cookie into his tea. Another philosophical discussion was coming. Oh joy. They always ended with me in tears.

"Good point," he said, letting the discussion of Henry and his dubious endowments slide. "Let's talk about you deciding what type of person you want to be because that will reflect your business persona. What do you think?"

"Is that a trick question?"

"Maybe."

"I thought you weren't giving a quiz today."

"Life is a quiz, Joan."

Oh God, here we go. I couldn't even cross my legs yogi style anymore for the meditation. I picked a bad time to be out of shape.

"You have a choice. You can follow Machiavelli's *Prince* or *The Principle of Servant-Leadership*," he said, indicating two books on his desk.

I found this very inflexible. "Can't you be both?"

"You can try. But in the end you won't be true to yourself."

I sat, waiting for the other shoe to drop. Or levitate. There had to be more but nothing else was forthcoming.

"So," I said. "What do I do?"

"You can't divide yourself into two parts because you'll never be whole. My job is to help you discover who you want to be."

I tried not to laugh. "You're about nine months too late."

He handed me the books. "I want you to read them both. It's never too late."

I had to have whatever was in that tea. "You know I never asked you what your background is?" *Bait and switch. Good girl, Joan.*

"I create software programs to help businesses reach maximum productivity."

"So how does that help you create a business relationship? They buy your product and then they don't need you anymore."

Siddhartha took a sip of tea. "Not exactly. The software has a limited lifespan."

"So they buy the upgrade."

"I don't do upgrades. They corrupt the integrity of the program. I only create new generation software."

This was too much. The mahatma was explaining his sales technique for ripping off the public.

"So why don't they just buy something else?"

"My programs do what others don't."

"You're holding your customers hostage."

"I prefer to think of it as providing a unique value-added product that no one else can."

At that moment, I understood which person he had chosen to be.

"Joan, something is holding you back. I can sense it."

"Big accomplishment. I've been blubbering in your office for weeks."

"Read these books and find out what's holding you back." *If he calls me Grasshopper, I will not be responsible for my actions.*

I bet if I asked I'd find out I'm the only student he's mentoring. Everyone else ran screaming from the room. Or better yet, he doesn't really work here, he just wandered in and I happened upon him. He's not a mentor but he plays one in real life. I scooped up the books.

"How's your job going?" he asked.

"Fine. I still haven't met my boss."

"Where are you working?"

"New Technologies."

"Ah," he said. What that meant I didn't know. He thought for a minute, and then perked up.

"Who are you working for?"

I arranged my books, holding them in the crook of my arm. "Peter Duncan."

Gandhi went paler than usual.

"Do you know him?" I asked. Finally, a link, a connection. Who the hell was this Duncan?

He sat back, silent for a moment. "Yes, I do."

"Well, what's he like?"

He looked at me for a long moment, then picked up his cup and took a small sip of tea.

"Read Machiavelli first. You'll need it."

Oh damn . . .

At Duncan's house I checked the mailbox. Nothing. Not even junk mail. Inside, Sherlock lifted his head but made no move to greet me. I patted his head, scratched under his neck. Nothing. I put out food. He continued to lie there. I walked over to the side door and opened it. Sherlock didn't move. All of a sudden the dog had developed an iron bladder. I settled into a chair in the living room to look over the *Fortune* magazine; then I heard the noise. At first I thought it might be Sherlock, moving around or chewing something. Then I realized it was coming from upstairs. Oh shit, I thought, feeling frozen. Someone was in the house. We were being robbed! I bolted up—and had no idea what to do. So I called Carrie.

"Why didn't you call the police?" Carrie yelled.

The noises grew louder. Someone was moving around up there, opening drawers, closets. Why didn't Duncan just leave a sign: RECENTLY DIVORCED—WIFE TOOK EVERYTHING—MOVE ON. Why would they open a closet? Furs, that's why. Jewelry. They're looking for the good stuff. Okay, Joanie, think. *What the hell are you going to do?* I hadn't finished the company handbook but I was sure failure to defend the boss's property was sufficient grounds for termination.

"They'll never get here in time," I reasoned.

"In time for what?" she shrieked into my ear. "Let them take the fucking plasma TV, just get out of there."

Easy for you to say, I thought, ducking behind the couch. You won't be paying back a loan to your mother until you're on Social Security. I looked at Sherlock stretched out on the floor. I directed my venom at the useless animal.

"Why didn't you take them on a tour and show them where everything is?" I hissed through clenched teeth. "Someone lets you out to pee and all of a sudden they're your best friend." Rolling over on his back, he yawned. *The Hound of the Baskervilles* would be so proud. They probably gave him Valium-laced meat. They? What if there were two?

"Joanie," Carrie called into the phone, rousing me from my fright-induced paralysis. "You have to leave the house now."

"Don't I have a moral obligation to do something?" *And try to keep my job.*

"You don't have a moral obligation to a DVD player, Joanie."

Footsteps were moving along the hallway above my head. He was done. He was coming down.

"You know, apathy is the leading cause of lack of progress in this world. How can we be humans, part of humanity, and deny our own humaneness?"

"You're babbling philosophy now? Okay, riddle me this: if a moron stays in a house that's being robbed and there's no one there to see it, is she still a moron?"

"Huh?"

"Get the hell out of the house!" she screamed.

Footsteps on the stairs. I clicked off the phone. Okay, I needed a plan. Spying the dog's blanket, I snatched it up. Sherlock lifted his head in momentary curiosity. The footsteps on the stairway were moving toward the landing. My mind raced. I couldn't hide behind the couch. I'd have to get him from behind. I crept silently to the wall at the side of the staircase. Sherlock looked at me like I was a moron. I didn't care for that.

He lingered on the steps and for a long moment, I didn't hear anything. Then it sounded like he went back up. I waited, gripping the blanket with sweaty palms. I had to go to the bathroom. Why do crises make me want to pee? Another footstep. He was definitely coming down now. He was at the bottom of the stairs. Sherlock picked up his head. What's the matter with him? Why doesn't he bark? *Memo to me: Get down on knees before Marty's sister and beg forgiveness for that whole trespassing and assault episode.* He walked into the living room. My reflexes kicked in. Throwing the blanket over his head, I pounced.

"I've got you now, you bastard!" I cried. Sherlock began barking as the perp, with me on his back, crumpled to the floor. Muffled cursing came from under the blanket as he thrashed around, trying to grab me, but I gave him a vicious elbow in the ribs.

At that moment, the police arrived.

My Officer Krupke was the first one through the door.

"You again!" he cried. "That's it, you're under arrest!"

"Not me! Him!" I screamed, wrestling with the doggie-blanket-covered mass underneath me.

"Get off me," came a deep voice.

I gave him another elbow. "Stay down, hair ball!" I yelled.

A second cop ran in from the kitchen, gun drawn. "That's our line," he said.

"He was robbing the house!" I shrieked.

"Get off me," the voice said again. And quite authoritatively I might add. I loosened my grip.

"Get off him," Krupke ordered.

Rolling off, I pulled the blanket away. The man straightened up. All three of us looked him over. He was wearing a bathrobe. An expensive bathrobe. His dark hair was disheveled, and his eyes were black with anger.

"Thank you," he said through clenched teeth.

He directed his angry gaze squarely at me. My stomach flipped as I had an epiphany. It couldn't be.

"Suppose you tell us who you are," Officer Krupke said.

"Peter Duncan," he enunciated slowly, still glaring at me. "This is my house."

Krupke turned to me. "I know I'll be sorry I asked, but why were you attacking Mr. Duncan if this is his house?"

"He's my boss," was all I could manage.

"Of course," Krupke said.

I heard the screech of car tires outside. Terrific. There'll be a crowd to witness my latest humiliation. Pounding footsteps sounded as backup cops rushed in. I zoomed in on the first one through the door, tall and fair haired. Cute.

"What do we have here?" he asked.

"Crazy secretary attacked her boss in his own home."

"Hey," I protested, "I've never seen him before. How was I supposed to know what he looked like?"

"Better cuff her," Krupke said. The second cop approached. Peter Duncan stepped between us and explained why I didn't know him. The cop listened. Duncan had the look and sound of a man who could make you suck your thumb and cry for Mommy.

The fair-haired cop zoned in on me. "Joanie?" he said.

I took a closer look. "Steve?" I answered incredulously.

"I know this woman," Steve announced to Officer Krupke.

"I'm sorry to hear that."

Duncan addressed the group. "I think we can clear this up. After I get dressed." He turned and gave me a long, hard look.

I am so fired.

Peter Duncan was a man in control. He cut quite a figure in his black pants, gray silk shirt, and expensive tassled loafers. If I wasn't preoccupied with applying for unemployment, I might have taken more notice. And then of course, there was Steve.

Steve steered me away from the other cops after Krupke gave everyone the 411 on my unlawful exploits. We stood by his squad car. He was taller than I remembered. I wondered if he would be a personal reference when I went for another job. Probably not.

"This is the third incident in a year," he said.

"I know."

"You really need to stop doing this."

"I know."

After a moment of awkward silence, he tilted my chin up; he was smiling at me. "So what do you do when you're not involved with law enforcement?" he asked.

"The usual, weekends in Vegas, long walks on the beach, fine dining."

He laughed.

The police were leaving. I looked over at the house. Duncan stood on the front steps, arms crossed, waiting.

"I'm going to need to speak to you again, just to firm up details for my report. Maybe we can do that over coffee?" Officer Steve asked.

"Sure," I said. *So this is Steve.*

"And in the meantime, do you promise not to attack anyone, employers, family, or former boyfriends?"

"I've been scared straight," I vowed.

He opened the car door and then stopped and took another look at me. "You've changed since college," he said.

"I improve with age, like cheese."

He nodded. "I can see that."

I watched Duncan disappear into the house and followed after him.

I found him standing at his desk, flipping through the binder containing his bills. Sherlock was sitting at his feet. Stupid dog.

"What hours do you work?" he asked without looking at me.

"Eight-thirty to five-thirty," I said.

"I'll expect you at seven-thirty. We'll discuss whether or not you have any other skills beyond assault."

I stood there. He looked up at me. Oh, this conversation was so over. I decided a chirpy "See you tomorrow" would be overkill. I took my purse and left without a word to Duncan or Sherlock. I figured they would both get over it.

Chapter 22

"**Y**ou didn't notice he was wearing a robe?" Carrie asked.

I was trying to put a bra on while clutching the cordless phone between my shoulder and my ear. Not an easy task.

"No, Carrie, I didn't," I answered. "I told you I couldn't see him at all. He's probably making me come in early just to fire me, the sadistic bastard."

I had spent the previous evening speed-reading *The Prince* to gain insight into my boss's soul. If my calculations were correct, he didn't have one.

"My mentor clued me in. He fires his secretaries for fun. And always right before lunch. Like an appetizer."

"You defended his property. Besides, the dog loves you."

"I'm sure he told him that." Maybe he noticed I bought the really expensive kibble. That could make all the difference.

I ran the gamut from fear to outrage as I drove to work, finally settling on annoyance. If he was going to fire me, let's get it over with so I could move on. I had dressed in one of my best suits, its navy color giving off a sense of entitlement as opposed to the black one, with its aura of mourning. *Good, Joan. Clothes make the woman.* I decided to go straight from the office to file for unemployment. When I walked in, Mrs. Howard said, "Good morning," which was probably code for "It's been so nice to have you here." I could smell the change in the air. Somewhere between tense and scared shitless. I dumped my stuff on my desk and knocked on his door.

"Come in."

Duncan was seated behind his desk, his jacket draped over a chair. His hair was combed back, a trace of silver peeking through. While he continued to ignore me I took a closer look. He was in his late forties with chiseled features and a stubborn jaw line. He wore a pair of rimless glasses as he looked over a binder. Several other binders were open on his desk next to a laptop. I stepped forward.

"You're late," he said.

"It's seven-thirty."

"Seven-thirty means be here by seven."

"My crystal ball is in the shop."

He looked up. Leaning back in his chair, he took off his glasses and studied me with those dark eyes. That stare must scare the shit out of people, I thought. What the hell. I'd had enough of this crap.

"Do you have a degree?" he asked.

"Not yet."

"Are we paying for it?" he asked.

"I'm enrolled in the company's tuition reimbursement program," I answered.

"Can you manage PowerPoint?"

"Yes, I can."

He refocused on his laptop and started typing. "I'm e-mailing you a presentation with a list of changes. Have it done by noon and order in lunch for six people for the conference room on the fifth floor."

He peered at me over his glasses. "Do you know how to order lunch?"

"Of course. Would you like fries with that?"

He ignored me and went back to work. I stood rooted to the spot.

"Something else?" he asked without looking up.

"I would like a list of people you want to speak with if they call."

"If Mr. Williams calls, tell him I'll be with him momentarily and find me. Tell Mr. Manning or Mr. Hanover I'm away from my desk and check with me."

I headed for the door.

"If Mary calls, I do not wish to speak with her."

I stopped. "What should I say?" I asked as I turned.

"You may tell her whatever you like." He looked up at me and took off his glasses. "Mrs. Howard thinks a lot of you."

The statement didn't require an answer so I gave none.

"You did a good job taking care of the bills. And the dog."

"Thank you," I said.

"So now you know everything about me," he said.

"What makes you think you're so fascinating that I would be interested?"

He raised his eyebrows. "I can still fire you," he said.

"Not before I bring in lunch."

"Fair enough. There's always tomorrow."

And that's how it began.

The hours were long but the work was interesting. His meetings didn't have the slightest resemblance to the one-man ego show Wells used to put on. Wells spoke; nobody listened. Duncan spoke; everyone hung on every word. And he never spoke unless he had something to say. There were weekly sales forecast meetings. One week, Johnson put on a twenty-minute performance that was all style and no substance. He finished with a bang, saying everyone would have to wait and see if the profit predictions panned out. Duncan asked if he couldn't be a tad more specific. Another song and dance ended with a no. Duncan said he was sorry to hear that, perhaps Johnson would learn to be more specific at his next job. That was at eleven forty-five. Just before lunch. Right on schedule. At one-fifteen Johnson was exiting the building carrying a cardboard box. Duncan was not a man to be toyed with.

If he ever lost his temper, which I'm sure he did, I didn't know about it. His armor was not without chinks. His anxiety level could be measured by his phobia for neatness. It spiked

when paperwork from various attorneys arrived in thick en-
velopes marked confidential. His soon to be ex-wife obviously
had no fear. She would call on his private line, he would close
his door but I could hear his voice elevated an octave, through
the door. After he opened the door, if I peered in I would see
him pouring a glass of water. At times he would assume the
role of teacher, explaining to me why he wrote letters a certain
way, or said something in particular to a manager or even a
client. I listened. I learned. Here was a man used to winning
and coming out ahead every time. I respected his intelligence
and realized that I liked him.

One fine, sunny Saturday afternoon after my third brush with
the law, I was sitting in Applebee's waiting for Steve to show
up. He had followed the usual procedure. First the "How are
you after the incident" phone call. I responded positively so he
followed with the "I'm just a friend checking in" phone call.
All I needed to do was wait for the strategic moment to casually drop the line "I'm really glad you called" and the deal was
done. He chatted about his cases, I talked about my job, and of
course, there were the always pleasant moments of dead silence on the line. So, I took my cue.

"I'm really glad you called," I said.

"Me too," he said. "It's been a long time."

"Yes, it has."

Finally, he found his courage. "Maybe we could have
lunch," he said.

Thank God. These intro calls were hell.

Lunch was good. Steve talked. He was funny. He told me
his amazing police stories. I had some time to take a closer
look. He was taller than I remembered, a little thicker, a lot
cuter, and a lot more outgoing. I didn't remember him being
this open and friendly. He was working hard, doing his best. I
tried to be in the moment instead of outside looking in but I
couldn't relax and just let things happen. I was analyzing the
ritual we were going through, missing what was supposed to

be the best part. I felt sorry for him and wondered if I had been ruined for the game.

He pulled his car up behind mine in front of my apartment and we went for a walk as the sun lowered in the late afternoon sky.

"We made it through lunch without you attacking the waitress. I think that went well."

"It's the new medication."

As we walked, he brushed his hand against mine until our fingers became intertwined. Well done, I thought.

"What do you think we should do next?" he asked.

"Well, since I promise not to order ribs, corn on the cob, or anything with a dipping sauce, I think we should move on to dinner."

He laughed and stopped walking. We faced each other. He put his hands on my shoulders.

Three thoughts raced through my mind: he's adorable, he likes me, my upper arms are getting flabby. I'd have to start exercising again.

"Why didn't we stay together in college?" he asked.

"I was a different person then."

"Which one do you prefer?"

Good question. Strange, everything I had ever wanted was finally here, only a new Joan was here to greet it. The old Joan was gone. And Jennifer? There were parts that stayed with me. The good parts, I hoped.

My mother's house had become wedding command central for Carrie's preparations. Not even having a normal fiancé and dying her hair back to its original color had been enough to satisfy her family into letting her back in the door. Ever since the psycho episode in Marty's basement, Carrie worried about any more freak-outs in front of Scott, wedding or otherwise. Mom stepped up to the plate.

Carrie was having a color wheel crisis as I came through the door.

"Which is worse, peach or pale plum," Carrie cried, tossing color chart strips at me. I looked them over.

"How do I make sure the flowers are coordinated with the dress?" Beads of sweat were clustering on her forehead.

"You know both of these are hideous, right?" I offered.

"And the food! What am I going to do for food? It's forty-two ninety-five a person for roast beef and vegetables or fish and vegetables. If you add the baked potato, it's forty-five ninety-five. Why is it three dollars for a potato? Is there a famine?"

"No one will miss the potato."

"These colors are ugly?"

"Only if you think so."

Carrie tossed the color strips onto the table. "They are ugly," she whimpered.

I brought her a glass of water and a tissue. "What does Scott think?" I asked.

"He says, 'Pick whatever you want, babe,' " she sniveled. "Until I pick the wrong thing and he hates it and his family hates it and then they hate me and tell him not to marry me!"

It was time for divine maternal intervention. My mom came up behind Carrie and put a hand on her heaving shoulder.

"I think a pale pink would look lovely on the bridesmaids. It's a very soft color. Then your flowers could be an assortment of pink gardenias or carnations with baby's breath. Either would be lovely."

Carrie snuffled softly for a moment, then nodded.

"Could we not have huge flowers or bows on the dresses?" I asked.

"For you—anything," Carrie said.

Two hours later we had made sense of the madness that was to be the happiest day of Carrie's life and put together a checklist. The veins in Carrie's forehead receded. Things were better.

"So Mrs. B," she asked, "do we like Steve?"

"He's a very nice young man," my mother said while pulling a cake out of the oven none of us needed to eat.

"So," Carrie said to me on the q.t., "if he's a nice young man, how come all I've been hearing about is the Beastmaster boss and the training classes he's sending you to."

"I talk about Steve," I defended. "I was excited about the classes."

"Yeah, you talked about Steve. But you talk more about work. And your boss."

I gathered up brochures. I looked over to find Carrie eyeing me.

"Absolutely not," I said softly. "I met my quota as moron of the decade. Besides, I'm sure he's a tad difficult to live with."

"That's not it," Carrie breezed. "She's divorcing him because he fooled around."

"Carrie, you haven't seen this guy. He's good-looking but he can make grown men weep. She probably just had enough of him."

"Joanie, didn't you tell me she's going in for the kill with the lawyers?"

"Yes. The divorce papers read like the Hatfields and McCoys." Okay, so maybe I did peek a little when putting the paperwork on his desk.

"I'm telling you, when a woman goes after the money he's had an affair. Taking the money equals cutting off his balls and shredding them like Bac-Os. And they only do that if there was another woman. Did we confirm the appointment with the band?"

"Twice." For a minute it was the old Carrie. I was getting confused.

"He probably had her stashed when he took his road trips."

"He travels to a lot of different cities."

"It's the one he goes to the most." She talked as if this was an obvious fact known by the entire world except for me.

"How can you tell?"

"Check the credit card receipts for his expenses, limo reservation slips—it's easy."

I felt exasperated, like this was the second shooter theory for JFK. Was there a grassy knoll we could check, too?

My mother came into the dining room and set about serving the cake. Carrie laid out her final color choices.

"What do you think?" she asked, looking up at my mom.

"I think they look lovely, dear. Good choices—all of them."

"Thanks, Mrs. B. By the way, why do you think Joanie's boss is getting a divorce?"

"He had an affair dear, of course."

Carrie raised an eyebrow at me.

We perked up at the sound of heavy footsteps and male voices coming in from the patio. Steve and Scott were talking and laughing as they entered. Scott draped his arms around Carrie.

"I like these," she said, looking down at the color strips.

"Me too, babe," he answered without missing a beat.

Steve came over and kissed me. I returned the kiss with enthusiasm. He gave me an open smile that said, "I am not freaked out that we are in a wedding zone." He gave me a hug and I leaned into his embrace. I had a momentary déjà vu of a Wells maneuver. I shook off the feeling.

"Is that cake for everyone?" he asked.

"Only close personal friends of the homeowner's daughter," I answered.

"You think she could sneak me a slice?" he asked, kissing my ear.

"I think I can work something out," I said.

"You haven't seen my home yet," Steve said later, when we were in the car.

"Then we should take care of that." We were holding hands, exchanging kisses by the car.

"Friday?" he whispered in my ear.

"Perfect."

Steve's house was a typical guy set up. Comfortable furniture. Standard large breed dog as faithful, devoted companion. Signs of recent, intense cleaning in the bathroom and kitchen prior to my arrival. He had a large piece of property with a huge backyard. He took me by the hand and gave me the ten-cent tour.

We settled on the enclosed patio for a pleasant dinner of cold salad and red wine for me, beer for him. The wine went down smooth and warm. I had a comfortable buzz as we settled into the overstuffed lounge chairs.

"I thought you were going for prelaw," I said lazily.

"I had a handcuff fetish I couldn't ignore."

"I'll make a note of that. Real reason please."

He looked up at the night sky. "I wanted to be out doing something. Not just sitting around talking about it."

He refilled my glass.

"Should you, a police officer, be contributing to my alcoholic state?" I asked.

"Don't worry. I won't let you drink and drive." His eyes were soft. I knew it was coming. Men didn't invite women over for dinner to have them look at their stamp collection. Unless they kept it in their shorts.

"Why didn't you finish college?" he asked.

"I'm finishing now."

"Why didn't you finish then? You were always so smart."

"I was, huh? I don't know too many geniuses who make all the wrong decisions by the age of thirty."

He went silent, giving me a sharp look. I had forgotten. Steve had been in tune with the softer side of the old Joan. He liked a little spice but only within bounds of reason. He didn't know what to do with the more acerbic Joan. I needed to curb my commentary. I chattered selectively about past jobs, even a few words about Michael; then I fell silent.

"Sorry," I said after a few minutes. "Sometimes reminiscing doesn't work for me."

He leaned over and gave me a kiss. His beer mixed nicely with my wine.

"You're going to be okay now. You know that, right?" he said.

I looked at him. "Yes, I do."

He offered his hand and I took it. We strolled into the house. He took the lead and I let him. He was sweet, putting the brakes on any Indie 500 action so I could enjoy myself as well. Afterward, I lay in his arms. It was refreshing to not have the other person leave. The fact that we were in his house may have had something to do with it.

"I'm glad Michael let you go," he said.

"Thank you," I said after a few minutes, and then I shed a few tears even though I had no idea why.

The next morning I waited for the kiss off. "I have to go to work," "I'll call you," "Duke has a terrible case of fleas and is going through a rough time," and my personal favorite, "I thought we could just be friends." What I got was breakfast, a kiss and, "What do you want to do tonight?" And that's how it began.

A pleasant if erratic routine of Saturday barbecues, weekend softball games, and quiet nights of Chinese food and TV began; everything depended on his rotating shift. My new life was cemented by the seamless integration of Steve and Scott. The two S's had hit it off immediately. How did I know this? The sight of two men sitting on a couch watching baseball in mind-numbing silence was a clear sign of the deepest of male bonding. This was a stark contrast to my daily routine at work— fast conversation, quick-witted retorts, limos, and meetings on the fly. I shuttled between the office and Duncan's house. If he had to travel he'd work out of the house until the limo showed up. He usually took late afternoon or red-eye flights. I would get to the house by three in the afternoon loaded down with files. Duncan would let me in while plowing ahead on the phone. His form of hello was motioning to the laptop on the desk. I learned by instinct what I was supposed to do, transcribing what he was repeating into the phone, making hotel reservations, paying his bills, or proficiently fixing whatever major screw up he'd just made on his laptop.

"Did you get me a suite?"

"They didn't have any suites available. I reserved a standard room with two double beds with a scenic view overlooking the alley."

"You're exceptional. Did you book the conference room?"

"I told everyone to meet you downstairs by the pretzel stand."

"I can still fire you, you know."

"Not while I have your plane tickets."

And so it went. The Tuesday he was leaving for Seattle he suddenly found his human side, albeit briefly.

"How's school?" he asked.

Ordinarily, I hated these questions, because bosses really didn't give a damn and it was simply an opportunity for them to tell an amusing anecdote about themselves. I played along.

"Fine. The maharishi thinks I'm right on track for graduation."

He gave me a quizzical look. "Your mentor is a spiritual person?"

"Absolutely. His greed exists on a higher plane." He smiled and held out the cup of peanuts he was munching as an offering. He was dressed in gray slacks, black shirt, and black loafers. He looked nice.

"Have you thought about what you'll do after graduation?"

"So you really are going to fire me?"

"Eventually."

"I haven't thought about it," I said. "I don't do much planning anymore."

He looked around the kitchen and gave a disgusted chuckle. "Neither do I."

That was the closest he'd ever come to a comment on his personal life. I think he'd grown as a person. There was a knock at the door.

"Take care of everything, especially Sherlock," he said. I saw him off outside.

I answered my phone one evening instead of letting the machine pick up. It was Louise. I hadn't heard from her and frankly that was okay. She insisted I stop by—probably because she'd been out of the loop. Lack of details was putting her in withdrawal. I stopped by—out of habit and curiosity more than anything else, I guess. And I mentioned Steve.

"Oh my God," she cried. "You have to tell me everything. I was just reading about something like this in *True Stories* magazine."

"He's still tall, still fair, still cute," I summarized. "And he ate my cooking and lived." No small feat, mind you.

"This is it," Louise announced. "He's the one. I know it. Forty-two percent of women say someone they knew was the one all along. And they popped up when least expected."

Somehow I wasn't prepared to trust my future to a survey about your life partner and soul mate "popping up." It just didn't feel right.

"I'm so happy for you," she said, and then raised her eyebrow.

I threw her a bone. "He hasn't proposed, Louise," I noted.

"I know, I know," she perked up. "But he will. Now aren't you glad you saw what Michael was and didn't stick with him?"

It was an interesting retelling of history, yet the sound of his name still annoyed me and I knew her motive wasn't to cheer me up. Somewhere out there, he was going to be the father of someone else's child, which I still thought about much more than I should.

"By the way, it's a boy."

I stared blankly as a response.

"Jennifer had a sonogram and blabbed to everyone in the salon."

So there it was. Michael was expecting a son with Jennifer. Maybe it bothered me because there was more finality in that than the marriage.

"You're about to have the life you always wanted, Joanie. It's all going to happen. Everything with Michael is so yesterday. You're going to have it all with Steve."

And that got me to thinking. Jennifers were the poster girls for having it all. And what exactly was that? If I were to consult my ideal inner Jennifer, I would've found she was no longer wearing lingerie and smoking a cigarette but rather dressed in a three-piece suit with short polished nails and her hair swept into a twist. But only during the day. At night, Jennifer would be strictly jeans and T-shirt, easy going, quiet, and prone to having the athletic sex of a gymnast. Okay, a slightly out of shape gymnast. Polonius would have said, "To Thine Own Jennifer Be True." Which Jennifer was that again? I decided it didn't matter. I could have both Jennifers coexist peacefully side by side. Finally, there was a solution.

Chapter 23

So I had reached nirvana. Okay, not nirvana but close enough. Duncan continued to send me to training classes; everything from finance to project management. I knew it wasn't all benevolence. The more I knew, the better for him. His divorce was heating up. There were more phone calls behind closed doors. Lawyers came and went at all hours with paperwork for Duncan that I never saw. Through it all he continued his commutes to Seattle every few weeks.

"You won't be in tomorrow so you need to sign all the letters in your in-box today," I said.

He sat slumped at his desk, dark circles blooming under his eyes. I decided he was having an affair and obviously she was in Seattle. Carrie was right again.

"I guess I have to do this, don't I," he answered.

"Yes, you do."

He took the stack of letters and began signing. "Can't you use the rubber stamp?"

"Original signatures required."

"Your efficiency is annoying," he remarked. "Appreciated but annoying."

"We all have our cross to bear. I'm yours." He looked at me and smiled. A real smile.

"By the way," I said nonchalantly, "Mrs. Howard is pregnant."

He threw his pen down. "Damn it," he said.

"I know, she has some pair not consulting you first."

"I think I bring out the worst in you," he said with a sigh.

"Quite possibly."

He looked away and chewed on his lower lip. "You wouldn't be the first."

I looked at him squarely. "Not to worry. You won't wear me down."

"Good, while you work on your inner strength, I won't worry about losing you to the HR department." He ran his fingers through his hair. "This is going to make things difficult," he said. "I forgot to tell you I'm going to be away for three weeks starting on the fifteenth."

"Seattle again?"

He nodded.

"How much longer do you think you'll be doing this?" I asked.

He looked away again. "Not much longer." It was tough working for a sphinx.

I was living more out of Steve's apartment than mine. My clothes were starting to find their way into his closet. He didn't care. He was always talking about his next set of home improvements, including the location for my desk. After dinner he watched TV while I studied. I chattered about work and what went on but it didn't take long before I noticed that his attention wandered as I spoke. The more vocal I became the more it seemed to put him off. I let it pass, shrugging off the feeling of unease. I kept to the topics of school and books or asked questions, letting him do most of the talking. He went on about the house, his plans to buy another house as income property, buying new carpeting for this house. I realized that he was softer than I was—that was good. One of us should be. He seemed happy. I was happy, too.

I was summoned to my mother's house by another of her world famous cryptic phone messages on my answering machine.

BEEP. "Joanie, I have to talk to you about something. It's very important. I'll make lamb chops for dinner. Bring your laundry."

She gave no clues. I didn't rule out the possibility of illness because my mother had once found a suspicious growth on her arm.

She met me at the door with an asphyxiatory hug.

"Mom, are you sick?" I asked.

"No, of course not, don't be ridiculous."

I broke her grip in order to acquire oxygen. "Then whatever it is, I'm fine with it."

"Joanie—"

"You're moving in with Randall."

"No."

"You're adopting a child."

"Joanie, be serious."

"You're adopting a dog."

"Joanie—"

"You're letting Randall manage the money?"

My mother chuckled and pinched my cheek. She's sweet, but no fool.

"Joanie, we're engaged. We're getting married."

My mother was engaged to be married. I saw the mixture of apprehension and joy in her face and a feeling of guilt rushed through me; my attitude had made her afraid to tell me. I wanted her to be happy. She deserved it. This is what she'd been waiting for. Somehow she had managed to preserve her heart and soul just in case her second prince came along. How she did it, I had no idea.

I gave her a bear hug and kiss on the cheek. "I'm so happy for you, Mom. Randall is great."

She hugged me back. "Thank you, Joanie. You're not upset?"

"No, Mom. Can I be the maid of honor?"

She started to cry. I guessed that meant yes.

My mother's impending marriage got me to thinking about my relationships. I realized I had not known what I wanted in a partner when Michael came along. I had been stunned that he wanted or appeared to want me as I was. I had never actually cared for myself in any form. As long as someone else did, that was all that mattered. I thought about my mother and how she had lived her life in the opposite way. She was completely comfortable with herself and the right man would have to come along and accept the package as it was. And he had.

Steve didn't quite want the package as it was. If I expressed an opinion too forcefully, spoke too much about business, or held my ground on a subject too long, he grew silent and withdrew. Sexy and sweet was all he wanted. I decided not to rock the boat, making little adjustments as I went along. Duncan could care less about Jennifer. A Joan by any other name had better be competent—that was all he cared about. I was a dual package, coexisting side by side. I knew as long as my life was settled, I could handle it.

"Where are they going on their honeymoon?" Steve asked as we set the table.

"I don't know. They haven't set a wedding date yet."

"They could go to Club Med."

"You're hilarious. My mother doing the macarena is not something I want a visual on."

He laughed and slipped his arm around me. "We could double with them."

I stopped. He stopped. I gave him a minute to realize what he had just said.

"You can take it back if you like," I said quietly.

"No," he said. "I'm fine, I'm not trying to pressure you."

"I understand."

"I'm just letting you know, I'm leaning in a certain direction."

I gave him a kiss. "I'll keep that in mind," I said lightly.

A week later, Duncan returned from his trip and came in on Monday morning, looking haggard.

"Morning," he muttered, or snarled, depending on how

you wanted to take it. He ditched his jacket on the chair and went straight for the coffee.

"Everything okay while I was gone?" he asked.

"Sales reports and forecasts are on your desk. The consolidation project is under way and Bradley's screwing around with the status reports again and no one on the team knows what's going on."

The usual fire in his eyes wasn't there. Was Duncan getting soft? It didn't seem possible, but Bradley had been screwing up nicely for some time and Duncan hadn't done a thing.

"I'll talk to him," he said quietly. "Thank you," he added. "You did a great job." That was it. I went back to my desk.

After another morning and afternoon buried in his office on the phone, he finally opened his door at four o'clock.

"Are you busy?" he asked.

That was my cue. I grabbed a pad and followed him inside. I sat down, turned to a clean page, and waited. Duncan sank into a chair across from me at the conference table. He looked like hell; sallow skin and dark circles under his eyes. Resigned, overworked, and slightly disgusted.

"Are you okay?" I asked.

He nodded. "Joan, the company is selling this division. I'll be relocating to the new corporate headquarters in Seattle."

I knew my mouth was open. I could feel the breeze.

He sighed. "Sorry, there was no easy way to say it."

I had to find my voice. *C'mon, Joanie, say something, anything.*

"When—when will it happen?"

"Not for another three months." He paused, giving me a measured look. "I'm offering you the choice of coming with me."

I think all the circuits broke. I wasn't computing.

"You would continue to work directly for me, full benefits, and a relocation package." *C'mon, Joanie, snap out of it. Pay attention.*

"What are my chances for advancement after graduation?" *Excellent, Joanie, clearly shows lucidity.*

"You know I can't give guarantees," he said. "But I will continue to give you every opportunity."

I didn't say anything.

"Are you interested?" he asked.

"Yes," I heard myself say. "When do you need my answer?"

"Two weeks. I have to tell the purchasing company whether you'll be here or not. Let me know as soon as you make a decision."

"Of course," I answered.

My life had settled. It was good. Now I had to decide my future in two weeks. What happened to two Jennifers coexisting in harmony? I guess that was shot to hell. Now I had to make a choice. I should have known. A Jennifer divided against herself is one screwed up woman.

Duncan went back to his all business routine but I sensed that he wanted to tell me more about what was going on. He would start to talk about things but then restrain himself. If he knew for sure I was going, he would have talked. Now he had the added pressure of selling his house, more meetings with more lawyers, and more settlement agreements drafted and rejected. Messengers and lawyers kept coming and going until I didn't know who the hell they were or why they were coming. I worked late one night waiting for yet another envelope. I didn't bother looking up from my proofreading when the door to the office suite opened. There were muffled voices and then footsteps. Another delivery had come.

I looked up when the footsteps stopped at my desk.

It was Michael.

He looked a lot older than when I had seen him last year. He had a little salting of gray coming in at his temples. He looked tired. I had imagined this moment for so long and in a split second I realized how ridiculous my practiced monologues had been. What do you say? How's it going, and thanks for breaking my heart and screwing up my life?

I saw the surprise in his eyes. "Joan," was all he could get out.

Emotions crowded in on me all at once—the hopeless attraction, heartbreak, the betrayal and the humiliation. But above all I felt anger. I forced myself to keep control.

"Do you have papers for Peter Duncan?" I asked, standing up.

"You look incredible," he said, finding his voice.

"Thank you. I feel incredible. I am incredible. I have a fantastic job. I'm on the fast track moving up the corporate ladder. I'm graduating college soon. I look, feel, and am, incredible. Now, do you have papers for Peter Duncan?"

Fumbling with his briefcase, he pulled out a manila envelope. I snatched it from his hand.

"Joan—I—I was worried about you. Wondering how you were—"

"Didn't you hear what I said? I'm fine," I said, cutting him off. Stalking into Duncan's office, I threw the envelope onto his desk. When I came back out, Michael was gone.

Which was fine. I was certainly fine. I saw Michael. Who cares? What was he to me? Nothing. Absolutely nothing. I had built an entirely new life, two lives, and in walked my old life. So what? Wondering how I was? How the hell did he think I was, the fool. He never bothered to call so just how much had he been wondering? I was shaking in the elevator all the way down to the lobby.

When I got to the parking lot, he was waiting for me.

"Get away from my car," I ordered.

"Please, Joanie, I just want to talk to you," he pleaded.

"What do you want to talk about? Your wife? Your son? Your nice, safe little job in your father's firm that you settled for because you're a coward."

"I'm sorry," he mumbled, staring down at the ground.

"About which part?" I retorted. "Stringing me along, seeing Jennifer behind my back, or having your mother dump me for you? By the way, the engagement was a nice touch."

"I wasn't stringing you along," he said, reaching for me. I pushed him away and crossed to the driver's side.

"I thought if we got engaged they couldn't stop it," he said.

"So that's the bullshit story now?"

"I told them I wouldn't break it off but—Joanie, I never thought I'd see you again." I looked at him. I knew him. And I knew it was true.

"All the things we talked about, the things you wanted to do—you never worried about your parents. We used to laugh about them. You made jokes," I said.

His shoulders sagged. "I owed them money. A small fortune, Joanie." He turned to me. "You don't think my father *gave* me the cash for the law school he insisted I go to, do you? What could I do?"

Looking at him, I felt the anger go out of me. *You could've been a man.*

"You're right," he said softly. "I'm a coward."

We stood there in silence for a long moment. He looked at me as if he was seeing me for the first time.

"You're so different, everything about you."

Yes, I am.

"I loved you just the way you were," he said.

At that moment, I finally understood that party and why I couldn't stop thinking about it. He was Don Quixote but not only wasn't I Dulcinea, I was never supposed to be. I *was* Sancho, his faithful partner, always there to help him fight the windmills. That party was the beginning of the end and he knew that. His parents had already decided he would marry Jennifer. She knew it when she smiled at me. And he knew he wouldn't do anything about it.

I stepped back. So here he was, my Michael. The man I thought was in control, and all along everything had been out of his control. Carrie had been right as usual when she said at least he'd had the decency not to sleep with me. It would have made the breakup so much worse.

I felt a momentary pang of guilt. Was there something I should have done, could have done? If I had been stronger, smarter, wiser; I could've helped him fight. Stop it, I thought. It's over. The one thing I can't do anymore is live in the past. It's time to put this to rest.

"Are you seeing someone?" he asked.

"Yes, I am."

"Is he nice to you?"

"Yes, he is."

We stood there in silence looking at each other.

"I miss you, Joanie. I always will." He kissed my forehead and walked away.

I unlocked the car door and got in, watching as his car pulled out of the lot. He had been happy with the original Joan after all—and I wasn't that person anymore. I sat there for a long while marveling at how time had already eroded the intensity of the feelings I once had for him. Eventually his features would blur in my memory and I would forget what he looked like. Then I cried. When I stopped I knew I had done all the crying I would do. I started the car and drove home.

Chapter 24

Each day the clock kept ticking. I had to make a decision. It was a choice between Jennifers. Or was it? Was it a choice between career and marriage? Maybe it was a choice between priorities. What did I want the most? Staying with Steve would include marriage and children. Would I regret my decision? Would I resent him? Suddenly all of my psychology and sociology classes were no help at all.

Maybe it was a choice between two men or two types of men and how they responded to Jennifer—who was now me, except not the "me" I was before. But that had to be wrong because I realized now I had always defined myself by someone or something outside of myself. Who was I if I wasn't trying to be someone else? I should've been a psychologist. I could've given myself therapy, but of course I would've overcharged myself so that would've sucked.

I hadn't told anyone yet—not even Steve. I had to mention it soon. If I didn't, I would be doing the same thing to him that Michael did to me. I knew as soon as I brought it up everyone would weigh in with an opinion. And that was only going to make the situation more complicated. I decided to tell my mother first.

Over dinner, my mother was euphoric. "Joanie, what a wonderful opportunity!" she exclaimed.

Okay, Mom thinks it's wonderful. That would be a yes vote.

"Will you have the same salary? Who will pay for the move? What about a car?"

No, wait—she's giving it more thought now. . . .

"What about Steve, dear? What did you tell him?"

"I haven't—yet."

"Well, you're not married."

Of course I'm not.

"Of course, he may want to marry you. Are you in love with him, Joanie?"

Excellent questions, however, before I could answer, "Do you know it rains all the time in Seattle?"

"Yes, Mom, but the foliage is spectacular."

My mother hugged me. I think she was winding up for the big finish.

"It's a wonderful opportunity, Joanie. I'm so happy for you. . . ."

And a one, and a two, and a three . . .

"Of course nothing can ever take the place of a good husband with a good life insurance policy."

She looked me in the eye. "So, what are you going to do?"

"I'll figure it out soon, Ma, very soon."

During dinner with Steve, I kept looking for the right opening. It didn't seem to be a good time after the discussion of the barbecue at his partner's house. *Great, I'll make the potato salad and I might be moving to Seattle.* He was talking about charcoal and lighter fluid.

". . . and then Jimmy's house caught on fire from the sparks and they had to live in a trailer for six months."

"Uh-huh," I said, coming out of my special place to find him staring at me. "What did you say?"

"Do you want to tell me what's bothering you?" he asked as we cleared away the dishes.

I cringed inside. I don't want to do this, I thought, but I have to. Actually I don't. I haven't yet given Duncan my decision. But I am considering it and that means I have to. My head hurt.

"The company's being sold," I said.

Steve put his arms around me. "Oh, babe, I'm sorry. I know you like it there but you'll find something else."

He held me in his arms. And they felt really good. Those were nice, good arms. *C'mon, Joanie, spill it.*

"They offered me a transfer."

For a second—nothing. Then he pulled back and I pulled back.

"The same job," he said.

"Yes."

"You could get that here."

Good point. "Yes, but there might be room for advancement."

"You can get another good job here, Joanie. You don't have to move to Seattle." He took me by the hand and we sat down at the table.

"Babe, you can get *another* great job right here."

I didn't answer. He squeezed my hand.

"Joanie, you're not really thinking about this?"

"Yes," I said finally. "I'm thinking about it."

His body stiffened and he pulled his hand away. "We just got everything together, Joanie. What about us?"

"I know. I know. I have to think about it but I didn't want to not tell you because it wouldn't be fair."

"But I love you, Joanie," he said, his voice rising.

"I know you do," I replied.

He got up, standing over me. "You have nothing else to say?" I heard the anger in his voice. *Congratulations, Joanie, you just hurt him.*

"I love you, too," I soothed. *How much, Joanie? How much do you love him?*

He stomped out of the room. I heard the sound of the TV.

Okay, memo to me: Decision-making skills, totally gone. Throw up hands, cry to Steve, decide to think about this tomorrow while helping Scarlett rebuild Tara. What the hell was I doing?

* * *

Two days later, Louise left me a message saying I needed to come over. Against my better judgment, I did. She was in a foul mood when I walked in.

"Fool," she was moaning, "he's fixing my sink. See how my sink is fixed." I noted the mess of pipes and tools on the floor. A Mikey flashback caused an involuntary shudder. "He's useless. All he does is complain and I can't get him off his ass to do anything."

Something crashed in the den. Without missing a beat, she screamed into the living room, "Knock it off or you're going to bed!"

"I needed an adult to talk to," she said, turning back to me. "At least you understand. How's Steve?"

"Steve's fine," I said. But I wasn't sure why I would understand Louise's problems. Steve didn't sit on his ass and my sink wasn't broken.

"So, when's the wedding?" she probed.

"Carrie's getting married in a month."

She waived her hand. "Not Carrie. You. When are you getting married?"

"I don't know. Duncan's going back to Seattle. He's made me an offer and I'm thinking of going to work for him there."

I could see the look of misery wash over her face. "And give up Steve? You're crazy."

Maybe I was. "I haven't made my decision yet."

"You've got a great guy who makes a good living. Women will kill for that. It's what you've always wanted. You'd leave Steve so you can type in Seattle? You can do that here."

"You seem a little annoyed. Thanks for caring. I know you'll miss me."

"Of course I'd miss you," she snapped. "I just think you're crazy."

"For wanting something different?"

She started bustling around the kitchen. "You always wanted to get married."

"Yeah, I always wanted a husband like you had, children like you had, a house like you had. Now I might want something different from what you have."

"What will you have?" she attacked. "Nothing. You're leaving yourself with nothing but a job. And what if you lose that job? What then?"

"I don't know. I'd have to decide what to do next."

"And as a matter of fact, I like my life, Joanie."

"As long as someone else wants it. As long as I wanted it."

The color rushed into her face. "If you leave and it doesn't work out, don't think Steve will take you back, because he won't. Seventy-five percent of women who chose a job over a man say that the man moves on and marries within a year."

"I gotta go," I said.

"Sure," she said. "I'll call you."

"Sure," I said.

I walked out of the house. My twenty-year friendship with Louise was now officially over. It had been over for quite a while. I drove home wondering if I could get used to a brand new city, a brand new life, being completely on my own. Or I could stay with Steve and play it safe. My state of vacillation was truly a joy.

I stopped in to see my mentor. He was featured in the *Long Island Business News* making some serious money with a new software program. I should've done a dual major in philosophy and business. Who knew the philosophy of healthy-well-adjusted-self-centered-capitalism would be a great combo?

"Did you say hello to Bill Gates for me?" I asked as I sat down.

"I take it you haven't made a decision," he said. He was wearing new beads. What better way to celebrate a monetary windfall.

"You're the mentor," I retorted. "Obviously, you're not mentoring properly."

"I've provided you with a set of tools, Joan. Remember, work is not life, and life is not work. Each is a part of you, therefore, you cannot separate the two."

Convenient. Don't they provide any cheese in this rat's maze? I'm partial to swiss myself.

"Your paper on Churchill and Roosevelt functioning as astute businessmen in their resolution of World War II was very interesting. But you didn't pinpoint why they succeeded."

"I said it was because of their superior intelligence."

"Not entirely."

"Because they knew they couldn't lose?"

"Absence of fear is not a guarantee of success, only a confirmation of stupidity."

"Okay," I said finally. "I give up and by the way, have I mentioned how I hate these conversations? Other students are studying Locke and Rousseau and reading *The Wealth of Nations*. Why am I not reading *The Wealth of Nations*?"

"We already have commerce and industry. The point is how do you function in commerce and industry. How do you view it, how does it view you? How do you want to be viewed?"

Memo to me: Mentor is babbling idiot. Cancel all plans to pursue master's degree, regardless of location.

"Your complaint is that I'm not teaching you about life. Your life is a business—what you construct, how you build, how successful your ventures with enterprise and people will be. How you see and how you're seen. Learn that and you will succeed no matter what you decide to do. That's the choice. The Prince or the Servant Leader—who do you want to be?"

"Does this mean you won't be telling me what I should do?"

"That's what it means."

"Thank you," I said. "Thank you very much. I value our time together."

I hated my mentor.

The work days were quiet. Duncan and I didn't chatter. We didn't even spar. He was waiting. I sometimes wondered if he was hoping for anything more. I caught his reflective looks at me but didn't respond. It was all business and I was determined to keep it that way.

I lamented my inability to make a life-altering decision to Carrie. We were sitting on the swings in the playground of my old elementary school one Sunday afternoon. The warm breeze felt good as I rocked back and forth.

"I'm pathetic," I finished.

"That's a little harsh, isn't it?"

I started to pump. Swinging in the breeze as a metaphor for my present mental state was not lost on me. Carrie twisted herself around, watching the chain tangle and untangle.

"What's my problem? I've spent half my life telling everyone it'll all work out. Why didn't you tell me that was an idiotic thing to say?"

"You were so nice, I didn't have the heart to upset you. Joanie, most people don't know what the hell they're doing. By the time they do know, they're too busy trying to fix the damage. I'm not just a spokesperson, I'm also a client."

Now I understood what she was talking about. So my theory of the meaning of life was correct after all.

"I saw Michael," I said.

Carrie stopped spinning. "When?" she demanded.

"Last week."

We were silent for a moment.

"Was she with him?" she asked.

"No."

"So, did you tell him you were having great sex with a gorgeous cop who couldn't wait to marry you?"

No, I didn't.

"I told him I was working my way up the corporate ladder and had a promising career."

Carrie smiled at me.

After I left the playground, I wandered the aisles of my old haunt, the bookstore, searching for answers. There were none. It was time to stop hiding myself away in books searching for the life I had to choose for myself. If it was a choice between two Jennifers, I chose neither. I was done with reinventing myself at will. As Polonius would've said, "To thine own *Joan* be true." After one year, Project Jennifer was officially over. I had to begin again.

BEING JOAN

Chapter 25

I dreamed of my father. He was wearing his overcoat and fedora. I approached him with tentative steps. He smiled at me with kind eyes.

"What did you learn today?" he asked.

"To be Joan."

He opened his arms and I melted in his embrace. He held me and kissed the top of my head. I held on tight for a long moment. In my mind, I knew I was on the outside of my dream, looking in, and that this was the last time I would see him.

"I'm proud of you," he said.

I opened my eyes. He was gone.

Carrie's wedding was loud, raucous, and pink all over. My dress was simple and stylish, free of flowers the size of triffids, mega bows, or bustles. The band was good and Scott actually spoke more than ten words together at the same time. Carrie was thrilled and I was thrilled for her. Louise didn't come. No one had heard from her.

Carrie and I hugged through our tears before she embarked on her honeymoon. I'd be gone by the time she got back.

"Don't take any shit, Joans," was her sage advice. She was right. She's always right.

Scott had asked Steve to usher when we had been a couple. In the end, Steve backed out. He came to the ceremony but skipped the reception. I saw him outside the church.

I hadn't spoken to him since the official good-bye at his house. "I have to know," I told him. He nodded, even though I don't think he understood.

Now we stood outside the church, looking everywhere but at each other. For a minute, we watched the crowd disperse, making their way to their cars to drive to the reception.

"Take care of yourself, Joan," he said.

"You too," I said.

He pulled me in for a quick hug and a kiss and then walked away without looking back. I looked after him, my stomach churning. The truth was that Steve was a good guy who loved me more than I loved him. He offered me everything I had ever wanted—ten years too late.

Saturday night, I made one last pilgrimage to my mother's house. In between telling me how happy she was, we did a lot of crying and hugging.

"Thank you for everything, Mom," I said, handing her a check for the last of the money I owed her.

"I just want you to be happy," she sobbed.

"I will be, Ma, I am, don't worry. Before you know it, I'll be back for the holidays." She and Randall were having a Christmas wedding.

On Sunday morning, I stood by the curb in front of my apartment with two suitcases.

My cell phone rang, pulling me from my thoughts. I flipped it open.

"Just checking to see if you're on your way," Duncan's low, strong voice came through the line.

A Lincoln Town Car turned down the street.

"The chariot is arriving as we speak," I said.

"Good. Are you ready?" he asked.

"Are you?"

I heard him chuckle. "See you Monday morning, eight A.M."

The car stopped, the trunk popped, and the driver got out to take my bags. He opened the door for me and I slid into the car. *I'm on my way.*

And that's how it began.

Can a man and a woman have equal power in a relationship? For three New York women, that is the question.

Summer begins as blue blood Emily Morton and hedge fund wizard Parker Davis celebrate their wedding. But every couple has their secrets, and Emily is about to discover the dark side of being a Park Avenue power couple.

Meanwhile, Emily is determined to play matchmaker for her friend and bridesmaid, Elizabeth Strait, who, despite her unflappable façade, still hasn't recovered from being jilted at the altar nearly a decade before. At the wedding, Emily introduces Elizabeth to Nick Reynolds, a brilliant Manhattan attorney. But even though Elizabeth knows a man like Nick can provide her with a safe, comfortable life, she can't keep her eyes off of gorgeous, elusive artist Ian McKay, with his twinkling eyes, alluring Scottish accent, and penchant for companionship without commitment.

Meanwhile, writer Karen Townsend wants to shout her engagement to brilliant playwright Robert Harris from the rooftops, but one thing stands in her way: her embattled, divorced parents. Karen's father famously attempted to strangle her mother with a Louis Vuitton scarf, and Karen worries the bad luck will extend to her own nuptials, with disastrous results.

Join these women as they navigate the politics and pitfalls of modern love and relationships in Jill Amy Rosenblatt's exciting new novel, *The Wedding Party*. Available in August 2009. Turn the page for a sneak peek.

Chapter 1

Ian McKay took a deep drag on his cigarette and exhaled a long spiral of smoke. Standing outside the gothic-style church in Midtown, he watched the parade of limousines as the stone saints on either side of the doors looked down upon him. The city was smothering under another day of oppressive heat, and he held his jacket carefully draped over his arm. As the limos discharged their cargo, a rainbow of couture paraded past him, the beautiful people casting cool glances at his jacketless form and open collared shirt.

"Isn't this delightful," a woman commented. "I told Emily, June is best, there is nothing more romantic than a summer wedding in New York."

Ian looked down at his hand, bare now, without his wedding band. Sometimes he could still feel it, like a phantom pain. He could still feel Sienna too, at night when dreams of her pulled him from his sleep. He wondered where she was, who she had chosen to take his place. Throwing his cigarette down, he ground it into the concrete with the tip of his polished shoe. Turning, he entered the church.

Inside the narthex, he inhaled a welcome blast of cool air and shrugged into his jacket as a bridesmaid emerged from a side door. His eyes traveled the length of her, lingering on the rose colored slip of a dress hugging her slim form. Her chestnut hair was swept into a neat French twist and she fidgeted with the small bouquet of orchids in her hand. She looked up, catching him in his scrutiny; her delicate features furrowed into a frown.

"Which side?" she asked.

"Sorry?"

"The bride's or the groom's side?"

"Neither," Ian said, amused to find himself the subject of her examination.

She pointed to a large book lying open on a stand. "Would you care to write a wish to the happy couple?"

"I don't think it will help."

She nodded. "Your accent—England? Scotland?"

"Very good. A little of both."

"You've come a long way to witness a wedding when you have no faith in marriage."

"I can't say that, as I've never been married."

"Uh-huh. Let me guess. You're not ready—still trying to find yourself?"

"I'm not lost."

"Perhaps you're feeling crowded and you need your own space."

"My flat is quite roomy." He smiled and waited.

She straightened, the humor fading from her face.

"A man who knows his own mind, how refreshing," she said, once again fingering the flower petals.

He loves me, he loves me not, Ian thought.

She waved the bouquet toward the chapel. "Sit anywhere you like." Turning on her heel, she disappeared back into the room she had come from.

Entering the church sanctuary, Ian spotted Robert maneuvering his sturdy six-foot frame through the clusters of guests chatting and laughing in the aisle. Grasping his friend's outstretched hand, Ian received a firm handshake.

"So what's your prediction? Twenty years of wedded bliss—thirty?" Ian asked.

"Not even close, and you know I only predict happy events."

Among their friends, Robert's uncanny aptitude for fore-telling felicitous events was an urban legend.

Ian glanced over his shoulder toward the narthex. "Did you notice the girl I was talking to?"

Robert nodded. "That's Karen's friend, Elizabeth, a money manager. Did you notice she's not your type?"

"You don't know what my type is," Ian shot back.

"You're not wearing a tie," Robert said after a long moment.

"I was hoping they'd ask me to leave."

"Not a chance," Robert said, leaning to whisper like a conspirator in Ian's ear. "The bride loves you."

"If she truly loved me, she would've bought three of my paintings and not two."

"I'll let Karen know to tell all referrals there's a three minimum buy."

"There's a good lad," Ian said with a chuckle.

Elizabeth crept back out into the narthex, peering into the sanctuary. Karen came up behind her.

"Who are we looking at?" Karen asked.

"The player talking to your betrothed. Who is he?" Elizabeth asked, enjoying the opportunity to study his slim, wiry frame. She felt a smile creeping across her lips as she took in the slicked back blond hair curling over his open collared shirt and the short, trimmed beard.

"Robert's best friend, Ian McKay," Karen answered. "I don't know that he's a player; he seems like a good guy."

"And he wears the most divine cologne," came a voice from behind them. They turned in unison to find Emily, the bride, glowing in a Badgley Mischka princess ball gown. It was perfect for her, the scoop neckline revealing just the right amount of cleavage, the dropped waist making her five-foot-nine-inch frame seem even taller, more regal. A descendant of a founding father and subsequent captains of industry, Emily's money was as old as her lineage and it showed; she didn't walk, she flowed, her elegance a hallmark of her birthright.

"And, his beard is like velvet," she added.

Elizabeth feigned a look at her watch. "You have twenty minutes. Do you want to switch grooms?"

Emily laughed, her cheeks coloring. "I had him over for tea a few times, strictly business. I kissed his cheek. Both cheeks, actually. It's the European way. You know I'm a sucker for an accent."

"And why didn't I hear about him?" Elizabeth asked, turning an enquiring eye on Karen.

"He only arrived three months ago," Karen said. "You were busy at the office, I hardly saw you."

Elizabeth waited.

Karen sighed. "He's an artist."

Rolling her eyes, Elizabeth gave a disgusted laugh, and headed back to the dressing room.

"You can't judge all artists against Peter," Emily said, trailing after her.

"I do not judge all artists. I just have an intimate understanding of their basic nature."

Emily embraced her. "Right. I'll stay with my original statement."

Back in the dressing room, they stood in a circle. Taking their hands, Emily gave them a benevolent smile. "Now, my dearest friends, this is it. This is Act Two of our lives."

She turned to Elizabeth. "I told Nick Reynolds he is going to meet one of the youngest directors of private banking in the history of New York's financial institutions, so he'd better be on his best behavior." She squeezed Elizabeth's hand. "This time it's going to work."

Yes, it is, Elizabeth thought. *I will make this work.*

As if bestowing a birthright, Emily turned and held up Karen's hand, with its glittering diamond ring. "You're next. Robert is your soul mate, just as Parker is mine."

Karen stared at her, her almond eyes suddenly dark and troubled. Elizabeth gave her a comforting pat on her shoulder.

"Now Karen, your wedding will be perfect," Emily continued. "What would Lao Tzu say?"

"He would say live in the Tao and be at peace with the Ten Thousand Things," she murmured.

"Exactly," Emily soothed as the wedding planner blew into the room, flanked by her team. They whisked her away while clucking at Elizabeth and Karen to take their places.

"Have you told your parents you're engaged?" Elizabeth whispered to Karen as they fell into line for the processional.

Karen shook her head. "Not yet. Since their—incident— there hasn't been a right time."

"Incident? Attempted strangulation with a Louis Vuitton scarf is now an incident?"

"I'm a playwright. I'm expected to take poetic license with the truth. That's my job."

"You're going to have to tell them soon."

The first bars of music began. There was a palpable rustle as the crowd turned in unison.

Elizabeth counted silently to five as Karen started out down the aisle, then she took her first tentative step. The old memories came rushing back, the embarrassment, the humiliation. Even though more than ten years had passed, she still remembered every step *she* had taken to the altar, drawing closer to Peter; watching his face pale as she took her place beside him; his urgent whisper, he needed to talk to her—alone. She stood frozen, unable to answer as he said he wasn't ready, he couldn't do this, he was sorry, he didn't mean to hurt her. She had the minister announce there would not be a wedding. She couldn't face anyone.

Pursing her lips, she kept walking, counting the rhythm in her head, step, wait, step, wait. She caught a glimpse of Ian McKay as she passed by, the blond hair and neatly trimmed beard. She could feel his eyes on her.

At the reception she would meet Nick. And she would make it work.

* * *

Ian wandered the dimly lit Rainbow Room, a hum of voices swirling around him. A singer crooned Sinatra in front of a twenty piece orchestra. He sidestepped the beautiful people, catching snatches of conversations about charity lunches, vacationing in Mustique, someone rhapsodizing about Thailand, an estate auction at Sotheby's and isn't it a shame so and so's marriage ended so publicly?

He watched Emily flit about, making introductions, chatting and laughing, mixing authors, professors, and artists to create a salon atmosphere. Although for the many tea and chat sessions she had insisted on, they were always alone. She sat next to him on the settee, almost whispering, drawing him in. He bided his time, allowing her to rest her hand on his knee, waiting for the right moment to discuss the canvases he had shipped from London that were hanging in her living room, on loan, for months. Emily hadn't been in a hurry to make a decision until he told her he had another buyer. *The price of doing business*, Ian thought.

He caught Robert's eye, motioning for his friend to make his way to the bar; it was the least they could do to salvage the evening. Ian passed Parker; the groom had a glass in one hand, its contents slipping over the side as he waved his arm, describing his new domain.

"Twenty thousand square feet," he was saying, "and that's just the main house. I'm putting in a thousand-square-foot poolhouse. You walk in, the front entrance will be all marble. Get this, I had some Ivy League prick in my office last week who said he didn't know if he could run money. Don't we have a moral obligation to be fiscally responsible or some shit like that. What the fuck? I told him—you go ahead, be fiscally responsible. Spend your life putting in eighty hours a week at some plain vanilla mutual fund for a shit bonus check. He's worried about safeguarding the economy. I *am* the economy. Good luck with your fiscal responsibility, shithead. I'll be at my compound in Greenwich, stepping out the door to the helipad to bring me to Manhattan."

The men surrounding Parker laughed as they clicked glasses in a toast.

Ian squeezed in next to Robert at the bar and they hunkered down with their drinks. Ian had just let out a sigh of relief when a heavy slap on his back made him jump and slosh his drink on to the bar.

"Hey, thanks for coming to my wedding," Parker said.

Elizabeth and Karen lounged at a table by themselves, but Elizabeth only half-listened to Karen. Her eyes were glued on Ian.

"Are you sure this thing with Nick is a good idea?" Karen was saying. "Emily shouldn't be matchmaking. A woman who's had four broken engagements isn't a reliable judge of character. Are you listening to me?"

"At least she left them, they didn't leave her." *And it should've been five*, Elizabeth thought. How did a woman who made her society debut at Le Bal Crillon marry Parker Davis?

"Sometimes I think I made a mistake convincing you to come to New York."

Elizabeth turned to give her friend a sharp look.

"Maybe you would have been happier in California, after everything calmed down, of course. Maybe you should have gone to Colorado with your mom."

Elizabeth returned to watching the bar, her signal that the subject was closed. Guests moved in and out of her line of vision and then a pocket would open, revealing a glimpse of Ian McKay.

"There was nothing for me in Colorado. You gave me good advice and now I'm sure Emily's got it right with Nick. He's going to be the one."

A half hour later Ian's empty stomach was rumbling and Parker, who had elbowed himself between Ian and Robert, was gnawing on his nerves.

"I can't believe how happy I am," he said, giving Ian another robust slap on the back. "All I needed was marriage to the right girl."

As Parker began ticking off the benefits of marital bliss, Ian raised his hand, attempting to signal the bartender. He reminded himself that artists of small reputation could not afford to piss off the few clients they had—and lose any referrals that might come their way.

Parker gripped his shoulder. "You need to get married my friend."

What I need is a scotch neat and a smoke, Ian thought. Then he remembered they were on the sixty-fifth floor. *Shit.*

"Now I realize how empty my life has been," Parker was saying.

"That's not what I heard."

At the sound of the soft, even voice, the men turned to see Elizabeth sliding onto the empty stool next to Ian.

"I heard your *business* lunches at the Plaza Hotel were quite full and satisfying," she said.

Chuckling, Parker threw his arms around her, squeezing her to him. "Listen cookie, I'm a changed man! You're just jealous because you passed on your opportunity."

The lights threw colorful shadows across the planes of Elizabeth's face. Ian felt a rush of blood surge inside him and had a fleeting thought of Lady Brett Ashley draped on a bar stool in a café in Spain, waiting for her bullfighter to return. She could be Lady Ashley, Ian thought, she looks unhappy enough.

"I yielded to the better woman," she said.

Parker cackled. "You don't know what you missed, babe, on so many levels."

A passing guest caught Parker's attention. Stepping away from the group, he pointed at Ian. "You should see this guy's stuff Liz, it's not half-bad. The resale value sucks but maybe he has something for your new office."

Elizabeth looked at Ian. "My office is decorated."

"Something for your flat?" Ian asked.

"My apartment has everything in it that I need."

Opening her purse, Elizabeth took out a card, and handed it to him. "But, if you like, reach out to my secretary for an appointment."

Ian took the card, turning it in his fingers. "Reach out," he repeated.

"It's just an expression used in our working world," she said quickly. "Are you enjoying the wedding?"

"Fantastic party," he said. "You don't seem pleased. Don't you fancy weddings, Lizzie?"

"Elizabeth," she corrected. "Weddings are fine but in the end they have very little to do with marriage."

He edged closer, catching her scent, a warm, drowsy duet of delicate flowers and a sweet summer breeze. "Don't they? I believe you need one to have the other."

"What I meant was marriage isn't flowers, candlelight, and romance."

"But you're not married, Lizzie. How do you know this?"

"Elizabeth, and what I know is the principle of any successful endeavor is the same—it's work." She leaned back with a little self-satisfied smile.

"Perhaps. but I believe two people can simply enjoy each other's company without complications."

Elizabeth laughed, a short, bitter sound. "Ah, yes, I see the problem. You have commitment issues. In the colonies we have a term for your modus operandi, it's called a one night stand."

Ian smiled. "You Americans, always in a hurry."

"And you Europeans with your lovers, always chasing after romance."

"So if marriage is not romance, what is it?" Ian asked, his voice controlled, quiet. "Portfolios and property, profit and loss?"

Elizabeth slid off the stool. "I think in terms of mutual respect, understanding, and yes, working to build a solid financial future."

Ian nodded. "Ah, yes, I see the problem. You don't want a marriage, Lizzie, you want a merger. Except for your heart, of course. I suspect you'll keep that to yourself."

Elizabeth paled and Ian looked away, tossing back the rest of his drink. *Brilliant, you git.* He turned, intending to say something soothing but saw Emily approaching with a tall, clean-cut man in tow. His dark hair was salted with gray; his stride, easy and confident. Ian judged him to be in his late forties. His relaxed posture said he was allowing himself to be led.

"Elizabeth, this is Nick Reynolds, the most brilliant attorney in New York City," Emily said. "I'm sure you both will have a lot to talk about."

Nick offered his arm. "I hope you're prepared. Now I have to prove that build-up is justified by impressing you," he was saying as he led her away.

Elizabeth's soft laugh floated back to Ian, and he felt a knot in his stomach as he watched Nick walk her away into the crowd.